Water climbed past the prisoner's mouth and he tried to breathe through his nose, but inhaled water. The interrogator raised his hand and the water was sucked from the mask. The prisoner gasped, sputtered, and cried.

"Where in America? What type of attack?" the interrogator demanded.

"I do not know," the man gasped.

"What?" the interrogator snapped. The two CIA men gripped the prisoner's arms forcefully.

"I do not know! I only know it is in three days. I have heard 'Ronald Reagan' in connection with the target. We were to learn more in Cuba!"

The interrogator nodded his head and the mask filled with water. The prisoner howled, kicked, and bucked. One of the CIA men injected him with a small syringe. The panicking man immediately fell limp and the water was sucked from the mask once more. All three masks were removed. Pulses were checked. All three prisoners were still alive.

A voice said, "Get them out of here. We'll drown them again tomorrow."

Night Stalkers titles by Michael Hawke

NIGHT STALKERS
NIGHT STALKERS: COERCION
NIGHT STALKERS: HOMEFRONT

NIGHT STALKERS: HOMEFRONT

MICHAEL HAWKE

BERKLEY BOOKS, NEW YORK

THE BERKLEY PUBLISHING GROUP
Published by the Penguin Group
Penguin Group (USA) Inc.
375 Hudson Street, New York, New York 10014, USA
Penguin Group (Canada), 90 Eglinton Avenue East, Suite 700, Toronto, Ontario M4P 2Y3, Canada
(a division of Pearson Penguin Canada Inc.)
Penguin Books Ltd., 80 Strand, London WC2R 0RL, England
Penguin Group Ireland, 25 St. Stephen's Green, Dublin 2, Ireland (a division of Penguin Books Ltd.)
Penguin Group (Australia), 250 Camberwell Road, Camberwell, Victoria 3124, Australia
(a division of Pearson Australia Group Pty. Ltd.)
Penguin Books India Pvt. Ltd., 11 Community Centre, Panchsheel Park, New Delhi—110 017, India
Penguin Group (NZ), Cnr. Airborne and Rosedale Roads, Albany, Auckland 1310, New Zealand
(a division of Pearson New Zealand Ltd.)
Penguin Books (South Africa) (Pty.) Ltd., 24 Sturdee Avenue, Rosebank, Johannesburg 2196,
South Africa

Penguin Books Ltd., Registered Offices: 80 Strand, London WC2R 0RL, England

This is a work of fiction. Names, characters, places, and incidents either are the product of the author's imagination or are used fictitiously, and any resemblance to actual persons, living or dead, business establishments, events, or locales is entirely coincidental. The publisher does not have any control over and does not assume any responsibility for author or third-party websites or their content.

NIGHT STALKERS: HOMEFRONT

A Berkley Book / published by arrangement with the author

PRINTING HISTORY
Berkley mass-market edition / January 2006

Copyright © 2006 by The Berkley Publishing Group.
Cover design by George Cornell.

ISBN: 0-425-20739-0

BERKLEY®
Berkley Books are published by The Berkley Publishing Group,
a division of Penguin Group (USA) Inc.,
375 Hudson Street, New York, New York 10014.
BERKLEY is a registered trademark of Penguin Group (USA) Inc.
The "B" design is a trademark belonging to Penguin Group (USA) Inc.

PRINTED IN THE UNITED STATES OF AMERICA

10 9 8 7 6 5 4 3 2 1

It's not enough that we do our best;
       sometimes we have to do what's required.

                —SIR WINSTON CHURCHILL

The quickest way of ending a war is to lose it.

                —GEORGE ORWELL

A man cannot be too careful in the choice of his enemies.

                —OSCAR WILDE

Freedom is never more than one generation away from
       extinction. We didn't pass it to our children in the
       bloodstream. It must be fought for, protected, and
       handed on for them to do the same, or one day we
       will spend our sunset years telling our children and
       our children's children what it was once like in the
       United States where men were free.

                —RONALD REAGAN

1

She was owned by Mexicans, built by the Japanese, registered in Singapore, and headed for Cuba.

Her gross tonnage registered at 27,985; she was a dry bulk carrier. A freighter, with a raised forecastle and a flushed poop deck, and four large cranes between her hatches. As freighters go, she was young, built only five years before. She was the *Odette Debs,* making thirteen knots, and her crew had no idea what was coming.

They came in the dark. With speed and precision. With intensity of purpose and a sense of urgency tamed only by experience and professionalism. They came at nearly two hundred miles per hour, skimming the surface, and bristling with the tools of war. In their bellies, they carried some of the most competent and fearsome warriors on Earth.

The MH-60M Black Hawk and AH-6J helicopters of the 6/160th Special Operations Aviation Regiment. Known as the Night Stalkers, they were delivering their "customers" to a rendezvous with the *Odette Debs,* and this mission's customers were three squads of Navy SEALs, with eight operators per squad.

Lieutenant Colonel Jack Hartman was in one of the four Black Hawks, in the Command and Control, or C2, aircraft. He was the commander of the 6/160th, thirty-five years old, and still in great shape. He ran at least five miles per day, still had the cut abs he was proud of, and spent time every evening in the gym. He had not sacrificed his dojo time to the job yet, still finding a way to deal with his stress by throwing people around. In his face could be seen a career of tough missions. He had flown dust-off missions in Desert Storm and had worked his way up to commanding a battalion in the best army aviation unit in existence. He had made it because he was the best. He was here because the Night Stalkers were incomparable in skill and professionalism. But most of all, he was here for his soldiers. He loved the 160th SOAR.

His aircraft was flying on the same heading as the three other Black Hawks; he was able to look out at them through the grainy green of night vision goggles. He flew in the rear of the Black Hawk in order to command the fight, but he could think of nothing he missed more than having his own hand on the cyclic. Nothing except maybe having Cat to wake up with every day.

Up ahead, Hartman could make out the stern of the *Odette Debs,* her silhouette of black outlined with lights that appeared twice their normal size through his NVGs. It was time.

"All Arrow elements, insert your customers. Bullet elements, I want a steady succession of supporting runs. Everyone holds their fire unless fired upon. Execute," Hartman radioed over the air net.

The Black Hawks raced forward, noses down. Hartman's C2 bird and another Black Hawk overtook the ship along her port side, while the other two Black Hawks disappeared on the other side of the vessel.

"Come on McCall," Hartman whispered to himself as he watched the Black Hawk off to his right suddenly spin ninety degrees and bank in a maneuver that did not look unlike an expert stunt driver causing a car to skid to a stop.

McCall's aircraft, flying sideways, matched the forward speed of the ship.

Hartman's helicopter continued on its heading, and Hartman quickly lost sight of McCall's Black Hawk. CW3 Jeanie McCall was the only female Night Stalker. Ever. Her brown hair was streaked with gold, but it was invisible under her flight helmet. Her large hazel eyes and high cheekbones were obscured as well by the wear and gear of the soldier she was. As far as Black Hawk drivers go, she was one of the best and bravest.

"Come around Glenn," Hartman ordered anxiously into the intercom.

"Yes sir," the reply came, and the aircraft banked hard left to circle around and give Hartman another look. When he next saw McCall's aircraft, it was maintaining a fixed position over the deck of the freighter, hanging in midair between cranes number two and three. Ropes appeared, and then men, deadly like droplets of venom, streamed down to the deck below. The ropes fell away, and the Black Hawk backed out from between the cranes. Once clear, it spun and immediately took up a holding pattern, pacing the ship. The other two Black Hawks appeared, having deposited their own SEALs fore and aft of McCall's insertion point.

The *Odette Debs* was supposedly carrying an "unspecified cargo of high national interest to the United States." Hartman knew that meant the intel guys had no idea what she had onboard, but that a whole bunch of bad guys must have been talking about the ship on cell phones and e-mail. And just like that, someone says the magic letters W-M-D, and an operations order is written up, sending the Night Stalkers and SEALs out to assault a freighter in the Caribbean.

Hartman knew it could be anything. Maybe WMD, maybe conventional weapons. Maybe gold; most likely drugs in this part of the world. But ever since the nuke attack in Poland, on what had been Warsaw, and the biological attack in what was now the GQZM, or General Quarantine Zone of Manila, no one was taking chances.

Hartman could see flashes coming from within the deckhouses. The SEALs were sweeping them, going through every bulkhead, tossing flash-bang grenades into every point of entry. Hartman continued to be amazed at the skill of American commandos. Be they Navy SEALs or Army Special Forces, the latter including Delta Force, it simply had to be an enemy's worst day to be on the receiving end of an American Special Operations assault. The sheer ferocity of it still impressed Hartman after all these years.

The ship never perceptibly slowed, never altered course. The SEALs had to clear four deckhouses, the deck, and five cargo holds.

Inside the forward deckhouse, a SEAL squad led by Navy Lieutenant Brett Cade came to a locked bulkhead. Breaching charges were quickly set, the bulkhead was blown, and the SEALs streamed through. There was no one there. They moved on to the next one.

This one wasn't locked. Without orders or even words exchanged, the men took their positions, and one squad member tossed in a flash-bang grenade. Immediately following the bright flash and concussion, the SEALs rushed in to the sounds of men moaning.

"I've got one here," a voice said in their tactical communications headsets.

"I've got another one," a second voice said.

"Everyone, stand fast," Cade's voice ordered. He moved quickly over to one of the captured men. The flashlight from Cade's MP5 lit up the man's face. He was clearly just a sailor.

"Who are you?" Cade demanded.

"Ya ne rozumiyu," the sailor responded.

"Chesky?" a SEAL asked, wondering if they had found the rarest of things, a Czech sailor.

"Ni, Ukrayinsky," the sailor said.

"Ukrainian?" Cade wondered aloud, and then to the sailor, *"Vidyizd?"*

The sailor said nothing.

"Chysla?" Cade demanded, nodding to the next bulkhead.

The sailor still said nothing.

Cade shouted his question, *"Chysla?* How many men?"

"He cannot understanding you," said the other man.

"You speak English?" Cade said as he strode that way.

"I speak some English," the second man said, and then, gesturing to the other man, "He cannot understand when you try talk *Ukrayinsky,* because he is not Ukraine. He speaks just some word. He change his clothes. He is captain, he is Dutch. I am Ukraine."

Cade went back to the captain. *"U beantwoordde me niet. Kunt u me nu beantwoorden?"*

"Yes, I can understand you now," the captain said contemptuously in English.

"There is nothing in the hold. Why is your ship empty?" Cade demanded, more than a little annoyed at the initial deception.

"We are going to pick up our cargo," the captain said.

"That's horseshit, no one sails empty. Why are you here?" Cade demanded.

"De duivel kan u hebben," the captain said.

Cade kicked the captain in the thigh. "We'll see who the devil gets first," and then to the SEALs, "You two, stay here with them. You five, come with me, let's see if we can figure out what the hell is going on here."

They worked their way further forward, in just the same

way, tossing flash-bang grenade after flash-bang grenade. They approached the next bulkhead and heard a voice from within, speaking English: "Do not throw your grenade in here, we will not resist."

Cade held up one hand, and everyone froze. "Identify yourself. How many are in there?"

"We are three," the voice said, "and I am Ahmed ibn Khalid."

Cade heard the names, thought the entire encounter too strange, and nodded toward the door. Without the slightest hesitation, a flash-bang grenade was thrown inside. Ahmed, or whatever his name was, and whoever he was with, never made a sound. The grenade detonated and the SEALs rushed in. They found the three men seated on the floor, with their jackets over their heads and their hands clasped against their ears. The SEALs quickly zip-tied them.

"I told you it was not necessary to throw your grenade in here," Ahmed said calmly, "and yet you threw one, just because I gave you an Arab name. What a typical American bigot. Instantly, you hear the name of someone from the Middle East, and you feel threatened. How very racist of you. And to come in here like this, with guns and overwhelming force. How very cowardly of you."

"I have a submachine gun and you are insulting me, and getting on my nerves. How very stupid of you," Cade replied. "What are you doing here?"

"Pleasure cruise," Ahmed said sarcastically.

Cade stepped forward, placed the muzzle of his weapon on Ahmed's forehead. Neither Ahmed nor either of his friends seemed the least bit unsettled by this.

"Is it just the three of you?" Cade asked.

"Yes," Ahmed answered, the muzzle still against his head.

"Where were you going?" Cade asked.

"Wherever the ship was taking us," Ahmed said.

"Are these guys on drugs?" asked another SEAL.

"No," Cade said. "Worse, they're true believers."

A full ten minutes later, Cade radioed Hartman, "Arrow 6, this is Moray 36. We have taken and cleared the vessel. We will conduct a more thorough search, but so far we have found nothing."

Hartman's brow furrowed. "Nothing?" he replied. Nobody sails an empty freighter, Hartman thought, it's a total waste of money; you can always fill a freighter with something.

The SEAL leader heard the incomprehension in Hartman's voice. "Yeah, I know. Nothing. We have a mostly Ukrainian crew, except for the captain, who is still whimpering something in Dutch, and three men of apparent Middle Eastern extraction."

A whole freighter to move three men? And leave them unguarded? If these guys are worth anything, why not post an armed company with them? "Good copy, Moray. The USS *Winston Churchill* and its entourage will be here soon. We'll stay on station until then. Keep me advised, Arrow out."

The helicopters circled the slowing *Odette Debs* and waited for the U.S. Navy surface ships to arrive. It doesn't make sense, Hartman thought, three unguarded Middle Easterners supposedly on their way to Havana in a freighter full of nothing.

It hadn't even been a month since the 6/160th had been out over the Caribbean trying to save Guantánamo from a nuke aboard a small boat hidden like a needle in the proverbial haystack among thousands of Haitian refugees. He had doubted there would be a nuke onboard the freighter, but to find that an entire freighter was sailing with a total payload of three men? They hadn't flown, so it was clear they didn't want their names appearing on any passenger manifest, and any Middle Easterner traveling in a suspicious and anonymous way was clearly someone worth talking to, but it still didn't make any sense to Hartman.

Maybe the bad guys are starting to become desperate, Hartman thought.

2

"Admiral, we've just received confirmation from ONI at Suitland. The three found aboard the *Odette Debs* are high-ranking members of the Hizb ut-Tahrir terror organization," the young ensign said.

Admiral Manfred's eyes narrowed, hearing the report, processing the larger meaning. Rear Admiral Greg Manfred, commander, Naval Security Group Command, was a direct report to chief of the Central Security Service at NSA. He was tall, African American, with graying hair. He had a seriousness about him that no one underestimated. If Manfred told you he believed something, he wasn't guessing. He was rounding up to the nearest fact, he wasn't playing a hunch. If he told you he believed something, then he was convinced.

He knew Hizb ut-Tahrir al-Islami had thirty thousand hard-core members, in the former Russian "Stans," Pakistan, Syria, Turkey, and Indonesia. A couple thousand of their number were already jailed.

Hizb ut-Tahrir explicitly rejected democracy, seeing it as the system of the infidels. The group had spread around the globe, and its primary characteristics included the fiery rhetoric of jihad, secret cells and operations, mysterious funding sources, rapid transnational growth, and goals that it shared with al-Qaeda and other organizations of the global jihad movement. Hizb ut-Tahrir had called for a jihad against America, its allies, and moderate Muslim states. The purpose of the jihad was "to find and kill all of the *kafir,* the nonbelievers."

It had been long suspected that Hizb ut-Tahrir was just one piece of a larger global effort, with a mysterious grand benefactor, because no clear link to any single state sponsor had been established. There were no clear answers as to who had been funding them, who controlled the funds within the organization, and how the funds got transferred. Were they using couriers? Had they employed the Hawala informal banking system?

There were rumors of a master plan, its execution scheduled over a thirteen-year period. The leader of Hizb was also unknown at that point, as were where he resided and the identity of his senior officers. Past leaders had included university professors and clerics. There were anecdotal reports that the organization was actually headquartered in London and staffed by Europeans, but there had been no hard evidence to prove it.

Whatever the truth, Admiral Manfred recognized that Hizb ut-Tahrir, up-and-comers, seemed to have arrived on America's very doorstep. By extension, it was evidence of the continued circling of outside Islamist terrorist forces. Like sharks.

The attacks of September 11 and then the barely thwarted attack at Guantánamo. The war on terror went on, and Manfred knew that so far the United States, even with more than three thousand civilian dead and with mounting military casualties, had thus far gotten off easy compared to Poland and the Philippines. Manfred understood that sooner or later, it was inevitable, the terrorists would get lucky. Perhaps just once. But just once might be enough to cause such destruction, such a fundamental shift in the psyche of America, such a cry for government action and such a loosening of protection of individual freedoms, as to leave America forever changed.

At this point, he wanted nothing more than to fly south and go shake the intel he needed out of the three men captured aboard the freighter, to save the weeks of work and frustration he and his people would now endure in trying to figure out what those captured had been up to.

3

**May 6
Campbell Army Airfield
Ft. Campbell, Kentucky**

"I'm telling you, Hill, I felt something," McCall said. They were flying a tight circuit around the airfield.

"What are your gauges saying?" Hill asked. He was sitting at his station on this maintenance-check flight, and was trying to listen to the aircraft through McCall's complaining.

"My gauges are fine!" McCall snapped. "It's my ass that's telling me something's not right."

Hill was considering McCall's backside when he felt something too. A strange vibration came and went. Hill had spent enough time in these aircraft to know the difference between the usual vibrations and the unusual ones.

"Feel that?" McCall said suddenly.

"Yes ma'am, I felt it," Hill answered, thinking, closing his eyes, trying to imagine what it might be.

"What did it feel like to you?" McCall asked.

"A strange vibration," Hill replied, still thinking.

"No kidding?" McCall replied, and then to no one, "See that? That's why we have crew chiefs on the aircraft. 'A strange vibration.' What an inspired diagnosis!"

Hill ignored her, and then they both felt it again.

"I'm taking the ship back," McCall said.

"Roger that," Hill replied. It was nagging at him. He

didn't recognize the vibration. It felt like it might be tail system related, but he wasn't sure yet.

It came again, and then again, the frequency and strength increasing. An incredibly loud knocking suddenly began, as suspected, from the tail. For McCall, the pedals immediately became difficult to manage.

"Put it down! Put it down!" Hill shouted.

"Doing it!" McCall yelled back.

The Black Hawk came down fast, and McCall executed a rolling landing. The main wheels were already down when she tried to slow the aircraft by pulling the cyclic aft. Even with the knocking in the tail growing more and more violent, a new knocking sound was clearly heard above Hill's head.

"Droop stop pounding!" Hill bellowed into the intercom. The Black Hawk main rotor was equipped with droop stops and flap restrainers to prevent extremely high or low blade flapping at low revolutions per minute. As rotor speed decreased to approximately 70 percent rpm, the droop stops rotated from their dynamic position to their static position. The audible knocking of droop stops during shutdown, especially in a roll-on landing with aft cyclic applied just as McCall was doing, caused the droop stops to pound as they were rotating between the dynamic and static positions.

"You're going to make contact with the countermeasures!" Hill said.

McCall cursed herself, centered the cyclic, and the new knocking faded away. They slowed, and as they did and the engines wound down, the knocking slowed and then was gone.

Hill jumped down and went to the tail. He couldn't see anything obviously wrong with it. He later would find a breaker bar in the tail rotor driveshaft access compartment on a tail pylon support bracket. The right-hand tail rotor cable guide was damaged, as well as a hyloc rivet, and a doubler hole.

As soon as Hill found it, he knew he had left it in there. He knew that it had been his error. A part of him wanted to just own up to it, but instead he put the breaker bar away, and wrote up the damage he found as inexplicable. He prayed the powers that be would not ground all the Black Hawks in the battalion.

"Any luck?" McCall asked, approaching slowly.

Hill was badly startled. "What? Oh, yeah, there's some damage here in the access compartment. Beats me what did it. Have to let the experts at it."

McCall laughed. "Experts? You're the expert. You seriously don't know what caused it?"

"Naw," Hill laughed a bit too much with her. "Cable guide is damaged, but damned if I know what did it."

McCall sensed tension. "What's wrong, Hill?"

"Wrong?" Hill said, the smile falling from his face. "Nothing. Why?"

"Hey man," McCall answered, putting one hand on his arm, "it's okay if you're still having a rough time. You've been through a lot. No one expects you to just forget about all you've been through. Especially when we have to put one of these things down hard."

Hill dropped his gaze; he felt terrible. Here he was hiding a mistake he made, which might have killed them both, and she's trying to comfort him. Trying to help him past the haunting images of a time he was putting behind him as well as could be expected. Still, before he broke his back in Iran, he would never have made an error like leaving the breaker bar in there. Hill wondered if he still had what it took to be in this unit, if he was still mentally sharp enough, or if he was just too preoccupied now.

"I'm alright, really ma'am," Hill said finally.

McCall looked at him for a moment more, dropped her hand. "Okay. If you need to talk . . ."

"Thanks," Hill said, looking up.

McCall nodded, turned, and walked off. Hill watched her go, and then threw the ratchet he was holding out into the dark.

4

May 6
Al-Istiqlal Mosque
Jakarta, Indonesia
Greater Islamic Consortium

The mosque was the largest mosque in Southeast Asia, built by the government in 1984. More than 120,000 people could congregate there at one time.

The rectangular main prayer hall building was covered by a one hundred and fifty foot-diameter central spherical dome. The dome was supported by twelve round columns, and the prayer hall was lined by rectangular piers carrying four levels of balcony. Staircases at the corners of the building gave access to all floors. The main hall was reached through an entrance covered by a dome thirty feet in diameter.

The latter structure was directly connected to the arcades, which ran around the large courtyard. The mosque also provided facilities for social and cultural activities, seminars, and meetings.

Twelve men in a circle. They sat around a large table in a subterranean room beneath the mosque. The light was dim, reflected from the walls. Most only saw the shadows of the other men with no defined facial features. They had come from around the world to represent their region and their faction of Islamists.

"The operation should be cancelled. They have captured our advance team. The Americans will learn of the entire plan," grumbled one.

A man with a deep voice replied, "No, those men will remain silent long enough. We only need a few short weeks. The true question is how do we get the operation back on its timetable. Do we need to send another advance team?"

"I say we cannot proceed," said the first voice again.

"We must proceed," said another. "Fahed bin Rahman still lives as a prisoner. We insisted before the world that he be released, or that there would be dire consequences."

"And there were dire consequences. Warsaw is gone, Manila is useless," said a nasally voice.

"But we have been unable to declare victory, because even in the face of this destruction, the Americans and their allies have not complied. They did not release Fahed bin Rahman," said another.

"As I have said before, bin Rahman and how terrifying we appear will not matter if we can make this final operation work," said a man whose voice betrayed decades of cigarette smoking.

"I agree," a deep voice said. "As we have discussed, all we have to do is kill four million Americans. One American out of every seventy. Their present form of government will collapse under a wave of fear and paranoia. Their so-called freedoms, which they hold so dear, have always only been made possible by a naïve innocence. The innocence of a young country, full of hope, saturated with the belief that they are special and blessed. But just as a child surrenders innocence with each new feeling of vulnerability, with each new fear, with each unique experience of the world's ugliness, so too will the United States. We will traumatize this child called America beyond its breaking point, and with Allah's help, it will destroy itself."

"We must consider," the nasally voice said, "that spoiled children often throw tantrums when disappointed or hurt. There is no nation as spoiled, as undisciplined, as the Americans. We must be prepared for what sort of damage a child with such raw power might inflict if in the full paroxysm of panic."

"America will only be able to do what is within the will of Allah, just as our success or failure will be determined with the indulgence of Allah. I believe that if our plan works, Inshallah, America will be left in fits, but after some initial lashing out at the world, the nation will retreat within its borders and turn on itself. Paranoid, whimpering, committing self-inflicted cruelties. In any event, we can agree that each at this table is willing to give his life to see America crumble," said another.

Around the table, they nodded, they agreed. Anything was worth the price of ridding the world of America's arrogance.

"And what of the Hizb ut-Tahrir al-Islami men?" a tall man asked.

"What of them? Surely we can find a few more reasonably bright and motivated servants of Allah somewhere?" the deep voice replied.

The meeting went on for hours. After it concluded, one of the council members, a tall dark man, walked out into the Indonesian sun and humidity and placed a call on his cell phone. He was not Indonesian, or an Arab. He was not Pakistani, Afghani, or Persian. He was Bulgarian. Only half of the members of the council were from the Middle East. The others were from around the world; there was one from Brazil, another from the Sudan, and yet another from Russia.

"Yes, everything is proceeding as planned. The objectives at Ronald Reagan should be full and will have maximum return on investment, if we can achieve success at the precise moment laid out. Yes, I have full confidence in our representatives in this deal, but keep me apprised of any late developments," the tall dark man said. He then hung up the phone and walked to his waiting car. Looking to his right and left, he could see other council members making phone calls. He trusted the encryption system they had purchased, but he hoped just the same that the others were as careful with their words as he was. A man in a Polynesian shirt opened the car's rear door, and the dark man slid in.

"My hotel," he said, and the car pulled away.

5

May 8
Camp Delta Detention Center
Guantánamo Naval Base
Guantánamo Bay, Cuba

First Lieutenant Tim Saffed was a chaplain in the United States Army working with Muslim detainees at Camp Delta. He was here to spiritually minister to people his government had locked up without charges or trial because they were determined to be just that dangerous to the United States. In fact, some of those considered the least dangerous had been released, and several had immediately returned to terrorism, killing Americans or allies within weeks of being freed.

He had lost much sleep to his dilemma. He was a loyal and patriotic American. He believed that in order to do his job correctly, he would have to find compassion and understanding for the detainees. However, the detainees were tough to love. Despite the best efforts of the liberal media and activist groups, Saffed was not convinced. Anyone who dealt with the detainees knew that these were not bewildered innocents rounded up on farms in Afghanistan. The vast majority of these people were evil. Monsters who would gladly trade their lives for the chance to infect an American elementary school with smallpox, or worse.

At first, Saffed was stunned that the outside world would object to something as tame as using sleep deprivation in order to coerce these terrorists to divulge what they

knew. Saffed was no longer stunned or surprised by anything. Saffed had come to believe that the media and those
looking for political advancement would criticize anything
if they thought their agenda would be advanced. Even at
the expense of American lives.

No, LT Saffed would minister to them, listen to them,
try to be there for them spiritually, and when they were
subjected to near drowning as a method of interrogation,
Saffed would refuse to feel sorry for them. One reaps what
one sows.

He stopped his pacing and sat in a metal folding chair.
He was on call. On the other side of the door, the three
Middle Eastern men taken from the ship were being ques-
tioned. They would not be struck, or burned, or cut. But
they were exhausted, and hard men were trying to break
them with fear. Fear of death, fear of being forgotten. Fear
of being on the wrong side.

On the other side of the door, where Saffed could not
see them, the three men sat side by side with large masks
fitted over their faces. Each mask was connected to a long
tube, the other end disappearing behind a small wall. They
sat on chairs with their arms bound behind them. Four interrogators from the CIA stood over them. The three men
had resisted all questioning, and had not provided much information. Their interrogators knew who they were and
that they were members of Hizb ut-Tahrir, but knew nothing else. The prisoners were exhausted, foul-smelling, and
hungry. They had been asked a thousand questions about
their mission or purpose in this hemisphere without giving
answers, but during this session they had not been asked a
single question. They had simply been sat down and
bound, and the masks had been strapped to their faces.

Then, the mask on the man to the far left began to fill
with water. He screamed until it was clear to the others that
the mask was too full for him to scream any longer. The
man's feet kicked and his body jerked. Two CIA men held

him down. And then he fell still, his head slumping forward. The remaining two men began shouting in anger and fear, until the mask on the man in the middle began to fill with water. He shrieked in terror and tried to stand but could not. The two CIA men moved quickly to him. Soon, his screams were muffled and then he stopped moving.

The lead CIA interrogator stepped in front of the remaining man. Water slowly trickled into the mask. The third prisoner urinated. The two CIA men moved to this one from the last.

Suddenly, the CIA interrogator spoke. "Why were you going to Cuba?" The Arabic was a bit rough but was clearly understood. The prisoner jumped, startled that someone had spoken to him, and not simply and silently watched as he drowned. This question seemed like a wedge of hope trying to crack open the black. His mind was racing, panic creeping in, and then the water rushed into the mask. He screamed, but then the water flushed out as quickly as it had entered.

"Why Cuba?"

The prisoner blurted out, "Attack, three days from now!"

The CIA man raised a hand and the trickle of water stopped. "Where?"

"On America itself," the prisoner said, beginning to cry.

"Bullshit," the interrogator replied, and gave a nod to one of his teammates.

Water rushed in and the prisoner screamed, "It's true! Like Warsaw or Manila!" The water climbed past his mouth and he tried to breathe through his nose, but inhaled water. The interrogator raised a hand once more and the water was sucked from the mask so quickly, the wearer thought his eyes would be sucked out with it. Cool air rushed into the mask. He gasped, sputtered, and cried.

"Where in America? What type of attack?" the interrogator demanded.

"I do not know," the man gasped, the mask fogging.

"What?" the interrogator snapped. The two CIA men gripped the prisoner's arms forcefully.

"I do not know! I only know it is in three days. I have heard 'Ronald Reagan' in connection with the target. We were to learn more in Cuba!" The fear rose again in the prisoner. The interrogator nodded his head again and the mask filled with water. The prisoner howled, kicked, and bucked. One of the CIA men holding the prisoner's arms injected him with a small syringe. The panicking man immediately fell limp and the water was instantly sucked from the mask. All three masks were removed. Pulses were checked. A quick succession of thumbs-up went around. All three still alive.

"Get them out of here. We'll drown them again tomorrow," one said grimly. U.S. Army MPs appeared and carried the men away, out past LT Saffed. He rose to his feet. The lead CIA interrogator followed the prisoners out, and said only, "Don't worry Padre, we didn't kill 'em. No matter how tempting it might have been."

Saffed sighed and looked at his feet as the other CIA personnel walked past. None of them laughed, or said anything more. The CIA men were not enjoying this; they were not sadists. They had a job to do, upon which the lives of potentially hundreds of thousands of Americans depended. Even the lives of the liberal editors of the *New York Times* and *USA Today,* who would no doubt be running a breathless exposé on all this within the next year.

6

May 8
Southgate Apartments
Christian County, Kentucky

LTC Jack Hartman had the Assistant Secretary of Defense for Intelligence Oversight on the phone. Cat Hartman and Jack had divorced, mostly because of stress brought on by their careers, but had begun dating again when they realized how much they truly missed and loved each other.

Still, Cat worked in D.C., and Jack was stationed at Ft. Campbell. They spent many weekends together and went on trips whenever possible, but they had come to a point where no additional "together time" could be engineered. It was wearing on Jack. He walked with a bottle of water in one hand, a salami on pumpernickel in the other, and the phone balanced on one shoulder.

"Cat, I just want a committed relationship, a real one. I'm not sure I can keep this up anymore," Jack Hartman said, circling and coming in for a landing on the short leather couch. He put the water down on the coffee table and grabbed the phone.

"We can still be totally committed. We have some miles between us, but we always had that even when we shared an apartment. You were always getting deployed," Cat said.

"Yeah, I know, but that was different. Seeing you a couple days here and there without knowing how long that will go on is different than me leaving for a three-month mission or even a field exercise," Jack replied.

"Jack, we can make this work. It's only for a few more years until retirement. No one needs to sacrifice their careers yet. We're both playing important roles in the service of our country. We can't turn our backs on all of it," Cat said.

"Cat, I don't want to turn my back on anything, but the whole arrangement is not working out." Jack took a deep breath. "I think I need a break."

There was silence on the phone. Jack winced at it.

"Is there someone else, Jack?" Cat said next, "If that's what this is about, just come out and say so. You want to take a break so you can test-drive another relationship?"

Her voice wasn't angry, and she wasn't crying, but there was pain there. He was surprised at how weak Cat sounded, what a lack of independence she was showing. Jack also felt guilty. Not because there was someone else—there wasn't. He just needed a break to clear his head, to try and understand what it was he was feeling and what he wanted. That's what he was telling himself anyway.

"Cat, there is no one else," Jack began carefully. "I just need some time to figure this out, at a bit of a distance."

Cat answered, "Well, does that mean I shouldn't call?"

Jack thought for a moment. He hadn't figured out every aspect of what taking a break really meant.

"Maybe you can wait until I call you?" Jack said, and then instantly wished he could take it back.

"What? You're expecting me to sit by the phone and hope in the next few weeks you'll call? I'll tell you what, Jack, you take as big a break or whatever as you like, and don't bother calling!" Cat said.

"Cat, stop it, I didn't mean—" and Jack was interrupted by a distinct click from the other end. Cat had hung up.

Jack's head fell. He pulled his hand down across his

face and let out a long breath into it. Sitting back, he threw his feet up onto the coffee table next to his sandwich and wondered if he had done the right thing.

There was nothing he wanted more than to have Cat in his life. He loved her deeply, more than he ever had. But he didn't want a part-time relationship. He thought of her and loved her all day, every day, but seeing her only on weekends felt like high school dating, not a real relationship. It was like she had become more a getaway from his life than a real and present part of it.

The worst part was the self-doubt. He had been without her before. He knew he had been lucky to marry her in the first place, and he had been damn lucky that she took him back for a second try. Now he was telling her that he needed a break from the second chance she had given them. What was he doing? Did he really need to think? Or was he trying to punish her for not being here?

"Psycho-babble crap," he said aloud. "Stop analyzing yourself, Jack." He stood, went to the fridge, and traded his water for a beer. He carried the beer back over to the couch and scanned the bookshelves for something to read, to take his mind off everything. He had read them all, but was looking for an old friend to revisit. He spotted it, went over to it, and pulled it down. A novel titled *Skate,* by Jon Appleby. It was worn, its pages yellowed and the red and white cover faded a bit. He carried it and the beer back to the couch, leaned into the cushions, and took a swig from the bottle. He opened the novel to a random page and hid in the book for a while.

7

May 8
Clarksville Jujitsu & Aikido Dojo
Clarksville, Tennessee

"You guys lock up when you leave?" asked a compact man as he reached the door.

"You bet," Captain Rick Sirois replied.

"Thanks, Will," McCall called after the man as he stepped out and the door swung closed behind him with a swoosh. She looked back at Sirois and grinned. Sirois tugged his *butoku gi* straight, set his feet, raised his hands, and smiled back.

The dojo was large, with a low wall separating the cushioned floor from the wooden one. One wall was completely covered with mirrors. The dojo specialized in jujitsu and aikido, but students of other styles often came to practice and work out. There were striking dummies on water-filled pedestals, and on the walls were photos of masters, including a photo of the late and then-elderly Morehei Ueshiba, the O'Sensei of aikido. His receding white hair and full and triangular white beard framed his kind face.

McCall stepped away, went to the CD player boom box, hit play, and returned just as the heavy guitars of "Black Helicopters" began playing.

Sirois winced. "This song again? You know, it's hard for me to find my inner peace like a good *aikidoka* with this stuff playing. Who is this band again?"

"The group is called 'Abdullah,' and with or without the music, your aikido doesn't get any better. But it's a mixed CD, Sirois, something more your speed will come along," McCall teased.

Sirois and McCall were finally, officially, and publicly a couple. They had long tried to pretend, mostly to themselves, that they were just "hanging out." But these days, it was clear, even to the two of them, that they were in love.

McCall set her feet and bowed slightly, scarcely perceptibly, to Sirois. He smiled and bowed a bit more graciously. Sirois stepped forward and swung downward at McCall's head with a strange and unnatural chop. No one would actually attack someone in a dark alley this way, but it didn't matter. They were practicing aikido, a martial art not designed to determine how many muggers one could beat up. Serious *aikidoka,* or students of aikido, eschew even the idea of competition. Aikido was, as its name suggests, a martial art concerned with harmony of energy. Still, it could provide for impressive defense, and when Sirois's odd chopping swing was midway between their heads it was met and crossed by McCall's forearm. She deflected Sirois's energy to her right, she pivoted on her front foot, her left foot, and swung her right foot wide. She grasped downward on Sirois's right wrist with her right hand, and wrapped the fingers of her left hand around the back of his collar. She turned 180 degrees to the rear.

A single thought entered Sirois's head: "Uh oh."

Sirois was "floating" now, not heavy on his own feet, his momentum now guided by McCall. Just as she wanted it. She continued her turn further, and Sirois was off-balance, pitching forward slightly. Had she just let him go, he would have skidded on his hands and knees. She had other plans. She released his wrist, made a fist, and struck upward into Sirois's face. Not especially hard, but quickly. He reflexively lifted his upper body, still stumbling forward, bent at the waist. At this point, with his shoulders raised, bent in the middle, struggling to get back his feet, he looked clumsy and almost silly. In fact, he was vulnerable.

She skillfully, effortlessly shifted her weight again, and slid her forearm across Sirois's throat. Time to finish it. Although Sirois's momentum had him stumbling forward, his balance was teetering on the head of a pin now, and McCall slid her right foot assertively forward in the opposite direction she had dragged Sirois. Her forearm clotheslined him, and Sirois went sprawling. He lay on his back for a moment.

McCall extended her hand to help him up and smiled. Sirois took it and while standing said, "What was with the *atemi* strike to the face? You didn't need to do that." There was no mark on his face—she had not struck him that hard—but his ear was ringing.

"Hey, you do things your way and I'll do things mine, *uke*." McCall laughed, bowed again, and said, *"Origato."*

Sirois wasn't done complaining. "And that stupid music . . . yeah, yeah, you're welcome." They both bowed quickly.

McCall set her feet again, and Sirois came with the same attack once more. This time however, knowing what she would attempt, he did not play along as a good *uke* should. He let her hand pass over his, and then grabbed her around the waist.

"Could we just dance instead?" Sirois asked as the music changed to "In Da Club" by 50 Cent. McCall grinned and let her hips swing with his and the music.

Sirois smiled back and sang, "It's your birthday, we gonna party like, it's your birthday . . ."

McCall laughed, and threw her arms over Sirois's shoulders. She was beautiful, moving with perfect rhythm.

"See? Isn't this better than fighting? Throwing each other around? Punching your boyfriend in the face?" Sirois laughed.

"No." McCall shook her head, still smiling. She bit her

lower lip; loose hair fell into her face as she tossed her head with the beat. Her eyes closed, and she pressed her hips into him. Sirois felt the warmth of her, the curves of her. She slowly backed away from him, her eyes closed, dancing for him, their arms outstretched. Her hands slid down his sleeves, caressing, until she reached his hands. She opened her eyes, and Sirois was there, his hips swinging, grinning like a drunken monkey. She grasped his wrists, and turned them out until his palms faced upward flat. She twisted further, and Sirois's smile was gone. He fell to one knee. She released one of his hands, holding onto his right wrist, now with two hands. She bent her own arm, so that her elbow and his came together, never releasing his wrist. With a great deal of leverage and very little force, she turned his elbow over this way. Sirois went down on his face on the mat. She manipulated his arm so that it was extended out straight to one side, with the wrist viciously bent in and the elbow pushed flat to the floor.

The music changed—"Hey Now" by Xzibit—and Sirois tapped out. This time he didn't get up. It wasn't just the beating he was taking. That time, it was just disappointment. In one moment, she had been about the sexiest thing he'd ever seen in or outside of a dojo, and the next thing he knew he thought his joints were being pulled apart like the overcooked wing on a Thanksgiving turkey.

Sirois sighed, rose, bowed, and they exchanged their thank-yous.

McCall was grinning ear to ear. Sirois said, "Okay, now you be the *uke*, I'm tired of having my heart and hinges broken."

McCall shrugged. "Okay, whenever you're ready."

Sirois set himself, becoming serious. McCall came in, very slowly, her hands down at her sides, her face grave.

Sirois became nervous, he didn't recognize this, didn't know what defense might be best. She came at him. Sirois caught on in the last second, just before she kissed him.

Deeply, passionately. At first he thought this might be another one of her tricks, his eyes wide, but it became quickly obvious that it wasn't. They'd had enough aikido for one day.

They had met when she was flying for the 10th Mountain Division, and he was an instructor at the 101st Airborne Division's school on advanced Air Assault Insertion techniques. At first they had not gotten along very well. She thought he was arrogant, and he thought she was affirmative action suspended from a rotor, but respect grew both ways, and then when they both ended up in the Night Stalkers, a friendship had taken hold. Now, they were in love, a first for each of them.

The song ended and "The Weight" by The Band came on next. Sirois smiled, and said, "Now we're talking."

"I told you something your speed would come along." McCall smiled back, and kissed him again.

8

ECHELON intercepted communications. Phone calls, e-mail, faxes, and more. It was an automated global interception and relay system operated by intelligence agencies in five countries. The United States and its National Security Agency, or NSA, were in primary control. The United Kingdom, Canada, Australia, and New Zealand rounded out the rest of the partnership.

ECHELON's listening stations were directed at the Intelsat and Inmarsat satellites, which were responsible for the majority of communications traffic around the world.

After capturing the data ECHELON sifted through the data using "Dictionary." Dictionary was a complex network of computer servers, using proprietary software suites called Silkworth and Sire, which found significant information by searching for keywords, addresses, and locations. It didn't watch a particular phone number or a specific e-mail account. It watched them all. Every e-mail, every phone call, every hour, every day, every year. Sifting. Prioritizing. Reporting.

Located 150 miles southwest of Washington, D.C., in the mountains of West Virginia, an NSA station at Sugar Grove covered Atlantic Intelsats. Keywords were gleaned from telephone traffic and a report was generated.

That report, in this case a summary or "gist," was in the hands of Rear Admiral Greg Manfred, commander, Naval Security Group Command. He read it, and immediately rose to share the intelligence with CSS Deputy Chief Army Major General Kira VanDuben.

Entering her office, Manfred went right to the point. "General, we're piecing together what seems to clearly indicate an attack at Ronald Reagan National Airport." VanDuben was solidly built, with red hair, and a gentle strength to her face. She looked kind, but not completely hidden was a seasoned intelligence professional. Someone whose successes and failures had cost lives on both sides, always hoping the tally favored her side, and who knew that was just the nature of the business.

"Greg, we've put together a lot of these," VanDuben replied calmly. "Why is this one different?"

"We've got the name 'Ronald Reagan' intercepted, and a target, or possibly even multiple targets, being hit 'full of passengers,' " Manfred said.

"How good is it?" VanDuben asked, eyes narrowing.

"Intercepts from these sources have always panned out, and it is backed up by a lot of other chatter," Manfred said.

"Why are we getting this now? Is it part of a trick to have up focus in Washington? I mean, you know the deal, we get nothing for years and then all of a sudden we intercept the location and the type of target. Seems a bit easy, a bit convenient," VanDuben said. It was her job to be skeptical, just as everyone in intelligence should be.

"Yes, General, I know. But can we afford to be so cautious as to not take this seriously and pass it up?" Manfred asked. "As you know, we don't have to decide what to do with it. We just pass it up and let those making more than we are decide how, or if, to employ the information we've provided."

"You're assuming," VanDuben said, "that if the intel is bogus, they won't act. You have to remember, Greg, that even when they don't believe us, they will when useful, employ us as political cover. You and I don't face a reelection. We can give them real intel, developed by patriotic and hardworking people, with all the caveats that intelligence gathering is not a science. That some of what we collect and analyze is gold, and some of it isn't. And when their policy starts taking hits, they will point at what we gave them and say it wasn't their fault, that they were misled by the intelligence they received."

"Yes, General, I know, but it is still the conclusion of the first-line analysts that an attack was planned for Ronald Reagan National Airport. We can't sit on that," Manfred countered.

He was right of course. It was the primary risk of working in the intelligence field during an era of liberal press and intelligence-hating pseudo-intellectuals. If you pass up the intel, and it's wrong, you become the whipping boy for the administration and Congress. If you're right and you withhold something, then it becomes a storm of a different kind. At least in the former scenario, fewer Americans civilians were likely to die.

Manfred continued, "Combined with other sources of intelligence, including the interrogations of the men captured aboard the *Odette Debs,* it seems undeniable that there is an attack planned. Thanks to the hard work of dedicated and talented people, we are confident we know where and roughly when it will be. We have to pass it up."

VanDuben nodded, but said, "Either way, there's going to be a price to pay. Especially if you're only half right, if you only have half the information correct."

Manfred nodded. Discovering the planning of an attack but then getting the method or location incorrect went over worse than not predicting the attack at all. Americans seemed to forgive much more readily when an attack was a complete surprise than if the intel services only got it partly right, or if they had the slightest inkling and kept it quiet.

"Pass it up," VanDuben sighed.

"Right away," Manfred said, and walked out.

9

May 9
6/160th Mission Briefing Room
Ft. Campbell, Kentucky

Lieutenant Colonel Hartman stood at the podium as the pilots of the 6/160th SOAR took their seats. The room was filled with row after row of metal folding chairs, occupied by pilots and crew members. Hartman stood in front of them, on a small stage made of plywood wrapped in gray commercial-grade carpet. He leaned on a podium on the stage and a projection screen hung behind him.

He waited, even after the small talk had subsided, letting the pause get pregnant. "We have been given a combat mission within the borders of the United States."

The small bit of whispered, back-of-the-room conversations that had persisted through the pause ceased. There was no sound, just a shift. Everyone leaned in just a bit to hear what was coming next.

Hartman continued, "Intel says that there is going to be an attack on an aircraft at Ronald Reagan National Airport. We will deploy to Washington, and fly around and over the airport in defense against a shoulder-fired antiaircraft weapon. You will have clearance to fire on anyone or anything you decide is a threat. The rules of engagement are liberal on this one. Before I turn this over to Major Ryan for the specifics, are there any questions?"

A hand went up. "What about *posse comitatus*?"

Hartman had anticipated this. "*Posse comitatus* does not apply. The *Posse Comitatus* Act of 1878 proscribes us from making an arrest, from seizing evidence. In the simplest terms, we the military are forbidden to act as law enforcement in this country. We are not undertaking anything of the sort. This mission is much more along the lines of an enemy hitting our shores, and we must repel him. Understand this . . . if you see someone with a shoulder-launched antiaircraft missile at Ronald Reagan Airport, you are not to attempt to arrest him, nor are you to attempt to seize evidence. You are to take that target out, with extreme prejudice. Is that clear?"

A chorus of "Yessir" went up from the Night Stalkers.

"Outstanding. Here is Major Ryan," Hartman said, stepping back to make way for the XO to take the podium. Major Mike Ryan began the more detailed briefing as Hartman strode to his office. He picked up the phone and did something he'd never done before. He compromised a mission.

When he was finally put through to Cat, everything he had planned to say seemed to vanish.

"Hello? Jack?" she said again.

"Sorry, Cat," Hartman began. "Got distracted for a second. Listen, I'm going to be in D.C. for a couple days, arriving later today. I feel terrible about the phone call yesterday. Let me buy you dinner."

There was a pause, and Jack knew he was going to be turned down. "Jack, I can't. I've just got too much to do. I'm catching an early flight out of Dulles tomorrow and I—"

"What?" Jack interrupted. "Don't fly, Cat!"

Another pause, and then Cat asked, "What are you talking about Jack?"

"Listen, Cat, check it out. Don't fly." Jack wished he could just blurt the whole thing out, but as it was he was compromising the mission, the intelligence, everything. But this was Cat, how could he let her fly knowing what he knew?

"Okay, Jack, I'll check it out. Give me a call tonight when you can," Cat said, reading something she could not remember before in his voice. Fear.

A wave of relief washed through Jack Hartman. "Okay, I will, I'll call as soon as I can. Love you."

"Love you, too," Cat said, puzzled and a bit shaken.

They hung up. Air rushed out of Hartman as he put the phone down. Loving this woman is making me older by the minute, he thought. He returned to the briefing.

"Sirois, you'll lead off and be circling here; you've got a key piece of this mission. If someone were going to take up a firing position on this airport, my guess is it would be in the shrubs close to the river," Ryan said, pointing to the area on aerial photographs he had projected on the screen behind him.

Sirois's hand went up. "At that point, sir, won't we be the only aircraft flying over the airport? What is it I'm protecting?"

There was some grumbling, some chuckling.

Ryan turned square to Sirois. "You're right, Sirois. You'll be the only thing up; the only target the bad guys will have in this sector. You won't really be protecting any aircraft at that point. But aren't you a bit angry at the thought of it? Can't you imagine it? Some maggot with an antiaircraft missile, unable to shoot down military aircraft in Afghanistan, choosing instead to shoot down a plane with hundreds of civilians. Women, children, the elderly. In our own capital city. Doesn't it make you mad? Don't you want to send a message? Isn't that enough reason to get up there?"

Sirois nodded his head slowly. "Yes sir, it is."

"Good. I hope you all feel the same way," Ryan said to the room.

The was a shout of agreement from the audience.

"Alright, let's continue . . ." Ryan said, turning back to the photos of the airport.

10

Sirois swept in a low circular orbit. It was hard to imagine that he was on a combat mission as he passed the airport tower on his left and off to his right, closer than he imagined they would be, the Jefferson Memorial and the Washington Monument. The proud structures were stark white within the green landscaping. Sirois wondered how long it would be before the terrorists started making a real effort at hitting the monuments instead of office buildings. While the human tragedy in the attacks had been enormous, the office buildings could be rebuilt. Monuments were never the same. He pictured tour guides saying things like, "And this is the third Washington Monument, since the first two were knocked down by terrorists. You'll notice the concrete barricades and minefield, not to mention the antiaircraft emplacement built into the top of the obelisk."

Sirois swung around and quickly passed over three terminals, each with a litter of large passenger aircraft seemingly nursing on extended gangways. Off to his left, a series of odd S-shaped buildings bordered on a large area of shrubs and trees.

"There could be a missile every ten feet in there." Sirois shook his head.

As expected, Sirois's AH-6J and the other Night Stalker

helicopters were the only aircraft moving. All flights into and out of Reagan National had been cancelled, to the great economic detriment of D.C. and even to the country. Every minute this airport was not functioning cost the nation millions of dollars. Still, a 757, blown out of the sky and turned into a tumbling fireball, plowing into the Mall, would have far more dire consequences.

Nothing was moving below. From his seat in the C2 Black Hawk, Hartman knew that if someone had come to knock down an aircraft, today would not be the day. No targets, save his people. He also realized that circling the airport would not have been enough. A terrorist could just as easily stand in the trees on the far side of the water, or get out of a car on the bridge, or hide in countless other places. His pilots were there to put on a show of force, with the hope that they would act as a deterrent to today's and future terror plans.

Hartman knew, however, after the first ten minutes, that nothing was going to happen here today. It was just after 0700h when he settled back and prepared himself mentally for what was going to be a long, boring day.

Sirois centered the cyclic and turned his head hard to the left, hearing a loud satisfying click in his neck. In the corner of his eye, he saw it. Someone in the shrubs, off near the river. More movement, and then light reflected off something.

"Arrow 6, this is Bullet 13," Sirois radioed Hartman. "Unknown target, at our eleven o'clock. We're going to check it out."

"This is Arrow 6, roger that," Hartman's voice came back instantly. Sirois lowered the collective. He pushed the cyclic left and applied a bit of left pedal. The nose of the nimble AH-6J Little Bird helicopter fell down and left, and the aircraft rolled left. Once his aircraft was pointed at the target, Sirois raised the collective, and centered the cyclic. He eased off the pedal and the helicopter was running nose-down at the person trying to hide in the vegetation.

In the FLIR, or Forward Looking Infrared, Sirois could see the clear outline of a man, pointing something back at him.

"This is Bullet 13, he's aiming something at us, but I'm not sure what. It doesn't appear to be very big," Sirois radioed.

"What is that?" his copilot said to himself, looking hard at the FLIR.

"This is Arrow 6, fire a burst into the ground far enough from the target to ensure not hitting him, but close enough that he gets the message," Hartman replied.

Hartman had scarcely said the words when he heard the report of Sirois's two 7.62mm M134 miniguns. The large rounds stitched through the grass close to the shrub line. Sirois's Little Bird then buzzed directly over the man. Sirois moved the cyclic to the right, increased collective, pushed gently on the right pedal, and the helicopter made a climbing right turn. He leveled off and straightened his course, and then executed yet another descending left turn. Beneath him he could see the man had sprung from the shrubs and trees, a camera with a long telephoto lens in one of the outstretched hands. Sirois circled him, shaking his head. It appeared the fourth estate was surrendering.

"This is Bullet 13," Sirois radioed. "Sir, I seem to have taken a member of the press as a prisoner. Can someone come out and get this guy?"

"This is Arrow 6, they're on the way. Keep an eye on him until they get out there," Hartman answered.

Sirois descended and circled the reporter low enough and quickly enough that while it would have made for great "art," the photojournalist just kept his hands up, flinching with his entire body with every lap Sirois made. The sound of the rotors prevented the reporter from hearing his own whimpering at each pass.

Not all that far away, beneath the surface of Washington, four nondescript men sat on four different Metro trains, all approaching Washington's Federal Triangle Metro stop. They each had a JanSport backpack between their feet. Three looked like college students. The fourth might have been a lawyer or a doctor, dressed down, but a person of some refinement.

The Federal Triangle Metro stop was connected to the Ronald Reagan Building and International Trade Center. Every day, a herd of federal employees packed the Metro trains for this stop and climbed up the escalators to their jobs.

Cassie Thompson had worked at CEEBIC, the Central and Eastern Europe Business Information Center, in the Reagan Building until last September. It was closed by sweeping cuts aimed at slashing an impossibly large budget deficit, but she had found work one floor up with the U.S. Department of Commerce. She had been able to continue to put her business and language skills to use in the service of her country, and she loved her new job. She had short red blonde hair, styled with a touch of gel, and she had an easily provoked smile. On this day, she was riding into work, just another day, when she noticed that the older man next to her was preoccupied with the backpack between his feet. His movements were not the same bored movements everybody who was awake made on the Metro. His hands had purpose, darting in and out of the pack. He looked up at the map for the third time, tried to see something out the window, went back to the pack.

On three other trains, all coming into the Federal Triangle stop, the three younger men were behaving in exactly the same manner.

In each of the backpacks were two half-gallon containers, each holding a household cleanser. One full of chlorine bleach, the other full of ammonia. As the trains began to slow, approaching Federal Triangle, the containers were opened inside the packs and the men kicked the packs over beneath the seats. They then rose and moved toward the doors. It was 7:45 A.M.

Cassie saw the whole thing, and in the next split second knew something was very wrong. A man so intently working with the bag would then kick it over and forget it? Instinctively, she reached for the bag, and saw immediately that it was leaking. Something noxious seared her nose and throat, and she gagged. She stumbled away as the fumes rose and those sitting closest to the bag began choking, and also trying to escape.

In the bag, and running out onto the floor, on all four trains coming into Federal Triangle, bleach and ammonia mixed. A concoction that had overcome many housewives hoping to combine the cleaning power of each chemical, but instead the toxic brew killed them and left them dead on their kitchen floors.

The ammonia liberated chlorine from the bleach. Chlorine gas was released. A gas with eight electrons in its outer shell was inert. Largely harmless. The chlorine had seven electrons in its outer shell. It was absolutely desperate to get that last electron, and literally ripped other atoms apart to get it. Nasal passages, trachea, and lungs were torn apart at the atomic level, causing massive cellular damage. For those exposed, chlorine gas caused a great deal of pain and, often, death.

Cassie signaled for an emergency stop and the train ground to a halt still in the tunnel, short of the platform. The door was forced open by the man who had kicked the bag over and he stepped out, followed by a rush of passengers. On the three other trains, much the same was happening.

People were trampling each other in an effort to get off

Cassie's train. There was not enough chlorine gas to make the tunnel itself deadly, but there was hysteria, and people were killed trying to get out.

Survivors emerged from the tunnels and into the Federal Triangle station shrieking, crying, and shouting about a chemical attack. Those on the platform saw passengers emerging from four different tunnels, vomiting, carrying the unconscious, running each other over. Panic ensued, and there was pandemonium as everyone rushed for the surface.

Cassie was knocked to her knees twice, and then strong arms lifted her to her feet. She heard a couple of words in Russian as the powerful stranger hustled her to the platform. She barely glimpsed her benefactor before she lost him in the crowd, the swell of people carrying her to street level almost without her effort. She'd never see the Russian again, but thereafter the sound of a Russian accent would feel safe to her.

In all that morning, hundreds were killed. Much of the public transportation in the nation's capital was halted. Much of the city's business was disrupted. The capital of the United States of America had been attacked. Again.

11

A FedEx truck, white with the patriotically colored logo painted along its sides, entered the Brooklyn Battery Tunnel bound for Manhattan. Traffic packed the roadway, and the FedEx truck was packed with six fifty-five gallon drums of diesel fuel. Entering the same tunnel from the opposite direction was another FedEx truck with an identical cargo. Rassim Mgani was driving the one headed into the city, although his New Jersey driver's license read Anthony Ramona.

There was another pair of FedEx vehicles, entering in exactly the same way at exactly the same time, with exactly the same payload, at the Holland Tunnel. And at the Lincoln Tunnel. And the Queens Midtown Tunnel. And even atop the Queensboro Bridge. A fleet of innocuous, white trucks. Familiar to everyone, largely invisible to Americans wrapped up in their own lives. Delivering mayhem.

At the same time, three Ford F-250 pickups each approached the Brooklyn Bridge, the Manhattan Bridge, and the Williamsburg Bridge. In the rear bed of each of these trucks was a child's plastic pool set on top of a bed of cinder blocks and large terra-cotta tiles. Each pool was covered by a sheet of plywood, secured in place by bungee cords. Snaking under the plywood and into the powdery contents of the pools were strips of magnesium ribbon, easily purchased at three dollars per foot. The pools were goofy, green with large stuck-on eyes, and made to look like turtles.

Each pool was nearly filled with the contents of four fifty-pound bags of ferric oxide powder, a common alternative abrasive to sand for sand blasting. The two hundred pounds of ferric oxide were mixed with sixty-seven pounds of fine granular aluminum, ordered on the Internet without raising the least little inquiry.

At 10:30 A.M. the FedEx trucks slammed on their brakes and skidded to a stop. The drivers went into the backs of the trucks and pushed over the drums of diesel. The flammable fuel rushed out the back doors into the tunnels, and in one case across the bridge decking. Traffic almost instantly snarled. The FedEx drivers then calmly stepped into the lakes of diesel, sat down, shouted "God is great" in Arabic, and lit the fuel. A wall of fire erupted in each case, the driver disappeared, and thick, black, choking smoke was produced. In the tunnels, the smoke overwhelmed the air-changing systems. Thousands of people panicked and tried to escape the tunnels. On the Queensboro Bridge, the roadways were blocked as cars piled up and drivers and passengers ran from the burning diesel, fearing an explosion.

Meanwhile, just minutes later, the drivers of the Ford F-250 pickup trucks carrying the children's pools used small torches to light the magnesium fuses. The fuses sparked and hissed as they burned their way out of the cabs, into the beds, and into the pools of ferric oxide and aluminum.

There was a police presence at each of the three target bridges. They had been especially vigilant because of the attack in Washington a couple of hours before, but were now distracted by the storm of radio traffic reporting fires in the tunnels.

The pickups ran through the police protecting the anchorages of the suspension bridges. The startled police fired at the pickups, but could not stop them. The pickups crashed through to the anchorages, not far from the exiting cables that ran up to the tops of the bridge towers. The drivers did not exit the vehicles. They did not run. They simply sat in their seats, hands on head. Waiting. The police approached cautiously, guns drawn, shouting instructions that the drivers ignored.

The thermite reactions in the kiddie pools began. A pound of the mixture can burn through two-inch plate steel almost instantly. Beneath each of the cables holding the three bridges aloft, in each of the beds of the three pickup trucks, 267 pounds of materials reacted. The glow was white-hot. The temperature in the beds of the pickups reached over three thousand degrees Fahrenheit. The massive cables were not in contact with the reaction, but they were too close. The beds of the pickups became molten. The drivers and the police caught fire or even melted before they could react. The cables themselves reached over one thousand degrees Fahrenheit, and their tensile strength was sapped away. The cables failed.

Thousands of steel strands, each normally capable of supporting tons of weight, ripped apart, like brittle pasta, until the entire cable tore loose. Each of the bridges was at this point asymmetrically supported, with one cable running the length of one side, while the other side had nearly no support at all. This applied horizontal torque to the deck and vertical torque on the towers. The bridges were ripped apart by their own massive weight. The Brooklyn Bridge roadway, first opened in May of 1883, fell 135 feet into the river below. Fifteen thousand tons of the landmark structure collapsed before witnesses could process what they were seeing.

Cars from all three of the crowded bridges plummeted into the water below, along with masses of concrete, Maine granite, and steel. People could be seen tumbling, and there were many bodies in the water, as the deadly rain of debris and vehicles fell from above.

CNN and other news outlets were filled with nearly apoplectic journalists, many of whom were on the island of Manhattan. Millions began to realize they were being cut off from the mainland and they panicked. They remembered what happened to Warsaw and Manila. They were aware of the attack in the capital just that very morning.

It started slowly at first, but soon there was a stampede of millions of people headed to the ferries and all manner of boats and ships, and north into Harlem, trying to get off the island. Thousands were killed, crushed by their fellow New Yorkers. It was nothing short of chaos. A mob brawl broke out near Penn Plaza, in the shadow of Madison Square Garden, as the desperate fought over cabs and entry to Penn Station. Fires, broken windows, sirens, with courageous and yet frenzied first responders trying to decide what to do next. At the corner of Hudson and King Streets, a fire truck was stolen and driven down West Houston toward the Hudson River.

On Fifth Avenue, at the corner of East Fourteenth Street, a rotund man brained a cabbie with a tire iron and then proceeded to try to drive north on Fifth, hopelessly snarling what little traffic had still been moving.

The population of Manhattan, once well over a million people, in the following days was exceeded by the population of Hartford, Connecticut. Those who came to be known as "the Manhattan refugees" would spend days being rescued. The business of Manhattan, the pulse of the U.S. economy, was stilled, even though not a single building within the borough had been directly touched by the terrorists.

12

May 10
San Francisco, California

At 9:30 A.M., an earthquake struck San Francisco. It measured a moderately strong 6.4 on the Richter scale, and did only minor damage. But, coming at 12:30 P.M. Eastern time, during the coverage of nightmarish scenes from New York and reports of a chemical attack in Washington, D.C., the earthquake itself caused undue fear.

Even CNN was asking its "expert" guests if the earthquake could actually be yet another attack. This was all the people of San Francisco needed to hear; they were panic-striken and clogged the streets in an effort to escape the city. No one went anywhere near the suspension bridges. The Golden Gate Bridge stood empty, where normally over one hundred and ten thousand cars crossed daily. Its tall orange towers cast shadows onto a deck devoid of any activity.

The earthquake was not, of course, a terrorist attack. It was bad luck, unfortunate timing. But the damage, loss of life, and terror it caused had not been seen in San Francisco in decades.

13

May 10
Evening
Alban Towers
Cathedral Heights
Washington, D.C.

"It's awful, Jack," Cat said, leaning up against him on the sofa. She lived in an imposing and beautiful Gothic revival building, once a dorm for Georgetown and directly across from Washington National Cathedral. It had been converted into a more than comfortable apartment community.

He had arrived at her apartment shortly after dark. The patrol of Ronald Reagan National Airport had been called off shortly after the attacks in the Metro. It became obvious that they had been guarding the wrong mode of public transit.

Jack and Cat Hartman sat and watched television, transfixed as night had settled in over Manhattan. News helicopters circled as boats were still helping people off the island. It looked like a new Dunkirk. A few of the tunnels off the island were open again, but they were already jammed with vehicles trying to get out, and many people were afraid to use them anyway. There was no way of knowing the exact number of dead in Manhattan. Soldiers, the National Guard, had been brought in to help establish order and to aid in the evacuation of those who wanted to leave.

"With all the extra intelligence, with the new law enforcement powers, even though we took the war overseas to the terrorists, they can still hit us in such a coordinated and organized manner. How did we not see this happening? The amount of communication it must have taken to set this up, why didn't we get wind of this?" Cat said, sweeping her hand at FOXNews.

"Cat, we always knew we'd get hit again. You can't fight a war without getting hit back at least occasionally," Jack said softly.

Tears welled into Cat's eyes as she spotted a mother carrying a small boy, trying to get onto a rocking boat.

"Jack, I'm going to resign," Cat suddenly announced. "I'm missing the important things in life. I'll move to Ft. Campbell with you. Maybe we can start a family, do what we should have been doing from the beginning. You were right, a total commitment."

"Cat . . . ," Jack started to say.

"No Jack, you were right. What am I doing all this for? We've only got a short time here and I'm spending mine clawing my way through the Pentagon bureaucracy?" Cat insisted.

"I can't let you, Cat," Jack replied. "Not like this. You can't come join me at a time like this. They need you more than ever now; people will get overzealous again in the name of intel collection and national security."

"No, Jack, that's not it. I've had it—I've had enough. Let's just start new," she said.

Jack took her face in one hand and said, "I'll make you a deal. Wait. Wait a few months. Put some time between you and today. Then we'll discuss it again, okay? A few months won't make any difference if you are really supposed to resign."

She looked deep into his eyes, saw the calm there, the reassurance, and silently nodded. He smiled, and wrapped his arms around her. He'd like to see her get out of this city. The capital would always be a target. It was next to impossible that anyone would come to the interior of the country to attack Ft. Campbell.

She pushed gently, and they separated.

"I love you, Jack," Cat whispered.

"I love you more." Jack smiled, and they kissed. Lightly at first, and then deeply. She fell back onto the sofa, and their kisses never broke. His fingers were in her hair, her hands around his back.

"You can spend the night, right?" she asked into his mouth, never opening her eyes.

He said nothing, and kissed her even more passionately.

14

May 11
New York Field Office
Federal Bureau of Investigation
Temporarily relocated to
Office of Drug Enforcement Administration
Newark, New Jersey

The New York Field Office of the FBI was normally located at Federal Plaza, but since the attack on the bridges, they had moved temporarily to Newark, sharing space with the DEA. There wasn't a lot of space, but the FBI was grateful to have it.

"From the residue at the anchorage points and reports from survivors, we suspect that the explosives used to bring down the bridges were crude but large and obviously effective thermite devices. We believe detonation was achieved by simply lighting a magnesium fuse, based on eyewitness accounts," Special Agent Danny Clough said as he flipped through PowerPoint slides of the devastation left by the attack. Clough worked out of the New York office, but was a coordinator of antiterror task forces, put together locally wherever they are needed, comprised of FBI and state and local law enforcement.

"We immediately began looking for odd or suspicious shipments of the materials necessary to make such large thermite mixtures, in such quantity, and we have narrowed it down to three locations. Three locations have had large inexplicable shipments of ferric oxide powder and fine granular aluminum. One is a plant in Arkansas that makes pottery, one is a warehouse in Oregon, and the third is a farm in Vermont. We are assembling strike teams and warrants for all three of these places, and we will hit them tomorrow, early."

"Clough," said one of three figures sitting partially obscured in the dark room, "we could not narrow it down any further than this? The plan is to storm the Pottery Barn of Goat's Knuckle, Arkansas, to see if some hayseed knocked down the Brooklyn Bridge with a kid's science experiment gone Frankenstein on us?"

"Sir, it's the best we could do. We have narrowed it down from a list of over one hundred potential targets, but we are left with three," Clough said confidently, proudly. "We are going to seize control of those properties, search them, and hopefully we'll have some answers."

"The press will begin their chant about civil liberties. The conspiracy-nut wackos actually thought this bureau was taking sides in the last election, using our task forces to intimidate the president's opponents and critics," said another dark shape.

"Yes, sir, there will be bad press," Clough said flatly.

"What answers do you hope to have?" The first voice, Assistant Director in Charge Henry King, spoke up again, leaning into the light.

"We'll have the next step, sir," Clough replied. "With some luck, we'll be one step closer to knowing who planned, financed, and coordinated this attack."

There was silence for a moment, and then King said, "Very well, Clough. Go ahead with this, but you keep me apprised of every detail along the way."

"I will," Clough said.

"Are you going out to one of these sites?" asked the one man who hadn't said anything yet.

"Yes," Clough answered. "I'm going to Vermont."

"Thank you, Clough, that's all we need. Keep safe and keep us updated," King said.

Clough nodded and exited the office. After the door

closed behind him, King turned to the other men and said, "They changed America yesterday. Although the number of dead won't get anywhere near the 9/11 death toll, and we have seen nothing like the attack in Poland, those images combined with the pictures of Manhattan refugees being pulled off boats onto New Jersey shores have inflicted one more scar on the American psyche. These bastards keep hitting us, and with every blow, they change who we are. They increase what we are willing to pay, in treasure and freedom, to stop them. It's become so cliché that no one will say it anymore, but if their goal is to be rid of the America that existed in the summer of 2001, they are succeeding."

"Stop being so geocentric, King," one of the other men said. "The whole world is changed, so it is only natural that we change. We as a nation adapted our national character to the aftermath of the Civil War. Our culture and our national psyche, as you put it, was changed by World War I, and again by the Great Depression, and again by World War II."

"That doesn't mean I can't be saddened by the change I'm seeing," King said. "It doesn't make me less patriotic if I don't like the change I'm living through."

"Doesn't it?" the man said from the shadows. "Hasn't history judged harshly those who criticized necessary shifts in the natural culture, made to better enable America to survive in whatever new world in which she found herself? Charles Lindbergh was a hero to many, but history now records that he gave a speech two months before Pearl Harbor, on September 11 ironically, in which he claimed that, along with the British and the Roosevelt administration, the Jews were pressing us into war. And that the only victors in World War II would be chaos and prostration."

"But today, people still think of Lindbergh as a patriot and hero," King countered.

"Ah, but that was because back then, the press could be controlled a bit more by convincing people not to advertise in papers that ran antiwar columns and stories. Not today," the man said. "Today, you sell more papers, and more advertising, by being antiestablishment. The only problem is the establishment is actually America itself. They are against change, even if the change is necessary to preserve the American way of life."

King said nothing; the conversation was spiraling into the fruitless. His two guests from Washington had seen their briefing, had had a chance to pontificate, and now King had had enough. He said nothing, and the men rose to leave.

King went to the intercom on the table, pressed a button, and said, "Helene, the congressmen are ready to leave."

A voice came back, "I'll be very happy to show them out, Mr. King."

"Thanks, Helene," King said. He stepped toward the door, meeting the two men and shaking their hands formally.

"You keep your head down, King, and after what we've been through, we need a few victories in the war on terror," one said sternly, making eye contact.

"Yes sir," King said, and then closed the door behind them. Once, King thought, I was just a cop. . . . How'd I end up in politics?

15

May 12
Al-Istiqlal Mosque
Jakarta, Indonesia
Greater Islamic Consortium

"I had hoped for more casualties in Washington," said the nasally voice. "We were led to believe that chlorine gas is more deadly than it proved to be."

The gravelly, cigarette-ruined voice answered, "There were hundreds killed in Washington, with only a few gallons of chemicals purchased in a supermarket. The capital of the world's most powerful nation was brought to a standstill with cleaning products."

"And that combined with watching the bridges of Manhattan fall . . . Allah was generous indeed," added the tall dark man.

The man with the bass voice: "I must admit, when the cowardly Americans suspected we created an earthquake in California, I found it rather amusing."

There was no laughing at this. The men around the table smiled thin smiles, but no one laughed out loud.

"That was the contribution of Allah, the just and merciful," said the nasally voice.

There was a murmuring of agreement, and then the gravel-voiced man again: "Where are we with the next phase? Is everything in place?"

"Very nearly," said the deep voice. "The assets are believed to be in place, although our advance teams have gone silent now. Nothing will be confirmed until the next men we have sent verify that everything is ready in the coming days, Inshallah."

"And the Hands of Allah?" The nasally voice. "Are they in place? Is our goal still to kill four million Americans?"

The ease with which they spoke of killing four million Americans, or any people regardless of nationality, would have been chilling to anyone. Except these men.

"They are in their primary staging locations. We will kill at least four million Americans, Inshallah, and the world will be free at last from their tyranny," replied the deep voice.

There was silence and then a light, almost courteous applause from all those present. The room fell quiet once again, and then the Muslim call to prayers could be heard filtering down from above.

16

The latest videotape was reportedly from Qaedat al-Jihad,
an arm of Al-Qaeda that originated with resistance to the
American liberation of Iraq.

"America must withdraw its infidel military forces immediately to within its own borders. The attacks on Washington and New York were mere demonstrations of our
presence," the video played out to millions of the satellite
television station's audience. "We will next attack with
weapons of mass destruction as we did in Warsaw and
Manila."

At this point, images had been crudely cut in of the utter
nuclear destruction of Poland's capital city and the anarchy
that had followed the biological attack on the Philippine
capital.

"If the American people are truly in control of their
government . . . if the Americans do not live in merely the
illusion of democratic rule, they must rise up and demand
their soldiers be moved back to within American or at least
NATO borders within one week. Else, Allah willing, we
will destroy entire American cities in reprisal for the con-
tinuing occupation of our holy lands," the tape concluded.

Outside the Al-Jazeera compound, poking into a dumpster with a length of rusty pipe, Martin Bragdon was actu-

ally watching and waiting. This approach had worked well
for him in tracking down where the tapes had come from
once before, and after the attacks stateside he was more
than willing to try it again.

Bragdon's clothes were ordinary, his eyes hidden by
sunglasses, and he had grown a scraggly beard. His hair
was ratty, in dire need of washing.

Three floors above him, in the Al-Jazeera building, a
purple towel appeared in a window.

"Purple?" he asked himself. He had been expecting
white. Purple meant nothing, at least nothing they had
arranged. His gut told him to abort, but just then an old
man came out into the street. The courier of the videotape
Bragdon had been waiting to follow? A white towel would
have been the signal that his target was exiting, that the old
man was the quarry. What did purple mean?

"Screw it," Bragdon hissed, tossing the pipe in the
dumpster, and hurried to pace the old man. Just as the last
courier had, the old man zipped back and forth through the
alleyways of Doha. The last courier had been a kid, less
cautious. This old man kept looking back, without being
obvious. Was he checking to see if he was being followed?
Was he checking to see if he was STILL being followed?
The old man climbed onto garbage cans and then went
over a seven-foot wall.

Bragdon stopped. He was surprised the old geezer even
made it on top of the cans, but then to slip over the wall?
Sirens were going off in his head. He had no idea about the
one-week deadline on the videotape, he hadn't seen it, but
he had been waiting for thirty-six hours after the attacks in
the United States, poking around outside Al-Jazeera, to
pick up this trail. Now the trail just led over the wall.

Bragdon looked around, took a deep breath, and hopped
onto the garbage cans. He slowly, cautiously looked over
the wall. Just as his line of sight cleared it, he was struck in
the forehead by a heavy piece of hardwood. He went

sprawling backwards into the dusty alley. The pain went straight through to the back of his head. He was incredibly dizzy and nauseated. He could see them, like rats, coming over the wall. Down onto him. He forced himself to his feet just in time to have two men grab his arms and a third start delivering punishing body blows to his ribs and abdomen. The punches, coupled with the nausea, were more than his stomach could take. He vomited, splashing the attacker punching him. In revulsion, that man stepped back.

In a flash of clarity, Bragdon understood it was then or never. He spun his right arm free and behind the man to his right. Grabbing a fistful of the man's greasy hair, he flung him forward at the vomit-covered puncher. The two men came together, not hard but off balance, neither wanting to smear the vomit any further. That left a full second for Bragdon to cut his opposition down by one. His right hand flashed hard and fast, his thumb rigid on top of his fist, striking the man holding his left arm in the throat. There was a crack and then a gurgling sound. Bragdon drew back the same hand, flattened it, and drove it up into the man's nose. It was crushed, the man's eyes rolled back, and he fell twitching.

Bragdon staggered backwards, still unsteady on his feet, blood trickling down his face, and faced the other two. They had stopped and stared, shocked at their comrade. Bragdon didn't think he had much of a chance. If they jumped on him and dragged him to the ground, he'd be finished. He tried to set his feet as best he could; his vision went double in waves. The man who had been holding Bragdon's right arm actually took a step backwards, and Bragdon thought for a moment they might run, but the puncher smelled Bragdon's weakness through the vomit. He rushed at Bragdon, shouting.

Bragdon tried to focus, stared at the man's right knee as the man approached at a run. Step, still bent, and then locked. Step, still bent, close now, and then locked. Just as the man's knee locked this time, Bragdon fell straight down. As Bragdon's hands hit the ground, both of his feet lashed out. One completely missed, but the other connected in a satisfying crunch. The puncher's knee folded completely backwards like a flamingo's. He went sprawling and screaming in the dirt. Bragdon rose to his feet, trying to find the third assailant, and saw him running away.

Bragdon looked down, and walked wide around the man writhing in the alley, as blood soaked the man's pants and pooled around his ruined knee. People were beginning to peer out of windows and doorways to see what had happened. Bragdon kept going, trying to focus, trying to stay out of the street as he made his way to the safe house. He vomited twice more on the way, but he made it. Unfortunately, he had lost the courier. If the old man had ever actually been the courier.

The safe house this time was not a house at all. It was a small apartment, with sparse furnishings. There was water in the refrigerator and canned fruit and beans in the cupboard. As would be expected, there was an impressive first aid kit, but aside from stopping the bleeding from his lacerated forehead, there wasn't much in the kit for Bragdon. He never even retrieved it.

He knew his nausea was not a result of being punched in the stomach but instead came from the concussion he suffered at the end of the piece of hardwood. He lay down, wanting to fight off sleep, but could not. He knew he might not wake up, but his eyes were so heavy, he couldn't resist it. He was not even sure what had really happened and what was imagined at this point. He just knew he was safely behind locked doors, and he collapsed on the couch.

17

There were eight barns on the two-hundred-acre property, but he was looking for one in particular, one with a hip roof. The ranch was idyllic. Trees, corrals, buildings, and the occasional water tank broke up a patchwork of green and brown landscape.

In this part of Colorado, where property was still somewhat reasonable, his associates had purchased the entire ranch, including a three-thousand-square-foot house, for half a million dollars.

Until now the man known as Manuel had never seen the place, and he would never see most of it. He had never even been to Colorado before. He would never see the inside of the low-profile but expansive house. All he needed to do was find the correct barn.

He checked his map again, trying to decide which of the two barns in the distance was the right one. He selected one and jogged most of the way to it, looking around on the way as if he might be spotted on the large plot by something other than the wildlife.

Pulling open the door, he saw it immediately, and knew he was in the right place. Amidst the streaks of sunlight coming in between loosely spaced barn wall-planking, with a cloud of incessantly moving hay dust, sat an air-

plane. A small airplane, a Piper PA 25 Pawnee crop duster
to be more precise, was hidden inside the barn. It was
white, with a broad red stripe running down its side. Its
wings were slung low beneath the fuselage and the boxy,
turret-like cockpit sat like a pimple on top. Its wings were
broad and rounded at the ends. The length on top of the
fuselage from the front of the cockpit to the propeller in its
nose was painted a flat black. Hanging down all along the
trailing edge of the wing were small nozzles.

He wanted to take it up, get a feel for it, but he didn't
even dare start the engine. Instead, he walked around it
once, and then locked the barn up again.

Everything here was in place. He just needed to be patient.

18

"We haven't been to your mom's in awhile," Sirois said from the kitchen. He stood in a pair of black nylon running shorts, bare feet, and a long-sleeved gray T-shirt. Across the chest of the shirt were navy letters spelling out "Check. Shoot. Score. Montreal Canadiens."

He was making them a couple of omelets, and he was tired of discussing the attacks. The television had nothing to offer but footage of the Brooklyn Bridge coming down. Sometimes in slow motion, sometimes in real time. But the media was already talking about tucking the videotapes away, just as they had after the attacks on the World Trade Center towers, saying it was too troubling to watch, too painful for the families, too commercial. In actuality, the liberal media wanted to stop giving airtime to the attack footage, then and now, because every time Americans saw the footage, the remembered why the nation was involved in the war on terror and support for the Republican administration grew. The major news outlets wanted to stop playing footage of the attacks, then and now, because the truth of it, the brutality of it, reinforced support for Republican-controlled foreign policy. It wasn't about taste, it was about politics.

Sirois had stayed at Ronald Reagan National Airport for

a day after the attacks, but the Pentagon knew as well as he did that they had been scored against and there was nothing left to do but go home and regroup.

Now with the ultimatum video played live on Al-Jazeera, the Night Stalkers were prohibited from going more than one-hour's drive from Ft. Campbell. Still, Sirois wished they could go visit Maggie McCall in Alpharetta, Georgia. There was something reassuring about Jeanie's mother. She was tough, funny, smart, and still attractive. She teased Rick Sirois mercilessly, which of course meant she was fond of him.

"It's too far. One hour, remember?" Jeanie McCall said from the living room.

"I know. I wasn't saying we should go today, I was just saying we haven't been in awhile," Sirois called back.

Music came in from the other room, Reyo Bikkin's cover of "Back in Black." The AC/DC rock classic was being played on an acoustic guitar and a sexy but soft woman's voice was ripping out the lyric. McCall came slinking, smiling, and singing into the kitchen. She danced up against Sirois as he tried to fold an omelet just right. She was wearing a white button-down men's dress shirt, of his, her legs bare, toned, and slender. Her curves beneath the shirt were obvious. Her hands were up above her shoulders, and she was snapping with the music. Her eyes closed, she continued to smile and sing along. Sirois had been in a funk for the past few days, since the attack, and she was trying her best to get him out of it. Sirois wished there was more that he could do, that he could get personally involved, not just as one part of the Night Stalkers, but that he could fight the terrorists every day. To be "on mission" twenty-four seven.

Sirois reached around her with a spatula in his hand, pulled her close awkwardly and throwing off her groove, and then let her go. She turned and danced away, just as the music ended and Kravitz's "American Woman" started.

"Do you own any music performed by the original artist?" Sirois laughed.

She disappeared into the living room, dancing the whole way. She was beautiful and too good for him, he thought.

Before he knew what he was saying, he blurted out, "Hey Jeanie, you ever seriously think of getting married?"

She reappeared. This time not dancing, walking slowly, her arms at her sides. "What did you say?"

Sirois fought to draw up some courage. Combat was one thing, but the "married" conversation was only approached by masking it in a joke. Sirois had used the word *seriously*. They were in unchartered territory. But the attacks put into focus how silly hiding from it all was.

"I asked if you ever seriously consider getting married," Sirois said, staring at the omelet.

McCall was quiet for a moment and then asked, "Are you proposing to me? Or to the omelet?"

"Proposing?" Sirois looked up: time to run for cover. "Who said I was proposing? I was just asking you a question."

"Proposing is just asking a question," McCall said.

"What, do you want me to propose?" Sirois offered.

"Well, I don't know, are you?" McCall asked.

Okay, this is ugly now, what a mess, Sirois thought, and then said, "I was just asking if you think about it. Did you want onions in your omelet?"

"Were you proposing?" McCall asked.

"I'm proposing eggs in your onions," Sirois stammered.

"Eggs in my onions?" McCall smiled.

"Forget it!" Sirois snapped. "You'll eat what I make you."

McCall grinned and slowly started to walk away, but looked back over her shoulder as she started to dance again. "If you get the nerve sometime, give a real proposal a shot. I promise to try not to laugh. It'll be a hoot." She danced her way back into the living room, and then really picked up the step. She stomped her feet and pumped her arms in glee at the idea that Rick Sirois might actually propose soon, the shirt riding up and exposing light blue underwear, and as she turned in the tight circle, she saw him. He had followed her, spatula in hand, and he stood there grinning at her celebratory jig.

"Breakfast is ready," Sirois announced.

McCall stopped dancing, her smile faded a bit, and she walked past him and into the kitchen. "I didn't want onions, you know."

Rick shook his head and returned to the kitchen.

"How long do you think the one-hour recall order will stand?" Rick asked, dropping the omelet onto a plate and handing it to her.

"I don't know," McCall said, shrugging her shoulders. "Until we either get a mission and execute it or until they give up on trying to figure out who to hit in retaliation for the latest attacks."

"I don't think they'll ever give up. They'll make something up first. Not with those bridges falling," Sirois said, starting on the next omelet. He watched as McCall squirted ketchup onto the plate beside her eggs and winced. She caught him.

"Oh, you don't have to eat yours with ketchup," she scolded, "so don't make faces at me eating it the way I like it."

"I just don't know why I put any effort into the omelet at all if you're going to just cover up the taste with that stuff," Sirois said. "Or maybe I could just blast some ketchup into the omelet while I'm cooking it?"

"Ick, gross!" McCall laughed. "Who would put ketchup inside an omelet?" She dragged the first bite through the condiment and put it in her mouth. Sirois shuddered in revulsion and looked away.

"Big baby," McCall chuckled.

19

Mike Ryan stood behind Lydia, his arms wrapped around her, looking out from the deck. The breeze was relaxing, gentle.

"I'll discuss it with him," Ryan said.

"He's going to think you're awfully fickle," Lydia teased, but she was thrilled he had made this decision.

"Let him. It's time," Ryan said, and pulled Lydia in a bit tighter. Ryan had made the list a month ago, and the Department of the Army was cutting the promotion orders. He would've been promoted to lieutenant colonel already if he hadn't asked Hartman to find a way to stop it. While the promotion up from major would have normally been a reason for celebration, for Ryan it meant a transfer out of the 160th SOAR. The promotion orders were coming with orders to take a command at Fort Rucker flight school. Ryan had asked Hartman to intervene because Ryan wanted to stay with the Night Stalkers. Lydia had been less than pleased, but Ryan was sure enough at the time to defy her.

After the latest round of attacks, however, Ryan was no longer sure. After all the work and the losses suffered in places like Iran, Syria, and Tajikistan, Ryan was ready to take it down a notch. He was ready to take a command where he could still serve, but where the chances of him

actually retiring, fishing, and traveling with Lydia someday, rather than traveling with his crew chief Derek
Cooper, were a bit better.

Lydia smiled, and then changed the subject. "Oh, hon,
there's a meeting of the Night Stalkers wives on the nine-
teenth. I'm going to go, especially to meet the younger
girls. I know it's deadline day, but where could I be safer,
right?"

"Sounds good. Will you be the old hen there?" Ryan
asked. Lydia turned to stone in his arms.

"Old?" she asked slowly.

"Just kidding, just kidding," he said, trying to get them
gently rocking again.

"I can still kick your ass you know," Lydia laughed, and
then started rocking with him. "I'm small, and maybe a bit
older, but I'm still way meaner than you are."

Ryan laughed, "Yes dear, I know. You're ferocious."

She slapped his arm. "You better remember that."

He laughed and kissed her neck.

"I just thought I'd go hang out a bit, talk some girl talk,
teach the younger ones about shoes none of us can afford
to buy," Lydia said.

"And how to cook various flora as a substitute for good
ol' fashioned meat?" Ryan teased.

"Hey," Lydia said, "you know I don't cook. That's what
I have you for, although I'm not sure you're still worth it."

"No one cooks the soy simulated steak somethings like
me, baby," Ryan laughed.

"I know. I'm very lucky," Lydia said, rolling her eyes,
her voice dripping with sarcasm.

Ryan froze. "What's with the nastiness?"

"You started," Lydia chuckled.

"Take it back," Ryan said, tickling her.

She screamed and ran into the house.

Ryan chased her, laughing. "Take it back or I'll substitute your veggie crap for some honest to goodness critter meat!"

She squealed with laughter as he caught her and they fell to the sofa. She had hair in her face and blew it away. With his fingers, he pulled hair back into her face.

"Aw, you brat," Lydia laughed.

"That's me," grinned Ryan.

He tried to kiss her, but she snapped at him with her teeth.

He laughed and moved her hair out of her face with the same fingers.

"That's better." She smiled.

"That's better?" he asked.

"Yeah." She continued to smile, and this time met his kiss with one of her own.

20

Derek Cooper came out of the bathroom with wet hair, a towel, and his dog tags hanging around his neck. His girlfriend Lara walked past him in the hallway. She smiled and said nothing, but patted the dog tags against his chest.

Attached to one of his dog tags was a St. Christopher's medal, held in place by an elastic Lara had pulled from her hair long ago. Derek considered it good luck, that it acted as an amplifier for the St. Christopher medal.

Back in Rowan, Iowa, Derek Cooper had never been superstitious, had counted on faith more than luck, but combat would make a new pope superstitious. There may be no atheists in foxholes, but in every occupied foxhole there are sure to be a few good luck charms as well.

He walked into the bedroom, grabbed a brush, and pulled the hair on top of his head to one side with two strokes. He passed the brush over the hair in the back and on the sides of his head as well, but it had no effect on the tightly cropped stuff.

"You slept late," Lara said behind him. Cooper turned and smiled. Lara leaned against the door jamb, her arms folded in front of her, smiling back at him. She was wearing a baggy T-shirt with "Noble High School" printed across the chest, and flannel pajama pants. Her blonde hair was tied back, and her bare feet had a single ornament, a silver toe ring around the middle toe of her left foot. It matched a ring she had around her right thumb. There were no rings on her fingers. She always said she was waiting for one ring in particular, but she always added a quick "no pressure" and a smile for Cooper whenever she brought it up.

"Do you know how much I love you?" Cooper asked, raising his hands to her arms.

"No," she smiled. "You never tell me."

Cooper grinned at her lie. "I loved you first, I love you more, I'll love you always."

Lara's eyes fluttered involuntarily, and her smile faded a bit, but then she quickly recovered. "Go eat something. There's some Cocoa Puffs left."

"Skim milk?" Cooper asked.

"You bet." She smiled as he walked past. He moaned at her answer.

"White water, that's what that is. Couldn't we go 2 percent at least?" Cooper whined.

"This is still my place. I'm still in charge, until you make an honest woman of me at least. We drink skim milk here," Lara said, in a false-scolding tone.

"Yes ma'am," Cooper said.

"That's more like it," Lara said, following him into the kitchen.

Cooper opened a cupboard and saw nothing. "Hon, we have Cocoa Puffs but no bowls?"

"Dishwasher," she replied without looking back. "Which reminds me, that dishwasher is still making that clunking sound."

"Tell the landlord," Cooper said, digging out a particular cereal bowl from the top rack inside the appliance.

"You fix helicopters and you can't fix a dishwasher?" she teased.

"If it ain't got rotor blades, I don't fix it," Cooper answered and then poured the cereal.

Lara turned on the television, saw the Brooklyn Bridge coming apart, and turned it off before the picture had been completely illuminated.

"You're going to get deployed again, aren't you? Now that this attack has happened, you're going to go overseas again, huh?" Lara asked softly.

"Well, honey," Cooper said around a mouthful of Cocoa Puffs, "I imagine even without this latest attack, I would have been deployed again, but this probably speeds things up."

Lara was quiet, walked over, and joined Cooper at the small table. She sat down hard, a sad look on her face.

Cooper stopped eating. "Come on, Lara. It'll be okay. I always come back in one piece."

"I just worry so bad when you're gone. It's hard to concentrate at work, I don't eat, I don't sleep," Lara said.

Cooper stood up and moved behind her, and then draped himself over her shoulders. "I'll be fine, hon. Really. I have St. Chris looking out for me, wearing your hair elastic seat belt."

She chuckled at this.

"There we go. Besides, you have to concentrate at work, or else some poor woman's going to end up with a bald spot because of your daydreaming," Cooper joked.

Lara giggled a bit more. She knew what he was doing, and she'd miss him all the more for it.

"Do you know how much I love you?" Cooper asked.

"No." She smiled, his breath tickling her ear. "You never tell me."

"I loved you first, I love you more, and I'll love you always," Cooper breathed into her ear. She squealed and pulled away from the tickling.

"Get off me and eat your Puffs!" she laughed. "They'll get soggy."

Cooper ran around to his cereal in an exaggerated manner and sat down. "You know I like my cereal soggy."

Lara crinkled her nose at him. "Disgusting."

21

He walked beneath fifty-foot trees and along a pond he had never seen before, and yet his name, or one of his names, was on the deed to the eighty-five-acre property. The name on the deed was *Larry Burns,* but he wasn't even very adept as pronouncing it.

There were pastures and fences, but no animals and no farmhands. Just him, and he was intently studying a hand-drawn map, trying to find a particular barn.

Finding the barn, he opened a small padlock on one door, carefully hung the lock on the hasp, and pushed his way in. The upper reaches of the barn were filled with swallows, dipping and wheeling and climbing.

On the floor of the barn, alone, there it was, just as planned. An airplane. A small airplane, a Piper PA 25 Pawnee crop duster parked inside beneath the loft. It was yellow, with a broad black stripe running down its side. Along the trailing edge of the wing hung small nozzles.

"Larry" walked around the aircraft, patting his hand on the side of the fuselage once, and then left after locking up the barn. Everything here was in place. He just needed to be patient.

22

May 13
New York Field Office
Federal Bureau of Investigation
Temporarily relocated to
Office of Drug Enforcement Administration
Newark, New Jersey

Assistant Director in Charge Henry King sat at a desk, with three FBI special agents sitting in chairs around the office, waiting. A speakerphone sat on the center of his desk as he leaned back in the chair.

"Yes sir, we're ready," Clough's voice came out of the speakerphone.

King rubbed his face with both hands.

"Ready here, sir," said another voice, with a slight hint of a southern twang.

"Ready in Oregon," said a third voice from the phone.

King nodded to himself. "Go."

Immediately, the voices ran together on the speakerphone, indicating understanding that they were all a "go."

In northeast Portland, Oregon, the FBI and the Oregon State Police SWAT team, with support from several other law enforcement agencies, stormed an ordinary-looking and unexpectedly small warehouse.

They threw in flash-bang grenades, broke windows, ripped open a panel in the roof, and entered the building like a mudslide.

Elsewhere, in the city, the owner and his wife were terrified as men dressed tactically, with MP5s, stormed into their home and bedroom and zip-tied them both before the elderly couple were even fully aware of where they were.

There was no one inside the warehouse. They searched the premises and found every bag of ferric oxide and granular aluminum shipped to the location.

Back in Newark, Henry King was growling already. "Nothing suspicious? Why does he have that stuff out in Oregon?"

"He says for sandblasting and other legal uses," the speakerphone came back. "Right now the paramedics have an oxygen mask on each of the individuals. They've had a scare—subjects are an older couple."

King looked at the other two men. "Dammit! So far, we've scared the shit out of Grammy and Grampy out in Portland. If there's nothing in Arkansas or Vermont, I'm going to choke Clough for talking me into this."

The three men sitting in King's office shifted uncomfortably.

In southern Arkansas, in a small town called Liberty, the FBI, along with the Arkansas State Police SWAT team, stormed a fifty-year-old family-owned pottery studio that produced plaques, vases, sculptures, and planters. Family members of the founder and the twenty-one employees were first subjected to flash-bang grenades. Then the SWAT members swarmed in with automatic weapons aimed, shouting commands to the stunned workers. Most looked like they had been dropped off at work by Greenpeace. Sandals, long hair, tie-dye. Each one of them was zip-tied or handcuffed. The manager was identified from among the employees.

"Do you know anything about a large shipment of ferric oxide?" Special Agent Boyd Criftin demanded.

The manager, his ears still ringing, squeaked out, "Of course."

"Why did you order ferric oxide?" Criftin asked.

"It's one of the most common colorants used in pottery!" the manager choked out.

"And granular aluminum?" Criftin went on, closing his eyes.

"We were spraying it on some of our special-use pieces, makes it non-slip," the manager said, starting to whimper. "Why are you doing this?"

Back in Newark, King was furious. "I'm going to kill Clough."

"What do you want me to do with this mess down here?" Criftin's voice asked from the speakerphone.

"Clean it up as best you can. Apologize and get a list of damages. Explain that this was part of an ongoing investigation, and that we're sorry," King said to the phone, and then into the office, "So help me, if Clough shoots up a dairy farm . . ."

In Vermont, Danny Clough pulled the goggles down over his eyes, and nodded. Men rushed forward, dressed in black and MP5s and AR-15s across their chests. The farm was incredibly tranquil. The house was off in the distance, and was completely overgrown. The front door was missing. It was empty. But the barn was in remarkably good shape, with a new metal roof recently installed. It was freshly painted a bright red, and the trim was as white as snow. It looked almost too good to be a working farm. Large vehicle tracks scarred the ground in every direction, but there was no engine running this morning. No sound at all, except the boots crunching the gravel as they made their way to the edge of the barn door. There, the men stacked, preparing to go in. Other teams closed on the barn from every side. Clough rushed to cover behind a large, green, John Deere tractor, taking up a vantage point where he could maximize what he could see.

He put his hand to his mike and was about to give the order to go in, when all hell broke loose. The men who were stacked at the barn door, standing toe-to-heel with the men in front and behind them, with the first man gripping a bulletproof shield, just as they'd been trained, were suddenly cut down by heavy machine-gun fire coming right through the wall of the barn. Every man was hit. Some were clearly dead. The tactic that they had been taught would save their lives had made them easy and clumped together targets. Men from all sides of the barn began spraying it with automatic weapons fire. Holes were appearing all over the barn. Still, what Clough thought must be .50-caliber machine-gun fire was still coming out of the barn, accompanied by long rifle and assault-weapon fire as well. Whoever was in the barn could not see very well, but they could see enough. Or at least their return fire was being directed somehow.

"Withdraw! Withdraw!" Clough was shouting, but many of the men were pinned down. Then, with the tractor between Clough and the barn, a heavy round snapped past his head from an angle the men in the barn could not have used. He fell flat, and jerked his head around, searching, and then he saw him.

"Sniper!" Clough called into his headset microphone. "East of our position! Up on the berm!"

A second sniper round threw dirt in his face before he heard the shot, the bullet ricocheting over his shoulder. The berm began coming apart near the crest. SWAT members, unable to clearly see a target in the barn, were turning on the threat they could see.

Clough jumped up, knowing he had to do something.

They were caught between the withering fire from within the barn and the sniper who would pop up again as soon as he could. More than likely, the sniper was changing positions right now. Clough searched for the ignition on the tractor, and finding it, tried to get the thing to start. It made a sound like it was turning over, but just not firing up. A bullet popped past his head from the sniper's direction. Clough looked back, and the berm was still being shot up, but then yet another round came by. The sniper was no longer on the berm. Clough had no idea where he was, but was grateful that, for a sniper, he was not a particularly accurate shot.

Clough tried the ignition again; again at first the whirring sound, but then with a bark and cough, the tractor came to life. Clough fought it into gear and got the John Deere rolling, and quickly steered it toward the barn door. The shooting from within the barn gradually focused. It seemed everyone in the barn was shooting in his general direction, and Clough decided it was time to get off. The tractor clearly had the momentum and speed to hit the barn with or without him. He rolled back and off the back of the tractor, allowing himself to fall flat in the dirt. Bullets whizzed past him, just a few inches over him. He could feel them stirring the air. Most were hitting the tractor, but the tough old John Deere kept right on going. Right on through the barn door and disappearing inside. Clough heard, even above the shooting, the tractor, being silenced, but now he could see inside. Within the barn, in the corners, were rings of sandbags, machine-gun pits. He jumped up and sprinted to find cover, diving into a drainage ditch, and then he called for help.

"This is Special Agent Clough." His voice filled the room from the speakerphone, heavy gunfire clearly audible in the background. "We are pinned down here! We are outgunned. Many men down. The barn at my location contains protected firing positions and at least one .50-caliber machine gun. Request immediate assistance!"

"What assistance can we give you?" King asked. "We'll never get an armored vehicle up there in time. We can't even get a helicopter up there in time. I'm sorry, Danny, but you're on your own with what you've got for the time being. We'll get more men out to your location, locals. Do what you can until then. Consolidate your men. Hunker down."

Back in Vermont, it all sounded much easier said than done.

"Yes sir," Clough said, rounds whistling over the ditch. He looked out at the situation and tried to make some sense of it. It appeared his men had formed two small defensive perimeters. One group seemed intent on chopping the sniper's former position away with steady fire, even though the less-than-deadeye sniper was no longer there. The other group seemed to be firing blindly at the barn. Clough still couldn't tell where the sniper was, nor could he see into the barn itself. Along one side of the barn, he noticed something. A fuel pump, as yet undamaged. But how could he get there? He looked out at the squad of men cut down by the initial burst of fire near where the barn door had been. Lying in the dirt was the shield. The shield would not stop a .50-caliber bullet, but it would be better than standing out at that pump completely unprotected, with nothing but his tactical vest. Unfortunately, he'd have to get to the shield, and then to the pump.

Clough looked at the two groups of men once more. With every passing minute, there was another spray of blood, and another man falling still or writhing in pain. He decided he had to try. Clough slung his MP5 across his back, pulled his SIG Sauer P229, and checked to make sure a .40-cal S&W round was chambered. He released the slide, took a deep breath, and jumped out of the ditch. He sprinted across the loose gravel, past the gaping hole in the barn where the tractor had entered. He slid to the ground like a Hall of Famer stealing second base. The .50-caliber machine gun was firing through the other side of the barn at the second defensive position his men had taken up, forcing them to keep their heads down.

Clough grabbed the heavy shield, sprang to his feet, and ran toward the pump. He was beginning to draw fire, and two rounds struck the shield, nearly ripping it from his arm. He did not fire back, not wanting to draw even more fire. A round struck the inside of the shield, from the opposite direction, throwing him to the ground. The sniper. Clough looked back, and could see him now, in the tree line. His men spotted him as well, and shifted their fire to the new position. Clough jumped up again and ran to the pump. Getting there, he realized he didn't know how to work the antique, nor was he even sure this pump would have fuel beneath it. He pulled the hose free and nothing came out. He searched frantically. Another round hit the shield, a seemingly wild shot. They were not shooting at him in a concentrated or directed way.

Clough found a lever, and flipped it upward. Fuel streamed out of the hose's nozzle. Clough tossed the hose aside, fuel pouring out onto the ground. He knelt beside the barn and fired four quick rounds from the SIG at the base of the wall. A hole, like one a rat might have chewed, opened up in the barn wall. He grabbed the hose again, and crammed the nozzle into the hole. Three rounds, and then four more, struck the shield. The shield in turn struck him in the head and Clough was driven to his back, onto the MP5. He groaned in pain, and tried to get his bearings.

He glanced across the ground, past his feet, and could see the hose and nozzle still in place. He could hear the faint "ding ding" of the old pump as more and more fuel ran across the barn floor. He wanted to light the fuel, but

wanted it to spread over a greater percentage of the barn
first. He looked up at the shield as it lay across him. He
doubted it would stop even one more round. He didn't want
to move. Bullets were flying directly over him now in mur-
derous numbers.

It was when the pump itself began to take many hits that
he decided it was time to go. Clough took three deep quick
breaths, threw the shield aside, and jumped to his feet. He
ran straight back for his drainage ditch. Bullets plied the air
past both sides of his head, and then he felt the heat of it.

The pump ignited in a ball of flame. The explosion
drove Clough the rest of the way into his hiding place. The
fuel that had poured across the barn floor ignited, and as
Clough looked back he could see men running out of the
barn in flames. They were shot dead as they came out.
Clough doubted any of the FBI or Vermont men were much
in the mood to take even one prisoner here today. Every
weapon outside the barn was blasting rounds into the burning structure, and soon there was no sign of any remaining
life. Rounds inside cooked off sporadically in the fire, but
there seemed to be no one left to resist. Off to his left,
Clough saw a man walking across the field with his hands
above his head. The sniper. Clough wanted at least one person to question. He jumped up once more and sprinted
across to the sniper, yelling for everyone to hold their fire.

"Get down on the ground!" Clough screamed. The
sniper complied. Clough zip-tied the man's hands behind
him, and then asked, "What's your name?"

No response.

"Fine, have it your way," Clough said, and then into the
radio, "Everyone fall back to the staging area. The ammo
in that fire is going to be going off for a while. Let's pull
back, get the wounded out of here, and wait it out. Sergeant
Saunders, call for immediate EMS, tell them to meet us
down by the old house, give them a count of wounded."

Clough walked past his prisoner, kicked him in the ribs

once, and then called back to King in Newark, "We have secured the barn. One in custody."

In Newark, King replied, "How many men down, Danny?"

"I'm not sure yet, sir, more than a dozen, quite a few dead; we're getting the wounded some help now," Clough replied.

"Understood," King said. He would have added a "well done," but he knew it was the wrong time. Clough was in charge of a scene where he had lost many young men. No one felt like celebrating, no matter how dangerous a terror cell had been discovered and shut down.

23

May 13
Arroyo's room in the barracks
Ft. Campbell, Kentucky

Sergeant Luis Arroyo was a short Puerto Rican, with full
black hair and thick eyebrows, proud to be an American but
never forgetting where he came from. If you needed to laugh,
or needed someone to watch your back, Arroyo was your guy.
He was a crew chief on McCall's Black Hawk. One of the
best, with medals in the shapes of hearts and stars, which was
no mean feat in an army that tended to save the more glam-
orous medals for higher-ranking and career soldiers.

The other crew chief on McCall's Black Hawk was Spe-
cialist Hill. He was enormous, his skin a warm brown. His
head was absolutely smooth and devoid of hair. He had es-
caped the Southside of Chicago and earned his way into
the most prestigious helicopter unit in the world. Still,
short months ago, he had outranked Arroyo. He was badly
hurt on a mission inside Iran, and after a lot of hard work
had recovered physically. Emotional and mental recovery
was an ongoing process, and in that process he had gotten
himself into trouble that cost him two pay grades and
nearly cost him his security clearance. That was why on
this night, while Arroyo was drinking Bud Light, Hill was
drinking O'Douls nonalcoholic near-beer.

"You sure this doesn't bother you?" Arroyo asked, holding up the Bud Light.

"Nah, go nuts," Hill answered without looking up, shuffling the cards. While, as countless Hollywood macho-flicks portray, some soldiers play poker, the most popular card games in the army were still spades, hearts, and cribbage. It was the last that had Hill and Arroyo huddled around a cheap coffee table.

The cards fell into place, the crib was created, and the calls began. "Fifteen for two." "Fifteen for four." When the cards were exhausted, scores were totaled, and this caused the predictable conflict.

"Who taught you how to count that?" Hill asked. "You can't count all that twice and three times."

"Kannenberg taught me, man," Arroyo answered, playing the ultimate trump card in cribbage expertise. Tim Kannenberg, a crew chief who had PCSed, had been from Connecticut, and that had only added to his cribbage resume. That and he just seemed impossible to beat.

"Well, you should have paid more attention to T.K., man, because he never counted cards like that," Hill said.

"Hey, you remember the time he fed you Ex-Lax gum all morning long?" Arroyo asked, grinning.

"Not funny," Hill scowled. "I was gripping the toilet seat with both hands all night."

Arroyo howled with laughter.

"I remember, when you first got here, that he sent you to get frequency grease for the antennas," Hill offered.

Arroyo remembered, "I spent all day rubbing silicone shit on that antenna."

It was Hill's turn to laugh. "Frequency grease, Arroyo? Too funny, man."

"T.K. was a trip," Arroyo chuckled, and then, "Fifteen two, fifteen four, fifteen six, fifteen eight, three pairs for six more, for fourteen." He moved the little peg a huge leap forward.

Hill shook his head. "You're cheating—I know it, and when I figure it out, you're ruined. I'll pound you."

Arroyo smiled broadly, thankful that the Hill he knew before the Iran mission was finally back, and then said, "Remember the time T.K. smeared that Anbesol crap all over the edge of your beer can?"

"Yeah, I remember." Hill half smiled.

"Your mouth went numb," Arroyo fought to get the words out, "and you were slurring." Arroyo held his stomach, laughing, falling over.

"Chemical warfare, man," Hill snorted. "T.K. kept going too far."

"Hey man, whah dijoo puh oh my bee-ah," Arroyo said, mocking Hill's formerly slurred speech, and then laughing some more.

"Yeah, real funny, you going to play or what?" Hill scowled.

Arroyo's laughing slowed, and he got up for another beer. He pulled the door open on the small dorm fridge he had in his room, and pulled out another Bud Light. Commanders were like anything else, they come and go. Not long ago, it would have been strictly forbidden to have beer in the room fridge. Now, the new post commander had quietly rescinded that order. Word had spread like wildfire. Morale had gone up, and the dreaded explosion in alcohol-related incidents had not materialized, and so beer was back to stay. Until perhaps the next commander. When Arroyo closed the fridge, the impact of the door caused a book to fall off of it. Hill looked over.

"Man. You are still reading that book?" Hill said. It was a paperback book, incredibly worn and well-traveled. Arroyo kept bringing it with him wherever he went.

"Listen, Hill, if you could read, you'd be able to appreciate it," Arroyo said, picking up the book and taking his seat. He tossed the book, titled, *Sympathy for the Devil* and written by Kent Anderson, onto the table next to the cribbage board.

"That is the best fictionalized war book ever written,

Hill. The author served in 5th Group in Vietnam," Arroyo said.

"I know, you've told me about this book a million times. And don't tell me about the drunken monkey or the dog named Hose again. I've heard it man, enough already," Hill said.

Arroyo laughed. "Oh, yeah the friggin' monkey! Too funny!"

Hill raised one finger, pointing it at Arroyo. "Don't, man."

"Will you read it someday?" Arroyo asked.

Hill just looked at him and then at the book. "Yeah, okay, someday."

Arroyo just grinned. "It's good having you back, man."

"Yeah yeah, shut up about it." Hill frowned back at Arroyo, and then smiled and dealt the next hand.

24

May 14
Notasulga, Alabama
West of Columbus, Georgia

The fifty-acre horse farm was beautiful. There were hay
fields and paddocks, with a stream-fed pond. A large barn
cast a shadow through which deer and turkey frequently
walked in the early morning dew.

He walked to the barn and pulled the door open wide.
Henry Lucci wasn't his real name, but in his wallet were a
driver's license, two credit cards, and a membership card
to a large discount store all in that name.

He stepped inside, and it was empty except for an airplane. As he pulled tarps away, a Piper PA 25 Pawnee crop
duster was revealed. It was blue, with a broad yellow stripe
running down its side. The telltale nozzles of a crop duster
lined the trailing edge of the wing.

He left it there without looking it over or replacing the
tarps. He locked the door, and walked out into the Alabama
sun. Everything here was in place. He looked east, out in
the direction of Ft. Benning, Georgia, some fifty miles dis-
tant. He just needed to be patient.

25

They waited on the stairs. American case officers from the CIA, along with a team of Bolivia's antidrug police, stood in the stairway leading up from Piccaso's to a one-bedroom apartment above the bar. The man leading the assault team was a veteran field officer named Sam Jordan, and his gut was telling him, as he stood in the foul-smelling and sticky space, that something wasn't right.

Cochabamba, a city of just under half a million inhabitants, had proven to be the next stop in an ongoing chase of those responsible for the chemical attack on the Washington, D.C., Metro.

The FBI had expected to find no evidence to tie anyone to the containers of bleach and ammonia, but to everyone's amazement, one container had a partial fingerprint. They ran it through the Automated Fingerprint Identification System, or AFIS. There were no hits. Under the new policies of sharing intelligence, the FBI shared the print with the Office of the Director of National Intelligence, which promptly distributed the partial print to all of its stepchild intelligence organizations. It was the CIA that came up with an identification. The CIA was less warm to the idea of sharing what it had, however, and so told no one and mounted a search to track the man down.

The man, referred to as Chuy in files, was actually Roberto Juarado, identified as a one-time agent for the CIA who was suspected of murdering his handler case officer and then disappearing. The Central Intelligence Agency had been watching for Juarado to pop up somewhere in the world. They were astonished to learn that he had come to Washington, D.C., had managed to stay hidden, had carried out an attack that everyone thought was Al-Qaeda's handiwork, and then . . . and this bothered them the most . . . he was able to slip away again.

So the CIA went hunting with a vengeance. They shook down every contact they thought might have the slightest idea where Juarado might be. The leads came pouring in. Most of them were crap. Until an old man, claiming to have heard of a bounty on Juarado's head, came in, chewing his leaves. The old man told them they would find Juarado in the apartment above Piccaso's. And then, he left. The locals to whom he had reported this let the wizened informant walk slowly right out the front door.

Sam Jordan looked down the stairs at the majority of the Bolivian antidrug troops, doubling as antiterror men this day, and then back up at the other two Americans and the Bolivian officer-in-charge. The Bolivian caught Jordan's stare and nodded a question. Jordan nodded in response. Time to go.

The Bolivian officer signaled for two of his men, and they immediately ran up the narrow stairs past Jordan. They never knocked, never shouted a word, nothing. They never even stopped running. The two Bolivian soldiers reached the top of the stairs, turned in the hallway, and immediately kicked in the door.

As they led the way in, everyone on the stairs followed. The Bolivians, well-practiced from years of hunting drug dealers, fanned out quickly. Just as Jordan entered the apartment, shouting could be heard from the bathroom. Jordan walked swiftly through that doorway as well, and found four Bolivians standing over the body of Juarado.

Lying in the bath, blood everywhere. His wrists had been slashed from his thumbs to the inside of his elbows. On the worn wooden floor lay a crusted straight razor. Juarado's skin was grey, with ugly bruises on his face and chest.

"Not a true suicide, eh?" the Bolivian officer offered.

Jordan stormed out of the bathroom. "Get your men out of the apartment. We'll get a team over here to tear the place apart."

"Not a suicide," the officer repeated.

Jordan reached down to the dining room table as he passed it and lifted a plate with a half-eaten sandwich on it. "Not unless his lunch was just that bad. Who stops midway through a sandwich to go carve themselves up with a razor? I want to know who did this."

26

"Hey new guy," Tom Phillips called across the room.

A young, underfed master's candidate, working the last few days of an internship, walked over, grinding his teeth.

"Who you going to call 'new guy' after next week?" he asked Phillips.

"Don't you know that there is an endless supply of new guys? Some form of you will be here long after I'm gone," Phillips answered without looking up at him, and then, pointing at the computer monitor screen, "Look at this."

The screen was filled with icons connected together in a fabric of brightly colored and shadowed lines. The software, known as PatternTracer, could take hundreds of thousands of phone call records and plot patterns. One of the patterns, outlining a web of phone communications that the two men had gone nearly blind observing, had shifted. Dramatically. The points tied together by the various lines had moved geographically. The tight hub-and-spoke effect had exploded. There had largely only been two hubs, one in Miami and one in San Diego. Now those same cell phones and sat phones were making and receiving calls in Colorado, Texas, North Carolina, and Alabama.

"They moved," the intern said absently and then winced at what he knew was coming.

"Sonovabitch!" Phillips immediately shouted, sitting up. "You're right! I hadn't noticed! See, that's why they bring you new guys in here. Otherwise old dumb guys like me would let the patently obvious slip past us."

"There's no need to get sarcastic," the intern replied. "You could cut me some slack. I've put up with your crap long enough I think." The intern never took his eyes off the monitor; there was something there, but what . . .

"Crap? You can't even curse properly. That's probably half your problem, you don't cut loose and really swear now and then . . ."

"Holy shit," the intern said softly.

"That's better," Phillips said. "But it's gotta come from the diaphragm. Project, son; a whispered curse word is a lost opportunity."

"No shut up, look at this," the intern replied.

Phillips turned to the screen. "What?"

"Colorado, Texas, Alabama, North Carolina," the intern said, pointing at each, and then, "Ft. Carson, Ft. Hood, Ft. Benning, Camp Lejeune. These places are close to those installations."

Phillips blinked at the idea for a moment and then, "Why not Virginia? Why not stay in San Diego?"

"We don't know where they aren't," the intern said, turning to face him. "We just know where they've sent people."

"Yeah, but attack these posts, bases, whatever? That's nuts. What hope of success could one possibly hope to have against a post like Ft. Hood? Can you imagine the ferocity the soldiers on a post that size, with the materiel they have, would bring to bear if you attacked them at home?"

"Any more crazy than attacking the Pentagon?" the intern added.

Phillips turned it over in his head, trying to guess at the probabilities. The currency of an intel pro was having a reputation of only passing up the good stuff. Phillips didn't want to run something up the chain that would come back to embarrass him or his department. He wanted to make sure the intern's intensity wasn't adding weight to something that was, in the end, just fluff. But, after a moment, Phillips decided the kid had made a good catch. His eyes narrowed. "Okay, nice job, Jason."

"It's Justin," he replied.

"Yeah, okay, let's write it up," Phillips said.

27

McCall and Sirois sat together in the rear of the briefing room, as they always did. They were wearing flight suits, each with a clipboard on a knee. The room was again filled with metal folding chairs, and in each sat another Night Stalker. On the stage at the back of the room, Hartman stepped up to the podium.

"Are we in iso, you think?" Sirois asked McCall softly. *Iso,* or *isolation,* meant that from this moment on none of those present would be able to see anyone or even make a phone call home. This would prevent even the smallest mission detail from getting out. It also got very tedious, especially if they spent days in iso, as they sometimes did. He was hoping that they were not. He and McCall were planning to go out.

By the look on Hartman's face, Jeanie McCall guessed, "Yeah, I think so."

The faint sound of Billy Squier was playing behind them in the hallways, covering their discussion from electronic eavesdropping.

"People, many of you are probably wondering if you are in iso," Hartman began, and McCall shot a look at Sirois. "Well, you are not. In fact, you are already at the objective. Our mission is to defend Ft. Campbell. With the deadline of May 19 quickly approaching, we will fly cover over our own post."

Hushed voices combined throughout the audience and built to a level Hartman chose not to try to speak over.

"People. People." The audience quieted. "Yes, I know you're wondering what terrorists in their right minds would attempt to attack this post, but intel indicates that certain military posts are under threat of what is mostly likely a VBIED, or perhaps multiple." A *VBIED,* or *vehicle-borne improvised explosive device,* was more commonly known as a car bomb.

Sirois shrugged. "What can that do? Blow up the gate?"

"It is our mission to provide cover. We will prevent anything suspicious from approaching Ft. Campbell," Hartman said.

There was murmuring again at this. What did *suspicious* mean?

Hartman held up one hand and said, "Every military installation in CONUS is being put on highest alert. Use your best judgment, call in if you have doubts or suspicions. Large vehicles, fuel vehicles, vehicles driving erratically or too quickly."

McCall shook her head. "This is nuts. We're going hunting for speeders?"

"Sir," CW2 Miles Morrison, McCall's copilot, asked, "How are we to distinguish between the driving of a terrorist and a teenager?"

Hartman's head fell. "Mr. Morrison, I can't pretend to have all the answers. This type of mission has never been flown before here in the States."

"But sir, what if we're wrong?" Morrison asked.

Hartman lifted his head. "Do you best: go with your training and your gut. I'll support anyone in here who does that. The rules of engagement include that you first make yourself seen and then you fire a warning burst in front of the vehicle. Having done that, if your target does not stop, you must neutralize that target."

"Sir." CW3 Glen Arsten, Hartman's own pilot, rose to speak. "Will the Apaches from the 101st be up also?"

"Mr. Arsten, every aircraft on this post will be involved," Hartman said. "Over the next few days, we will participate in a round-the-clock air cover mission coordinated by the post commander's staff. The gates will be guarded with additional troops. Barricades will be put in place. Ft. Campbell will indeed look like a fort very shortly."

Hartman then said, "Any more questions before MAJ Ryan gives you the operational details? MAJ Ryan." He stepped away from the podium, and Ryan moved up.

"Alright, situation: we have intel telling us that Ft. Campbell is under threat of imminent attack. While it is believed that a VBIED is the most likely method of attack, we will assume nothing. Most of you will join the other aviation units in protecting the high-value targets; such as the airfields, the headquarters buildings, the motorparks, the barracks, medical care facilities, etc. A few of you will patrol the perimeter searching for . . . speeders or whatever."

There was nervous laughter at this.

Ryan continued, "Anything looks out of place, you cannot afford to have the same patience or apathy we might normally have flying above Ft. Campbell.

"We know now that the attacks on New York, Washington, Warsaw, and Manila were only made possible by people not believing there was a present danger. Don't be the next person who lets it happen."

Silence fell heavy. Ryan paused and then, "Any questions?"

"Can we get word to our families in post housing to get out of the area? I mean, not everyone involved could be in iso right now?" asked CW3 John Lapis.

Ryan was surprised that the question had taken so long to be asked. "I'm sorry, for right now, you cannot contact your family."

"But sir, I'll be flying right over them. We'll be circling over the schools and housing. Why not get them out of here?" Lapis asked.

Ryan took a deep breath. "Mr. Lapis, consider it for a moment. If every service member's family, from every military installation in the country, suddenly ran to the country, what do you think would happen? What do you think the townies would do?"

Lapis mulled this over. If every family member and every civilian who lived within commuting distance of every military post or base tried to un-ass where they were, there would be utter chaos nationwide. Plus, where could they all go?

Ryan could see that Lapis, as well as those who shared his questions, had come to the only possible conclusion.

Ryan said, "We will stay here and defend this post. The terrorists are potentially coming to us this time. We all know it's a mistake on their part—let's prove to them."

28

McCall banked a hard left. The Black Hawk swung wide over the gate and headed away from Ft. Campbell. A Bradley fighting vehicle sat at the gate, its cannon pointed not quite up the road, but a few degrees off to one side.

"Seriously, ma'am," Arroyo continued in the intercom, "who the hell is going to attack a post like Ft. Campbell? I know they do the suicide bombing thing, these guys, but they usually hope for some effect, you know? Like, they don't do suicide bombings alone in the desert. They want to take someone with them."

"Arroyo, a bunch of us were there in Iraq when they blew a gate open with one suicide bomber and then three more rushed in," McCall said wearily. They had been up and down all night, and this discussion had gone on almost as long. It was almost time for them to be relieved. Just a little more than an hour left of Arroyo's incredulity.

"Yes, ma'am, but even then only one of the trucks reached its target," Arroyo said. "And it wasn't Ft. Campbell."

"One truck is one too many, man," Hill chimed in. "Guys died in that blast. Imagine if they came in and hit a barracks with people sleeping or something like that?"

"Yeah, yeah, you said that already," Arroyo said.

"You haven't said nothing new either," Hill replied.

"Okay, okay, let's just try keeping it quiet for the last bit," McCall pleaded.

"Ma'am," Hill's voice, and McCall winced, thinking the debate would never end, but it was something else. "On this side, I've got what appears to be a fuel truck, just ran a stop sign and is turning toward the gate. Really moving."

All the fatigue washed out of the four of them.

"We're coming around," Morrison said.

The large aircraft banked hard once more, Hill looking out almost straight at the ground. The truck was moving very quickly, rushing at the gate. Its red cab and chrome tank made it look like any of thousands of such trucks across America, but this one looked like it was on an attack run. If the fuel in the tank was actually a makeshift explosive, a lot of damage could be inflicted. The Khobar Towers were badly damaged and twenty-three air force personnel were killed by just such a setup.

The Bradley's crew picked it up also and the barrel of the Bushmaster cannon swung and aimed directly at the truck. Still it went on, just a bit more than a mile to go.

McCall's Black Hawk overtook the fuel truck.

"I got it," called Arroyo. "Right here, I can take it out right now."

"Hold your fire!" McCall ordered. "We have clear rules of engagement." She knew that if this were an attack, a fuel truck that size might stand a tiny chance of getting to the gate, even with the Bradley firing away, and if the tank were filled with explosives, the Bradley might be destroyed. She also knew that if this were not an attack, the chances of this driver surviving such a rapid approach on the gate and the Bradley were slim.

The fuel truck swerved, and threw some dirt up off the shoulder, and then corrected its course.

"Ma'am," Hill came in, "this has to be an attack. That truck is moving like a maniac is behind the wheel. We have to stop this thing."

"Stand fast, everyone!" McCall ordered again. She brought the aircraft around, dropping down to windshield level, and flew past the front of the truck. It swerved again, more violently, and slowed a bit, but then picked up its speed once more.

"Did you see that, ma'am?" Arroyo asked, knowing of course she had.

Morrison looked over at McCall and nodded his head. McCall nodded back.

"Okay Hill, I want you to fire across the path of that truck. Do not hit it! But make sure he knows you fired a burst across his path," McCall said. There was perhaps half a mile left, and the Bradley would not give the fuel truck the chance to cover half of that before opening up with its gun.

McCall came down again, low, past the driver's side. Morrison strained to see the driver, but could only make out a shoulder. Hill came up even with the driver and then past him.

"Do it," McCall said. Before the second word was fully out of her mouth, Hill opened up with his M134 7.62mm, six-barrel, air-cooled, electrically operated Gatling mini-gun. The rounds came out with the sound of some obscene zipper. The pavement and earth in front of the truck boiled. This time there was no mistaking the intent. The truck swerved hard off the road, came to a sudden stop. McCall climbed and circled a bit wider, not wanting to give the potential attacker something to blow up out here. Nothing. And then, the door swung wide and a blonde kid, maybe just a shade more than twenty years old, jumped out with his headphones still on, his arms out to his sides as if to say, "Like dude, what is your problem?"

He hadn't taken two steps when he was buried in a mound of MPs.

"He's going to have a long, hard day," said Hill. They wheeled once more and headed out away from Ft. Campbell.

29

May 18
Early morning
San Angelo, Texas

The Fleetwood Bounder 39z was forty feet long, had a diesel engine with 275 horsepower, and had an in-motion satellite system. It could cruise at seventy miles per hour, carried a microwave, and had its own onboard generator. It was an RV.

Built in 2000, it wasn't especially new, but it was in great shape. A couple sat up front, handsome people, the man behind the wheel serene with a floppy fishing cap. The woman wore a light cotton dress. They were in their forties, and looked as normal in an RV as anyone might.

The difference was, in the rear, where a queen bed should have been, there was a low-yield nuclear weapon. It was predicted to deliver approximately 150 kilotons of explosive power, based on how a similar device had performed in the terrorist attack on Warsaw. And this RV was heading out.

They turned out left onto Sunset Drive, pulling out of the parking lot of the small apartment complex where they had shared an apartment for the past four months. They would never return. The RV had been delivered that morning. They knew the device was going to be sent to them for delivery, and they knew it was to be in an RV. They had both studied maintenance on this vehicle extensively.

When they saw the RV, they were excited that their wait was over. The day of their operation had come and the day of deliverance was coming soon.

The man smiled at the woman, a warm smile as if from husband to wife, as the RV turned onto US-67 north.

30

"Sir?" Ryan said as he poked his head into Hartman's office.

"Come in, Mike," Hartman said, standing and motioning to a seat. As Ryan took it, Hartman twisted to turn down the radio.

"Gretchen?" Ryan said, nodding at the radio.

"Yup," Hartman answered. "I wonder what happened to Jack. When he left the 'Jack and Gretchen' Q108 morning show, I thought Gretchen would leave too."

"I'm glad she stuck around. Doesn't matter what mood I'm in, that voice can fix it. And this guy named Ryan is okay too." Ryan smiled.

Hartman nodded and smiled back, but then asked, "What's up?"

Ryan sighed, settled into his chair, and said, "Jack, you know those promotion orders for me? You can stop holding them up."

Jack nodded again. "Ready to move on?"

"No," Ryan said, but then, "Yes. We are going to take that command at Rucker, coast my last few years to retirement, and then go fishing. A lot. Maybe hang out with Lydia some too."

"You? Coast?" Hartman laughed. "Not likely. Besides, a command at Rucker is hard work."

"Yeah, I know," Ryan replied, sliding forward in his seat. "But no one tries to shove an antiaircraft missile up your ass when you're sitting at a desk at Ft. Rucker."

"Fair enough." Hartman stood. "I'll miss you around here Mike. It'll take a couple weeks before your oak clusters turn silver, and transfer orders will come immediately after that. Maybe simultaneously."

Ryan rose to shake Hartman's hand. "Thanks Jack, I appreciate you holding them up, and thanks for this too."

"Don't get all mushy on me. Besides, after a month at Rucker, you'll probably be cursing my name, begging to come back; but if this is what you want . . . ," Hartman said.

"Yeah, it's time," Ryan replied, nodding.

"Okay." Hartman smiled. "What will you guys do with that house out on Lake Barkley while you're down at Rucker?"

"Well, we'd need someone to keep it up, keep it lived in." Ryan grinned. "You interested? Or would you prefer to stay in that tiny little apartment of yours?"

"Me? Move in there?" Hartman said. "Naw, I was thinking the single Little Bird pilots might want to use it like a frat house."

Ryan raised one eyebrow. Hartman laughed. "Yeah, of course I'd be interested. Just let me know what Lydia wants for rent."

"Rent?" Ryan snorted. "You can just live there. You don't need to pay rent."

"Uh, yeah, can you check with Lydia just the same?" Hartman grinned.

Ryan smiled back knowingly. "Yeah, okay, I'll get permission from her to rent the place out."

"Thanks," Hartman laughed. "Let me know what the boss says."

31

May 18
Jeanie McCall's apartment
Clarksville, Tennessee

"Hey, what do you want for supper?" McCall called into the living room.

"What we got?" Sirois replied.

"We?" McCall's back straightened. "I'm the only one who buys food, goes shopping."

Sirois came into the kitchen and sat on an old pleather-covered stool at the counter. "That's because you're a picky eater, and I'm not. I'll eat anything, even your cooking."

McCall smiled at his teasing. "I'm not a picky eater. Name something I won't eat."

"Shrimp," Sirois offered instantly.

McCall shuddered.

"Because they look like bugs," Sirois laughed.

"It's not that!" McCall said. "I'll eat bugs, I can't eat shrimp."

"Why not?" Sirois asked.

"They look like they're in the fetal position, like a plate full of embryos or something," McCall said, making a face.

Sirois froze, and then said, "Where do you get these ideas? Only a sick, twisted mind could come up with the stuff you come up with. I've always loved shrimp, and I think you may have just ruined them for me."

"Picky eater," McCall teased.

"You don't like peas either," Sirois said, but then quickly added, "Wait, wait, don't tell me why."

They both laughed, and then McCall fell quiet.

"Rick, do you really think someone would attack Ft. Campbell? How far could they get? Arroyo was talking my ear off the other night, telling me there was no way someone would hit the post. He's right, isn't he?" McCall said.

Sirois stood, went to the fridge, and pulled out a Coors Light for himself and a Czech Pilsner Urquell for McCall. He twisted his cap off and pried hers loose with an opener. He placed both bottles on the counter between them as he returned to the stool.

"What I think, Jeanie, is that every time someone starts thinking they can't be hit, that's when they get pounded. It's like the universe gets pissed off at their complacency, at their arrogance. God has never been too forgiving of the arrogant," Sirois said, and then took a long pull on his beer.

McCall laughed. "This coming from you?"

Sirois fell quiet, then, "Yeah, I was arrogant, and then I got thrown in the cell in Iran."

"I'm sorry, Rick," McCall said. "I was just playing."

Sirois paused and then forced a smile. "It's nothing you did. It's okay. It's just part of living in this world of ours."

McCall took a drink from her beer, and said, "The world is changing. It started on September 11 for us, but that was just the beginning. I don't like where it's going. I mean, how do we come back from this? What are we likely to lose? What are we going to have to give up? Can we get to a point when we aren't all living in fear and still have a bit of our freedom left?"

Sirois didn't answer; he just took another swig of beer, put it down, looked McCall straight in the eyes, and shrugged his shoulders.

"How about we call for pizza?" he asked.

McCall held his gaze for a moment and then nodded,

acknowledging his need to move on. She didn't think she could bring kids into this mess, not that she wanted any right away. She just couldn't imagine worrying every day if her kids were safe at school, or on the playground, or even in their bedrooms. She had a brief flash of frantically duct taping a nursery, trying to keep a chemical agent out. She shuddered again, and this time it had nothing to do with shrimp.

32

May 18
Early morning
Nappanee, Indiana

The top two-thirds of it was cream colored, the bottom third a chocolate brown. Three parallel stripes of brown, bronze, and green ran down its forty-foot length. It was another Fleetwood Bounder 39z, just like the one that had set out from San Angelo the day before, and just like the other RV, it carried a nuclear payload.

Another couple in their forties, dressed like native Hoosiers, delivering a weapon of unimaginable destruction. The harmless-looking couple setting out in that most innocuous of all vehicles, the rolling symbol of an upper middle-class retirement. A vehicle of the pre-Yuppie generation nomadically roaming the country they still cared to see for the sake of seeing, and not simply for bragging rights.

She was wearing jeans and sandals, a light blouse, with hair too short to tie. He wore old khakis and a polo shirt, and a Chicago Cubs baseball hat.

Initially, they found themselves stuck behind a horse and cart driven by one of the twenty-five hundred local Old Order Amish, but they were finally able to turn left onto IN-19 north.

33

They had discussed canceling it, but that would have been like letting the terrorists win, someone had said. The Night Stalker wives' meeting was still on.

The Lady Night Stalkers took care of each other. Their husbands could be gone with a few minutes' notice, and gone for a month or more, to places unknown. What was known to every wife was if the missions weren't difficult and dangerous, they wouldn't give them to the 160th. If they were simple and easy to accomplish, they wouldn't go to the best. So every deployment for the Night Stalkers was a dangerous one, and the wives knew it all too well.

Lydia Ryan stopped at the gate, showed her ID, and was waved in with a "Have a good day ma'am." Talk about feeling old. Especially when the soldiers, who used to be her age, now all looked like kids. Mostly because they were.

She drove slowly, taking her time. It was actually a beautiful day. She was listening to NPR, National Public Radio, which several of their crowd had come to refer to as CRA, or Communist Radio Amerika, for its leftist lean, but she liked it. No one was shouting at her in the morning, no one was trying to gross her out. The interviews were with economists and leaders and authors, not rock and television stars.

"Today is Deadline Day, May 19. Many experts worry that once a terror group has given such a clear ultimatum they cannot afford not to deliver on their threat. Military installations across the country are on red alert," the radio said.

"Red alert?" Lydia frowned. "What is this, *Star Trek*?"

The broadcast continued. "And members of his administration are reporting to work as usual and urging the rest of the country to do the same. To do otherwise would be letting the terrorists win."

Lydia winced at hearing that phrase again. While there had been some truth in it, and perhaps there still was, it was becoming so overused it was losing any impact on thinking people. People would keep working, even without hearing that phrase to prompt them. What else could they do? Would they be any more safe at home than at work? Would they work harder if they thought production would hurt the terrorist cause?

"Who is John Gault?" Lydia whispered, remembering her Rand, but then shook it off. Surely, this really was a time for putting the public's needs ahead of one's own.

She pulled into post housing. Long rows of identical apartment buildings, placed impossibly close together. Just a bit nicer than a housing project. Bicycles in the front yards, brightly colored plastic toys fading in the sun. Children running after one another. There seemed to be a speed bump every few feet.

Lydia squeezed into a parking space. These were the lucky ones, she thought. Like many military posts, there was a housing shortage in this area. New soldiers could wait a year for off-post housing to open up, let alone on-post housing, their wives and children living with in-laws, waiting for an apartment to become available so that they could be reunited. And many of the youngest families needed food stamps to get by. It was a damn shame, thought Lydia. It was also one of the reasons she liked to come to these types of meetings. The wives of enlisted and officer alike mingling, discussing issues they all faced, supporting each other. Many officers' wives seemed to think they held the same rank as their husbands, but Lydia instead liked to just be someone the younger women could turn to, as an older sister perhaps. Never as a mother figure though—that just sounded too old.

She exited the car, walked across the lawn to the door, and buzzed the upstairs apartment of Mrs. Tiffany Pangelinan. Her husband, Scott Pangelinan, was a crew chief on a Black Hawk, relatively new to the Night Stalkers, and the young Guamanian couple had not had much chance to meet many people socially.

"Yes?" a tinny voice said from the little speaker near the door.

"Lydia Ryan," she answered.

The door buzzed and there was an audible unlocking click. Lydia pulled it open and was greeted by a flight of stairs. Climbing them, she was nearly run over by four boys scampering down, chattering amongst themselves and not looking where they were going.

"Sorry ma'am," they said almost in unison, but they never really slowed.

"That's okay." Lydia smiled. She'd never get used to the "ma'am."

The apartment door opened before she could knock on it, and she saw immediately that she might well be the last to arrive. The apartment was filled with young women, all dressed very casually, cups of punch all around. A cheer of greeting went up as she stepped in. The door closed behind her and Tiffany Pangelinan stepped forward to meet and greet her guest.

"I'm Tiffany." She smiled broadly, extending a hand. Her eyes were huge, and nearly black, but very warm.

"Lydia Ryan." Lydia took her hand, and then regretted adding the Ryan. She didn't want it to seem as if she were reminding people she was Mrs. Major Ryan.

"Come in, come in," Tiffany said at once. "Have some punch." She handed Lydia a small cup.

Lydia took a sip and said, "Got any vodka?"

Everyone laughed, suddenly feeling less like the chaperone had arrived, just as Lydia had intended.

34

May 19
Florence, Texas
South of Killeen

The man known as Larry Burns walked for a second time beneath fifty-foot trees toward the barn. Reaching it, he opened the doors wide. The yellow Piper PA 25 Pawnee crop duster was still there, unmolested, waiting.

He was an expert pilot, with countless hours in just this type of aircraft. He climbed into the cockpit, started up the venerable Piper, and taxied out of the barn. It was in superb condition for such an old airplane. Normally, he would have tested the spray distribution system, but not on this flight. It would work or it would not, he would leave that in Allah's hands.

He sat high, surrounded by abnormally large panes, providing the excellent visibility for which the aircraft was known. He increased the throttle slightly and taxied across the flat pasture and out onto the long, straight stretch of road. It was the runway-like roadway and the huge barn that had made this farm the perfect place to hide the aircraft, that and its proximity to the target.

Once out on the pavement, the Piper Pawnee did not require a lot of speed or runway to get airborne. He turned north, keeping just east of TX-195. He flew at treetop and rooftop level. When over flat Texas land, "Larry" was scarcely two yards off the ground. He was moving at nearly one hundred miles per hour, and the target was only twenty miles from his takeoff point. In less than fifteen minutes, he would be there.

He passed towns with names like Ding Dong, crossing rivers and creeks, and then flying impossibly low over Killeen itself. When he saw TX-195 cross US-190, he turned northwest, passing directly over the intersection. He was so low, and appeared so unexpectedly, several cars skidded and screeched to a halt on the busy highway interchange.

He crossed over Nolan Creek and descended even lower as he crossed the railroad tracks. He had arrived. He climbed ever so slightly as he crossed onto Ft. Hood.

The Apaches and other aircraft providing cover were centered on the high-value targets, and the armored vehicles and additional troops were focused on the gates. He knew he had precious few minutes, but he would make the most of them.

When he crossed Sadowski Road, he was flying just ten feet above the rooftops of the housing lining the many cul-de-sacs. The area was packed with short dead-end streets with names like Boatright, Whitson, and Patton Spur, and he flew over the housing and began spraying. The fine mist exited the many flat-fan nozzles lining the wing and fell among the children and families below. He adjusted his heading slightly and headed for McNair Village, the next clump of on-post homes, but he would never see them.

A pair of Apaches had come racing to this tiny corner of immense Ft. Hood, and with a single burst from the 30mm chain gun beneath the lead helicopter's nose, the Piper Pawnee came apart in midflight. It crumpled in a flaming mass on Tank Destroyer Boulevard.

"Target destroyed," the pilot reported. But behind them, the panic had begun. Soldiers and military police were already donning hazmat and chemical suits and masks to cordon off the housing area now assumed to be contaminated.

• • •

"Confirmed, Arrow 5, you are closest. Target is small fixed-wing approaching housing at . . ."

Ryan, circling on Ft. Campbell, couldn't process what he was hearing. A suspicious aircraft making a low run on the on-post housing on Ft. Campbell? Then his blood ran cold. Lydia and the Night Stalker wives' meeting. The Black Hawk stood nearly on its nose as Ryan applied everything the formidable aircraft had into making it move forward. He had no idea of the attack at Ft. Hood; all he knew was that a small airplane was a potential threat to the families of the soldiers of Ft. Campbell, and maybe even to Lydia. The helicopter raced over flat military buildings and the winding roads until the housing area loomed ahead, and above it was a crop duster clearly spraying the buildings below. Ryan never slowed, did not pace the airplane so Cooper could shoot it down. Ryan overtook the plane, and then drove the undercarriage of the Black Hawk down onto the cockpit, wings, tail, and fuselage of the red Piper in one devastating blow. The force of the collision was fantastic, and Cooper thought they would crash as well. But the Black Hawk was considerably tougher than the old fixed-wing airplane. The Piper Pawnee fell to earth as a bug might when struck out of the air. It crashed and burned in a parking lot below. Still, it was too late. The spraying had already happened.

Ryan circled back and tried to spot Lydia's car, but could not. He could feel a knot of fear building in his throat.

Cooper was searching as well. "Did Mrs. Ryan go to the wives' meeting today?"

"Yeah, she was supposed to," Ryan answered. "Did Lara go?"

"No," Cooper replied guiltily. "She said she was going to catch a movie instead."

Ryan did not respond. Cooper scanned the cars below, looking for Lydia Ryan's vehicle.

"Sir, did she take the Toyota?" Cooper asked.

"Yeah, she did, you see it?" Ryan asked in reply, his blood running cold.

"I think so, at three o'clock. Near those bikes," Cooper said.

The aircraft banked hard right, and then left, circling. Ryan saw it. Lydia's car, his Cardinal's baseball hat visible in the back dash to someone who expected it to be there.

"Dammit," Ryan hissed to himself.

35

Colonel Steve Briand was assigned to INSCOM, the U.S.
Army Intelligence Command. He had run to the office of
Cat Hartman, the ATSD-IO, and because she hadn't responded, he repeated his answer. "We don't know yet, we
don't even know if the attack is over."

"What do we know? What's confirmed?" Cat asked.

Briand hung his head, and started from the top. "We
know that there have been near simultaneous attacks on the
family housing and/or billeting on Ft. Bragg, Camp Lejeune, Naval Station Great Lakes, Ft. Benning, Ft. Carson,
U.S. Naval Academy, Ft. Hood, Ft. Drum, MacDill Air
Force Base, and Ft. Campbell."

Cat was horrified at all of it, but winced at the last one.

"We suspect that in some of the attacks a bioagent was
sprayed from the crop dusters. We have to test it, but we
also believe some of the spraying was harmless," Briand
continued.

"Not harmless," Cat interjected. "Those posts are in just
as much of a panic. Those family members are just as iso-
lated, quarantined; those service members just as out of the
fight."

"Of course," Briand admitted the poor word choice, "and
we are moving antibiotics, to be distributed to everyone."

Cat nodded. "Go on."

"In each case so far, ma'am, the attacking aircraft was destroyed, and destroyed quickly. At MacDill, the crop duster never made it over the base. Still, where the wreckage fell in Florida is being treated as a highest level hazmat site," Briand said, and then as almost an afterthought, "None of the terrorist pilots have survived thus far; we are working on retrieval of the bodies."

"Have any American lives been lost?" Cat asked.

"A few. Mostly car accidents because residents and service members are frantic," Briand answered.

"How did we not see this coming? How can we stop so many of the little ones, and we miss the two big ones? How can the Brooklyn Bridge be dropped and some of our most vital military posts be thrown into chaos by terror attacks we had no idea were coming?" Cat asked.

Briand's jaw worked. He had spent his entire adult life in the intel community. "Ma'am, as you know, the sum total of what we have prevented certainly dwarfs the combination of even the most terrible attacks here in the United States. While today's events represent a failure on our part, New York or Los Angeles did not go the way of Warsaw, and that's not for lack of desire or effort on the part of the terrorists."

Cat was quiet for a moment and then said, "So you're saying basically that we can't win them all?"

"That's exactly it," Briand sighed. "We can't win them all."

"Tell it to the soldier whose wife and kids are being quarantined down on Bragg right now," Cat said softly.

Briand said nothing.

Cat saw she had gone too far. "Sorry, Colonel. I know you and your people work very hard and are the best at what they do. It's just tough to lose one."

Briand looked at Cat Hartman and said, "You didn't lose anything. You're in here, looking over our shoulders, making sure we don't bend any of the rules while collecting the very intelligence you're now telling me we should have had more of. You aren't part of the intelligence community—you are one of the constraints on the intel community. So when we have a failure like today, don't sit there and sadly include yourself among us. Just sit back and appreciate the view from the cheap seats, ma'am."

Cat's mouth fell open, and before she could say anything, Briand grabbed his beret and walked out of her office. He was halfway down the hallway before Cat snapped out of it. She jumped up and jogged down the hallway after him, calling after him, and catching him at the corner.

Briand stared at the floor, the muscles in his jaw working; he was furious.

"Colonel, first of all, let me say to you that you had better never talk to me in that tone again, especially in that office," Cat said.

Briand stood frozen, not at attention, just not moving.

"Second, I want to apologize again for what I said, and for making it seem that I don't understand what a tough mission the intelligence organizations have. I want to talk about this. I want to know what you want to be able to do that this office, either with me or my predecessor occupying it, has prevented you from doing. Let's talk it over," Cat said, extending her arm back to her office.

Briand hesitated, and then turned back toward the office. "Sorry for my outburst, ma'am. I have no excuse for my loss of bearing. It's just so frustrating and I'm exhausted."

"Understood, Colonel," Cat said. They walked together back to her office, and Lucy watched them go in and close the door behind them.

36

"My God," Lydia said, looking out of the window and down into the far parking lot where the wreckage of a small plane lay burning, crumpled wings and a tail section clearly visible. Through the smoke, an occasional glimpse of what might have been part of the pilot. A Black Hawk circled overhead in a tight circle. Lydia of course suspected who it might be. The other wives pressed around her at the glass pane.

"It's not a helicopter, is it?" a voice came.

"No," said another. "Looks like a small plane."

Below, the residents of the housing complex began running for their cars, getting jammed up in a cluster of fender benders. The Black Hawk kept circling and Military Police Humvees began arriving. Men jumped out in MOPP-4, mission-oriented protective posture 4, with full protective suits and masks. And rifles.

Lydia said softly, "Turn on the television."

The answers came on almost instantly: CNN, with "And as of yet, it is not clear what the small planes were spraying over the military bases, but it is feared that it may have been a chemical or biological agent."

Lydia's eyes closed.

"Oh my God! We have to get out of here!" said one of the younger wives.

"No! We should wait here so the guys can find us!" cried another.

"My kids are at the sitters! I'm not staying here!" said a third.

Lydia turned around and said, "We have to stay put. Help has already arrived out there. Besides, the parking lot is already completely blocked, you won't get anywhere."

"I'll walk! I have to get to my kids!" the mother repeated.

"We're all scared," Lydia said in a calm voice, "but we need to stay here."

CNN continued, and all the women looked over. "There are reports of tens of thousands of military personnel across the country leaving their duty stations and massing outside the quarantined areas, demanding to see their families. Military Police are attempting to create some sense of order, but they have not been able to prevent determined soldiers, sailors, and marines from reaching contaminated areas. Those military personnel themselves then need to be left inside the quarantined area. Tests on what exactly was sprayed are ongoing, according to Ft. Benning public affairs spokesperson Captain Kara Kaiser just moments ago."

The screen was then suddenly filled with shaky camera work filming a pretty army captain. "We are testing samples of what was sprayed here at Ft. Benning. The same effort is being made at the other military installations. At this point, we do not know what was sprayed, so it is not helpful to speculate. We will have results very shortly. Until then, I would urge every family member to remain calm and every service member to stay at your post."

Lydia muted the volume as CNN launched into what was sure to be hours of repetition of the same information. She knew it would be dark before anyone was ready to announce what had happened, if they ever announced it. She walked into the kitchen, opened one cupboard after another until she found a bottle of orange-flavored Stolichnaya. This she took, opened, and poured into the punch.

"Okay," she announced. "Let's settle in for an extended get-together. Everyone get some punch, let's sit down, stay cool, and allow the professionals outside to take care of it. Leslie, lock the dead bolt please. We'll just hunker down, enjoy some punch, and get to know each other better. Tiffany, how about some of those cookies."

Tiffany stared for a moment, blinked her huge eyes, and then retrieved a tray of cookies and began distributing them. Lydia looked around at the faces. There were a few veteran wives here—they would hold up just fine—but there were many wives who were just kids. She took a deep breath and then slowly let it out. It was going to be an exhausting day.

37

Lara liked to attend movies by herself, especially romantic comedies. Derek Cooper wasn't a big fan of the genre, so every now and then she would steal away and catch one.

The door behind her opened suddenly and a man shouted into the theater, "Terrorists just attacked Ft. Campbell housing!"

He then ran off, allowing the door to close. No one was laughing; no one even moved. They sat stunned, looking to each other for some clue as to what to do next. It seemed everyone in Clarksville cared about or at least knew someone on post. Three rows in front of Lara, a man and his wife stood and hurriedly exited the row of seats. As they came up the aisle past Lara, she rose as well, and moved up the aisle to the light.

Who could she call? She doubted she could reach Derek on his cell phone. Call the battalion? Call Tiffany Pangelinan, the host of the Night Stalker wives' meeting?

She came out of the theater and into the light, squinting against its intensity. She lifted a hand to her forehead, shielding her eyes. There were people everywhere in the parking lot, streaming out of stores and the theater behind her. Two cars backed out at the same time, and then came together in a metal-crunching collision. The two drivers then began yelling at each other, while a third person was shouting that the collision had blocked her car in.

38

Dr. Alaina F. Thoshund was the director of the CDC, sitting at the head of a conference table, bracing herself for the news she knew was coming.

"Pneumonic plague," a lanky, birdlike woman announced. "Just like Manila. Thousands have become ill overnight. But the agent was delivered in only half the attacks. It appears that in the other half it was mineral oil scented with cloves. We don't know why, except if you try to wipe it off, it just smears and would raise the level of fear. Still, we quarantined those affected, just in case."

"Cloves?" Thoshund asked.

"Well," the bird-woman replied, "the scent of baby oil combined with cloves is a weird smell, it's foreign. Smells part medicinal, part industrial. It was meant to cause fear, and it worked."

Monsters, thought Thoshund, they're all just monsters, and then she asked, "The antibiotics?"

"They're out in large enough numbers and are being administered now," came the reply. "Most people will pull through just fine, and we believe all of it is now contained. The military is fit to be tied though, they say their 'combat readiness' has been severely compromised."

"If we let pneumonic plague spread through the troops, it would get much worse," Thoshund replied.

"I know, just thought I'd pass it along. Many troops broke through barriers to reach their families, and now they're taken out of the picture and quarantined like everyone else. The military is demanding their personnel be allowed to return to their posts until symptoms appear," said bird-woman.

"Absolutely not, I'll call DoD to confirm," Thoshund said.

The bird-woman paused, and then, "You know, if they need those soldiers to protect the nation . . ."

"When the enemy is landing en masse on our beaches, I'll pull the quarantine. Until then, we have this thing beaten. I don't want to create a situation where we are behind again," Thoshund answered, and then added, "Keep me up to date."

The bird-woman nodded and left as Thoshund picked up the phone.

39

May 20
Lara's apartment
Clarksville, Tennessee

Lara sat glued to the television, watching the mayhem created by the attacks on the military installations, edited together again and again with images of Manhattan bridges falling. Every time she saw a Black Hawk on TV or heard a helicopter outside her window, she jumped.

She sat with puffy eyes, a tissue in one hand and the remote control in the other. She had called Derek's cell phone a hundred times. It wouldn't even ring. The circuits were always busy. She couldn't get through to the battalion either. The Night Stalker wives were trapped on post, and she couldn't join them.

As she changed from CNN to MSNBC to FOXNews once more, the door opened behind her. It was Derek Cooper, still in uniform, coming in.

Lara shrieked, scrambled over the back of the couch, and fell into his arms sobbing. Cooper felt awful for her, for the fear she had been feeling.

"It's okay, we're okay," he kept whispering as he stroked her hair and held her. She cried that much harder.

40

"Utter chaos," said the nasally man cheerfully. "We've created utter chaos. Their military preparedness has been substantially degraded. Thousands of their soldiers taken off duty, all the way to the rank of colonel we've confirmed. An amazing feat, Allah be praised."

"There is panic among their forces, and among the civilian population in general. Nearly every newspaper in the land was crying out for answers this morning. 'How could this happen?' 'Homeland security?' 'Is anyone safe?' " the gravelly voice chuckled.

"The soldiers could not even protect their own families on military bases. The civilians feel especially vulnerable now. We have reports of a mass exodus beginning, Americans leaving their cities," said another.

There was a pause and then the deep voice said, "The Hands of Allah are in play. Just at the peak of this chaos, which as expected the American government seems to believe is the worst we can do, we will strike the final blow. New York is crippled, Washington is paranoid, every major military installation in the United States is turned on its head, and now we will strike across the American midsection and the world will finally be rid of them."

41

They were nearing Dallas. The Fleetwood Bounder, with its nuclear payload in the rear, and the pleasant-looking couple up front. She was driving, and he was dozing, when a confused look appeared on her face. The RV lurched a bit, nothing dramatic, but unusual. The man looked over. "What is it?"

"I don't know," she replied. "I've got it floored now; we have plenty of fuel, but it is slowing down."

He rose and looked at the gauges. "We're overheating! Pull over!"

As soon as they were stopped in the breakdown lane, he hopped out and ran to the rear.

"Dammit!" he yelled.

"What is it John?" she called back. She didn't know his real name, and as far as he knew, her name wasn't really Jane either.

"It blew the sight glass from our coolant reservoir. We're stuck," he said.

She looked at him for a moment and then said, "We have three options. Abandon the mission and the weapon. Detonate the weapon here and do what damage we can, the radiation alone will drift from here to the Atlantic Ocean within a couple of days. Get the vehicle towed to Dallas, and detonate the vehicle in the city as originally planned."

"The last sounds the best," John said, "but the most risky. Suppose the weapon is discovered?"

"We detonate it as quickly as possible," she answered. "Connecting the switch and detonation will take perhaps only ten minutes."

That they were so coldly discussing the murder of so many was lost on them; they'd set their minds to the act long ago.

John looked over the engine once more, steam rising from the rear of the RV. He was scratching his head when they heard the sirens.

A firetruck was approaching. John looked at her, and slowly nodded his head. She nodded back her understanding. The door closed and she ran to the rear of the RV. He walked to the front to meet the firefighters jumping down from their truck.

"We had a report of a vehicular fire," said the first fireman.

"No fire. Just overheated. Do you know of a place around here with a wrecker that can move this piece of junk?" John said with a smile.

Firefighters walked past John to take a look for themselves, but the first stayed with him. "Yeah, we'll call someone for you. Is there anyone inside?"

"Just my wife, she's getting her stuff together," John replied.

A state trooper pulled up in his cruiser, turning on his overhead lights. This was just getting worse, thought John.

"Overheated," the fireman said to the trooper before the latter could ask. John just shrugged and smiled.

The firefighters peered in through the steam and could not see any sign of flames. Walking back toward the front, two of the three kept moving, but the third paused at the door. He thought he'd check the inside, just to be safe. Pulling the door, he didn't get it but a few inches open when there was a blast. Not of gas or fire. The door was nearly blown off its hinges and the firefighter flew backwards from the blast of the 12-gauge shotgun she had fired through the door and into his chest.

The state trooper, John, and the first fireman spun to the sound and sight. The trooper drew his weapon and had taken three quick steps to investigate when John pulled a small revolver from beneath his shirt and shot the trooper in the base of his skull. Spinning to kill the firefighter closest to him, John nearly had the revolver aimed when an enormous fire axe came chopping down into his forearm. The fireman to his left, and out of his sight, had struck with the only weapon he had. Had his arm been on something stable, it would surely have been severed, but since it moved downward with the blow, it was left attached but badly injured. The gun was immediately dropped and both bones in John's arm were smashed. A large chunk of meat had been filleted nearly off, and blood was spurting. The firefighters piled onto John, pinning him, and one removed his belt to use as a tourniquet. They wanted John to live long enough to be executed by the great state of Texas. They were none too gentle, and John was screaming in pain.

The woman jumped out of the RV to come to his aid, and was immediately pounced upon by the firefighters who had gone to check on the comrade she had gunned down. They wrested the shotgun from her hands, and drove her to the pavement.

She was shrieking, "You will all perish in a sea of fire! You can't stop all of us!"

One particularly large firefighter took the shotgun into the RV to search for anyone else who might want to take a shot at them. Instead, he found a large cylindrical object where a bed should have been.

"Sweet Jesus save us all," he whispered. He left it alone.

As he exited the RV, he shouted "Call it in! We need a bomb squad out here, might be a dirty bomb or something from what she's saying. We need hazmat or some such for sure."

The call went out. First, back to the fire company, where a watch commander remembered the training coordinated by the National Domestic Preparedness Office, much of which was being piloted right there in Dallas. The FBI was notified immediately, and that was the first federal domino. Like a current surging upward and outward across the bureaucracies of the federal government, a whole alphabet soup of acronyms were getting the word: DoD, DoE, FEMA, EPA, NRC, and HHS.

A Nuclear Emergency Search Team, or NEST, was being assembled and would be onsite within a few hours. The NESTs are designed to provide specialized personnel and resources to search for, identify, assess, and disable any nuclear weapon directed against the United States for purposes of terrorism, coercion, or extortion. Unfortunately, when it came to disabling the device, no one knew if they had the time to wait for NEST.

Another team, known as a Lincoln Gold Augmentation Team, or LGAT, was also spun up. The LGAT was designed to provide near-immediate expert technical advice and aid concerning diagnostics, render-safe procedures, analysis of the weapon, and weapon-effects prediction to deployable U.S. military Explosive Ordinance Disposal operators. In this case, however, there was no EOD on site. There were a bunch of fairly shaken firefighters, a couple of near-dead terrorists, a pair of ambulances, and a rapidly assembling team of law enforcement personnel. The city bomb squad was still fifteen minutes away.

"Listen, Sergeant," the radio squawked at Sergeant Robert Nettle of the Texas State Police. "You've got to give me some eyes on the possible device."

"Alright, but shouldn't we clear this area?" Nettle radioed back.

"If that thing is a nuke, and it goes, it just won't matter. You can't clear an area large enough to make a difference right now. Get me some idea of what we're dealing with here," said the radio again. It was Rich Stalder, a member of the LGAT assigned. He had no idea what they were dealing with. A nuke in an RV just sounded too goofy to be true, but a firefighter and a trooper were dead, so things had evidently gotten pretty serious.

Nettle entered the RV and moved back to the rear. No one was inside; no one wanted to be anywhere near the device. As he approached it, he could see what seemed like nothing more than a long cylinder. It resembled a long aluminum oxygen tank to Nettle.

"I don't see anything except the smooth outside of this thing," he radioed Stalder, and then he froze. "Should I not be using my radio around this thing?"

"The time to worry about that has long past," Stalder replied. "I'm sure there has been a storm of radio traffic around the device for the past ten minutes. What's it look like?"

Nettle shook his head. "It doesn't look like anything. Just a long, metal tube."

"It's more long than round? More like a ball, or more like a log?" Stalder asked.

"Yessir, it's at least seven feet long and maybe three feet in diameter. There's no control panel or anything that I can see," Nettle said.

"There doesn't have to be big green numbers ticking down, Nettle," Stalder said. "This isn't James Bond. Check every side of it."

"Okay, but I doubt I can lift it. Should I try to roll it?" Nettle replied.

Stalder couldn't believe what he was hearing. "No! Don't move it!"

Nettle froze, his hands suspended above the device. Outside he heard the sirens of the ambulances as they pulled away. He wished he was on one of them.

"Nettle!" Stalder called, having no way of knowing what was happening.

"I'm not touching anything," Nettle said.

Stalder replied, "Good. Just look. Walk all the way around it. If it is completely sealed, we won't be able to do anything with it until we get you some onsite help."

Between the cylinder and the wall where a headboard for the bed might have been, Nettle pointed his flashlight and looked a bit harder.

"There's something here," Nettle radioed.

"What? What does it look like?" Stalder asked. He suddenly wondered why he had quit smoking, and couldn't wait to pick up the habit again.

Nettle strained to make out what it was, and he wasn't going to touch a thing.

"Maybe a simple metal toggle switch on a small box, hanging from two wires." Nettle was contorted, his breathing labored. "The wires aren't soldered on, they're just twisted on."

Hours to the south, at Ft. Hood, practically sitting on top of the large bank of radio equipment and with others leaning in over him, Stalder couldn't believe it. Almost surely a bomb, maybe even a gun-triggered, fission nuclear weapon, and it didn't have a timer. Just a switch, probably on a battery box, some dedicated mass murderer would flip on.

"Should I pull one of the wires free from the switch?" Nettle asked.

Good question, Stalder thought. If this was all there was to it, and Nettle could pull the wire from the switch, the device would be made somewhat safer. If Stalder were there, that's just where he would start. But he wasn't there.

"Stalder?" Nettle radioed again.

"Don't touch anything, Nettle. Good job. Should be good to go. Just make sure the area is secure. NEST will be on the scene soon," Stalder said, hoping he was right. The weapon, if it would work at all, was no safer now than moments ago.

Nettle was more than happy to comply. "Yessir, will do."

Stalder put the radio down. If it were as simple a device as he suspected, and the only method of detonation was a toggle switch, Stalder knew they should be set. Still, he couldn't believe this day had actually come.

42

"Apparently, it's being taken care of now," Cat Hartman said into the phone. It was a whisper, but of such intensity little wasn't overheard by Lucy.

"No, Jack, I guess it's a no-brainer. It's not a Rubik's Cube type of thing; cut a wire and then move it to safer location for dismantling," Cat hissed again, "but it's just the idea of it."

Cat paused, listened, and then closed her eyes and began shaking her head in response to what Jack was saying.

"No, Jack, I'm not leaving D.C. There is no truly safe place, and I have a job to do. The stakes are higher than the potential casualty count," Cat said.

Cat pulled the phone away from her ear, wincing, and then began to shout into the receiver, "Jack! Jack, would you shut up! Listen, it's bigger than the potential body count. This could end it all, the entire grand experiment called America. We are engrained with the idea that we as a nation are permanent, but look at how America changed. At its core, in its values and what it was willing to accept, from the deaths of three thousand people on 9/11. If these terrorists kill hundreds of thousands, if not millions, the America we grew up in will be gone. I need to stay here; first to help in the fight, and second if we miss one . . . if

God forbid one of these things slips through . . . I want to be here to help remind my small piece of the government who we were before the attack. What we stood for and what we would never have allowed, even in reprisal. I need to stay here to help provide a dose of national memory through the crisis."

43

"The waiting is more difficult that I thought it would be," said the man in the Chicago Cubs baseball hat. He took another bite of the sandwiches she had made for them both. He knew her only as Claudia, and she knew him as Todd. Those weren't their real names, and they were neither tempted to ask nor share. "Claudia" and "Todd" were all they required. They would soon have no need for Earthly names anyway.

She nodded. "Yes, I agree. And when we drove so close to the target on the way here, only to drive away from it, that was certainly frustrating."

He shrugged and said, "There is always a schedule to these things. Perhaps there really is another team. Perhaps the whispered rumors are true. Maybe twenty major cities will be hit at once."

"Let it be so." She smiled, and then asked, "Should we attach the switch now? It seems odd they do not want us to have the weapon ready to detonate at any moment. It will take me a few minutes to attach the switch."

"No," the man said around a mouthful. "We had strict instructions. Arrive at the target site, the parking lot, and only then attach the switch. If we were to have a mishap, we might not only waste our weapon but also ruin the chances for success if there are other teams."

She considered this, seemed satisfied with the logic, and pulled a piece of her sandwich off and ate it. They fell silent and stared at each other for a moment. They knew, looking into each other's eyes, that they were both equally and totally committed to their mission.

"Very well, I won't attach it until we're in the shadow of the University of Chicago," she said.

"We'll set out right after breakfast tomorrow, and that will put us on the target with plenty of time for the noon detonation time," he said.

The woman known to him as Claudia nodded, stood, stepped into her sandals, and then asked, "Would you like another sandwich?"

44

The woman known as Jane who just that afternoon had attached a detonator switch to a nuclear device just before blasting a fireman with a shotgun had fallen silent by dinnertime.

She sat handcuffed in a small interrogation room at the Texas Ranger company headquarters, the chain between her wrists passing beneath a metal loop in the table. The walls were an eggshell white, the ceiling a series of acoustic tiles. She sat on a metal folding chair with her elbows on a faux oak tabletop. The Rangers around her had comfortable padded swivel chairs on wheels. They leaned back in them at times, and at others leaned forward at her to shout. They slapped the table from time to time. She was not intimidated.

"Where did the nuke come from?" bellowed one of the Rangers. "Who else is involved? You told people when you were captured that we could not stop all of you. Are there other nuclear weapons?"

"You're going to tell us," said another. "We've been at this for hours. In a couple more, we're going to go home to our families, and you'll stay here with the next shift, who will start at the beginning again with the questions."

She sat silent, not moving. They were like schoolchildren. Another shift? So what. Another shift of clean-cut men who for the most part had never even committed an act of violence in their entire lives. She knew the limits of their interrogation techniques from the beginning. She and everyone like her had been trained from the beginning that if they were captured inside the borders of the United States, the police could do no real harm to them. The FBI was as fierce as law enforcement could get in this country. The CIA and the military were prohibited by law from getting involved domestically in such matters. Schoolchildren. She was winning, she felt, and she drew strength from that.

The door opened behind the Rangers, and Ranger Lieutenant Jim Burns strode in. He was tall, had put on a few since his high school football days, but was still a formidable looking man. Behind him, as if in tow, were many men in dark suits. The Rangers, mostly in white shirts and khakis with multicolored neckties, were suddenly outnumbered by the black and charcoal suits and black ties. None of the new arrivals said a word.

Lieutenant Burns pointed at the handcuffs and said only, "Take these off her, Sergeant."

The Rangers all stood frozen a moment in stunned silence.

"But, Lieutenant, what's happening?"

"Just take these off," Burns answered, his tone betraying his own anger and frustration with the entire situation.

Groans of exasperation and fatigue went up around the room and the Rangers begin to move again, not going anywhere, just shifting their weight, running hands over their weary faces and through their close-cropped hair.

The dark suits stood motionless. The sergeant unlocked her handcuffs. As soon as she was free, men in dark suits were clutching her arms near the armpits and she was hustled out of the room.

The Rangers did not follow, but looked back at Burns.

"Feds," Burns spit.

"Which Feds?" one asked. "Not FBI. Besides, why not work *with* us? They always have in the past. Why snatch her away? Something's rotten here."

"I called the FBI: they confirmed we were to turn custody of our prisoner over to those men. Their identification said they were from the Defense Department. The FBI said they were part of the Pentagon's Strategic Support Branch and that we were to turn her over. They had all the paperwork, prisoner transfer, custody, jurisdiction, all of it. Signed by our friend over at the U.S. District Court for the Northern District of Texas," Burns said, his face turning red. "She's gone. That's it."

"The military?" one asked.

"I guess *posse comitatus* doesn't apply when it comes to nukes," Burns said. "Come on, fellas, get back to work."

The men in dark suits hustled Jane to the parking garage and walked her roughly over to a large, white, and unmarked 1996 Freightliner twenty-four-foot van. The rear gate slid upwards, revealing several more men standing impassively in the cargo area. These new men were not wearing suits. Instead, they were wearing coveralls. She was lifted by some and pulled by others into the rear of the van, and the door slammed shut behind her. A red light filled the large box in which they were all now standing. It smelled like warm metal, diesel, and plywood. The men released her and grabbed handles hanging from the ceiling as the truck lurched forward. They swung and adjusted, but she fell hard to the floor. The truck made a few turns and then settled into a steady hum and a predictable rhythm. Arms once again reached out for her, dragging her toward the front. There, she was placed in a simple wooden chair bolted to the floor and her wrists were strapped down.

As she looked up at them, she could not find an ounce of

hope for herself in any of their faces. Fear came in waves, but she was confident that she would die the most horrible and agonized death before she told them anything. She knew that if she died at their hands, they were just finishing what she had set out to do anyway, martyring herself.

They rolled up her sleeve, and swabbed her arm with alcohol. The strong scent of it worked hard against the smell of warm metal and human breath. She struggled against the restraints, but they fell on her, pinning her. She could only move her head from side to side. She felt the stick of the needle and immediately sensed the scopolamine flashing out from her arm, throughout her body, and washing into her brain. The second stick was more painful than the first, but she already felt disconnected. The thiopental sodium in the second syringe ripped away the last bits of competitiveness she had. She was not sleepy, she was not afraid, she was not confrontational. Jane was not in any way giddy either. She was just slow, calm, soft-spoken. She looked from face to face, unafraid and compliant.

"What is your name?" a male voice inquired. She could not tell which face had asked the question.

"Jane," she replied.

"What is your real name?" the voice asked again.

There was a pause as she accessed the information, and then, "Malak."

A man in the back snorted.

"Malak, think about the weapons. About the nuclear weapons. You had one. Do you remember?"

"Yes, I remember," Malak answered.

"Good. Where were you taking the nuclear weapon?" the man asked.

"Dallas; we were going to detonate the device near the center of Dallas," she said calmly.

There were groans, and then the man asked, "When? When was the attack supposed to happen, Malak?"

"May 21, noon, catch many people on the roads, many

out of their offices but not home, children in school, maximum chaos, maximum damage," she said flatly.

"Cold-hearted bitch," one said off to one side. Malak looked in that direction, but saw three men. Her face remained expressionless.

"Are there any other nuclear weapons?" the man asked.

"Yes, many," she replied flatly.

There was a sudden shuffling of feet as the tension rose.

"Do you know where they are?" the man asked.

"Yes, the Israelis have them and the Pakistanis and the Indians, and of course the West and the Russians and the Chinese—" Malak began.

"No, Malak," the man interrupted. "I mean like the one you had. I mean in America. Are there more attacks planned with the nuclear weapons here in America?"

"I do not know for sure. We compartmentalize operations information for reasons of security. That way if captured, we cannot reveal that which we do not know," she replied. The irony was completely lost on her, but not on the men.

"Did you overhear anything? See perhaps a paper or hear a conversation about other attacks?" the man asked.

"Yes, I did hear of at least one other device, another RV, but I don't know where it was going, and I don't know if it is true. I was not told. We compartmentalize operations information for—" Malak said.

"Yes, yes, we know," the man said, frustrated. "Think, Malak. Where was the other attack going to be?"

"Indianapolis," Malak said.

Gasps, and then the man asked, "Indianapolis?"

"Or Chicago, or maybe Detroit," Malak said.

Disappointment swept through the men. The truck switched lanes, the highway-speed drone of the diesel engine never changed, and as men reached for something to steady themselves, the man asked, "Which one, Malak? Indianapolis, Chicago, or Detroit?"

"I don't remember, I'm sorry," Malak said.

"Bullshit!" one said. "No way she doesn't remember what city is going to be nuked."

"She's not lying," another said. "There's so much sodium pentathol in her, I'm surprised she's conscious."

"She doesn't know," said the primary interrogator.

Malak's head fell forward, and the man who had administered the injections stepped forward. He lifted her head, pulled open each eye in turn, pointing a small flashlight into the pupils.

"She's out," he announced. "She's not going to die, but she's not going to answer any more questions at this point."

The man who had asked the questions turned to his colleagues. "We know a potential time and three potential places. We're better off than we were when we got up this morning. Get this up to national level consumers ASAP and they can starting hunting."

"What about her?" one asked.

The lead interrogator looked back and said, "By the end of today, she'll be long gone."

When Malak did wake up, it was dark. She blinked a few times, her head pounding, and she tried to clear her vision. She was on a cot, staring up at chain-link fencing. It was disorienting. Focusing on the fencing, she felt like the world was turned ninety degrees. Up felt like sideways, and sideways was up. Turning her head slowly, painfully, she saw that the fencing had her penned in on all sides. The floor was sand, but the walls and the ceiling were ordinary chain-link fencing. She sat up, saw that she had been left a towel, an extra blanket, and a copy of the Koran. She could see there were actually a row of cages just like hers, with palm trees nearby.

"Welcome to Guantánamo," a voice said behind her.

She spun around and saw LT Saffed looking at her.

"I am LT Saffed, I am a Muslim chaplain in the U.S. Army, and I'm here for you," Saffed said.

"Traitorous pig," she spit at him.

Saffed nodded, turned, and walked away.

She jumped up, threw herself against the cage wall, and screamed after him, "Let me out of here!"

Saffed ignored her, and continued to walk until he disappeared around the corner of a small wooden building.

45

It was time to address the American people again. The problem was fresh attacks like those on the military housing units the day before didn't provide fresh words to use in the effort to reassure the American people. New attacks provided new casualties but didn't provide new diction and syntax to convince Americans that all that could be done was being done.

President Rand sat at his desk, makeup being applied, and the teleprompter glowed with words that sounded much too familiar. Still, the true purpose of this evening's address was not so much to calm nerves about the plague sprayed on the families of service members. A nuclear weapon had been dismantled outside Dallas, and there was reason to believe at least one other was on the move. Just the panic that such news would cause would kill thousands, especially in light of the recent string of terrorism here at home, not to mention the devastating attack in Poland.

Ten days before, in his last address immediately following the attacks on the bridges and tunnels of Manhattan, he had reassured the country that they were safe enough to go about their daily business.

With the plague attack yesterday, with vast stretches of military bases under quarantine, the people were not going to be as trusting of his words tonight. Already protests were springing up across the country, protests fueled by fear, and there were reports of near riots and looting in places like Philadelphia and Detroit. The people were demanding protection and the truth.

And once again, he was going to deceive them, or at least withhold the reality of the situation. He was going to try to comfort them in regards to the biological attacks, but he was not going to warn the people about the nuclear threat. He would not tell them that all was well and that they should go about their lives as they normally would, but he certainly would not tell them what grave danger an entire section of the country might be in.

A young man with headphones announced, "Ten seconds," and everyone backed off from the president just as he received the signal to begin.

"Good evening. Yesterday, we suffered yet another attack at the hands of terrorists. The cowards chose not to attack our military, but instead to attack the children and spouses of our brave men and women in uniform.

"Yesterday, at several military installations across our land, crop dusters came in very low and sprayed the housing areas where the families of our service members live. In some cases, the spray was a harmless mix designed only to create fear. In others, we have confirmed the presence of pneumonic plague, the same biological agent used in Manila.

"Unlike Manila, everyone, even those sprayed with what has been determined to be harmless, has been put on a rigorous antibiotic therapy. This disease is usually quite treatable when caught early and hopes are very high that the loss of life will be minimal."

President Rand paused, cleared his throat, and continued, "Early indications are that the crop dusters were purchased legally. Every crop duster was destroyed early in the attacks, and every terrorist pilot was killed. Still, we are following the money, and we will find out who supported this attack, and they will be brought to justice.

"Now, I would speak to those Americans who are allowing their fear to take over the better halves of their nature. Those creating unrest in our streets. The point of all terrorism is to create terror. To create fear. When a terrorist attack causes Americans to go out in unruly mobs and harm other Americans and their property, the terrorist has accomplished exactly what he hoped he might. He has, through fear, caused you to act less American. I ask you all to return to your homes and remember who you are and what we as a country truly represent to the rest of the world.

"You have heard me ask you time and again to go about your lives. To go to work, to go shopping, to be yourselves. To not allow terrorism to change your routine. Well, tonight, because tension and emotions and fear have risen to such an elevated level, I'm asking for something new.

"Tonight I am asking the American people to take a Great National Pause. I'm asking all of you to just stay home with your loved ones tomorrow. Stay off the streets and stay where you are for a national day of reflection. Not of fear, but of reflection. We need, as a nation, to take a deep breath and renew our resolve. So tomorrow, I ask you all to simply stay home, hug your children, and remember how lucky we all are to be Americans. Let's just take a Great National Pause tomorrow.

"I also ask for your prayers for our men and women in uniform and their families going through this difficult period. Thank you. Good night, God bless the victims of yesterday's attack, and God bless America."

There was the usual pause and then a voice announced, "You're off, Mr. President."

White House Chief of Staff Debra Pratt stepped up to the front of the desk. "Well done, Mr. President."

Jeb Gould, the National Security Advisor, joined Pratt

but then turned and watched the Oval Office clear. As the last of the technicians and staff members exited, and the curved door sealed the three and their secrets in, he turned and said, "We're looking, Mr. President, but perhaps we should consider martial law. Mobilize the National Guard, lock the civilian population down. It may freeze any nukes short of their targets."

"Jeb," the president began, "we've discussed this. The panic that would follow would kill too many. And how do we enforce it? Do you want stories of our own military firing on American refugees who refuse to comply?"

"Besides, the nukes, and we only have intel on one more, and it may not even exist, may already be in a major city. If we go Chinese on this and have our tanks rumbling through the streets to control our own people, whoever has it may detonate it immediately," Pratt offered.

"Mr. President," Gould said, looking past Pratt, "you don't honestly believe people will observe your 'Great National Pause,' do you?"

"Yes, I do, Jeb," Rand said, rising, half smiling, and pointing at Gould with the air of a salesman. "I think you are underestimating the patriotism and determination of the American people."

"Sir, with all due respect, I think you are underestimating the power of fear and are overestimating the trust people have in their government," Gould said, exasperated.

"That's enough," Pratt said. "You've had you say, Jeb, but we're not going that way."

Jeb Gould let his head drop and he thrust his hands into his pockets. He'd have to play the hand he was dealt. He nodded, signaling that his protestations had ended.

"Don't worry," Rand said, approaching. "The Lord is one our side. Let's just have faith."

46

The man known as Todd dropped into the driver's seat of the RV. He pulled his Cubs cap on and flipped on the radio. Another camper ran past in flip-flops, and Todd attempted to wave. The man did not wave back. He looked afraid, but not afraid of Todd. The man looked like he was trying to come up with a plan of life-and-death consequence. The truth was, that was exactly what the man was doing.

The news broadcast began with some odd jingle, and then a man in an impossibly Caucasian voice said, "Despite President Rand's pleas for everyone to stay home today, or perhaps because of them, Americans are doing anything but observing a Great National Pause."

"Claudia, come listen," he yelled back. "A Great Pause?" he wondered aloud. "What is that?"

Claudia arrived. "What is it?"

The voice on the radio continued, "The nation's roadways are jammed, from coast to coast. In light of the terror attacks on New York, Washington, D.C., and military installations, people are afraid. President Rand's Oval Office address last night, intended to soothe the nation's nerves, has seemingly accomplished the exact opposite. Rumors of pending terror attacks are running wild, even among first responders."

Claudia looked at Todd, concerned at the new development.

The broadcast went on, "Everyone is trying to either get out of the cities to hide in the country, or get into the cities to retrieve loved ones. The mad exodus is especially intense in the three cities of Detroit, Indianapolis, and Chicago where there are reports of police and even military roadblocks. The authorities seem to be checking every large truck. There are also unconfirmed and sporadic reports of violence."

Todd turned the radio down a bit, and twisted in his seat to face Claudia.

"We should just detonate it now," Claudia said.

"What?" Todd asked, surprised. "We are more than sixty miles from Chicago. The device will have no effect at all on the city. We'll have died in order to destroy Kankakee, Illinois?"

"We will never get close to Chicago," Claudia said softly.

"We will get as close as we can. Every kilometer closer is a kilometer better. Besides, it is way too early. Remember, we may not be the only team. They mentioned Detroit and Indianapolis as well. We do not want to go early and ruin their chances of success," Todd said.

"Fine, that is fine, but I will connect the switch before we go. I will sit with my hand on the detonator, and I will detonate the device the moment we are stopped," Claudia said.

"Agreed, but not a moment before we are stopped. It is absolutely imperative that we get as close to the target location and time as possible," Todd said.

Claudia nodded. As she began to connect the metal switch to the long cylindrical device, Todd fired up the engine. They headed out, headed north. Claudia sat in the rear on the floor with her hand a few inches from the triggering device. They still had an hour drive to the objective point, the University of Chicago. They were determined to try to get as close as possible. It was agreed and understood. If they were stopped, Claudia would set off the weapon.

47

"Time for antibiotics everyone," Lydia announced. They were still quarantined in the housing area. The Night Stalker wives had tried to turn the whole thing into a giant slumber party, but after two nights, they had all had enough and just wanted to return to their husbands, children, and home. They all began reaching for their ziplock baggies. No brown pill bottles with neat little prescription labels. Everyone had received a baggie containing her share of the medication from a man wearing a biohazard suit. A tad disconcerting to say the least.

Lydia washed the Cipro down with a bit of orange juice. She wondered where Mike was. Cell phone calls had gone unanswered last night and this morning. That wasn't like Mike, except when he was gone or in isolation before a mission.

CNN's *Breaking News* filled the television screen and someone turned it way up. "CNN has received several reports from highly placed members of Texas law enforcement that Texas Rangers recovered a crude but functional nuclear weapon during a traffic stop yesterday."

"Good Lord," Lydia whispered.

The women crowded around the screen.

"CNN has also learned that it is suspected that at least

one other weapon is currently in the United States, perhaps, according to sources, headed for Detroit or Indianapolis," the reporter continued.

"Oh my God," Lydia said. "Why report such a thing?"

"Lydia?" asked Tiffany. "Wouldn't you want to know, if you were living in Detroit?"

Lydia shook her head. "It won't matter. After that report, no one will be able to get out of Detroit except on foot, and if you are dealing with a nuclear weapon, you couldn't get far enough away."

Tiffany looked down and tears began to fall. "What's happened to us? It's all different now."

In Detroit and Indianapolis, within half an hour of the CNN report, there was utter chaos. People were trying to flee, and riots began when they could not. There was mass hysteria, there was looting, and entire sections of the cities were burning unchecked. In Detroit, looting and fires spread through the Northwest Side, then crossed over to the East Side. In Indianapolis, Capitol Avenue, Illinois Street, and Meridian Street were packed with three pieces of the same unruly mob. Military and police checkpoints added no stability, but were instead points at which the populace focused their rage. There were dozens of shootings. In coming months, there would be entire neighborhoods each city would have to rebuild from scratch.

Lydia Ryan, Tiffany Pangelinan, and the other Night Stalker wives watched the drama cranking up live on CNN. News helicopters, ordered grounded by the local authorities, were being chased across the skies of the two cities by police helicopters. All in all, the news media profited nicely from the mayhem they had created.

48

CPT Rick Sirois circled in his AH-6J Little Bird, looking down on and providing cover for CW3 Jeanie McCall's Black Hawk as it extracted the Delta operators. The highway traffic below was badly snarled, and the pair of Night Stalker helicopters was working its way north on this stretch of Interstate 57, seeking out large recreational vehicles, inserting the Black Hawk's D-boys and having them search the RV for a nuke. Sirois pulled away from his circuitous flight path, and the Black Hawk, just off to his east, climbed.

Three battalions of the 160th SOAR were searching highways this morning. The 1st of the 160th had been tasked with the Detroit area, the 3rd of the 160th had Indianapolis as their mission, and the 6/160th had been given responsibility for Chicago. The 6/160th was broken into pairs, just like the one Sirois and McCall were in, with the Black Hawks carrying Rangers and Delta operators.

McCall's two crew members, Arroyo and Hill, were manning their miniguns. While every mission was undertaken with the utmost professionalism and dedication by both soldiers, this one was different for Hill. The city they were protecting, Chicago, was where Hill grew up. It's where everyone he cared about, outside the military, still lived. For Hill, the stakes could not be higher.

Sirois could see McCall's Black Hawk slide back behind his Little Bird as they flew north, looking for the next
RV to search.

"Arrow 42, this is Bullet 13, I've got two up ahead,"
Sirois radioed, his voice betraying both the stress of
searching for a nuclear weapon on American soil and the
disbelief that either of these RVs was the RV for which
they were hunting.

"Good copy, take up your racetrack pattern, we'll bull-
horn them," McCall radioed back. Sirois climbed and then,
after passing the first RV, banked hard left. The Black
Hawk came alongside the slowly moving vehicle, pacing it
at less than ten miles per hour.

"This is the United States Army," Hill announced through
the loudspeaker system. "You in the blue and gold RV, you
are ordered to stop your vehicle right where it is. Your vehicle will be searched. Stop your vehicle and exit carefully
and slowly."

Hill then focused his gun on the RV. He was pretty sure
he could shred the thing to pieces with a minute's work. At
least rip it open pretty good, he thought. The Black Hawk
came down slowly, the Delta operators ready at the door.
The RV door opened and an elderly couple emerged, the
woman's hair in curlers, covered by a kerchief. When the
gear was a couple feet above the road surface, and with
cars now having to slowly drive around the low-hovering
helicopter, the Delta operators leapt out.

Sirois circled above, looking for external threats. Anything
that came out of the RV, Hill would rip up with the minigun, but a threat from without was Sirois's responsibility.

As the Little Bird came around to a northerly heading
once more, the second RV, the one further north, suddenly

lurched forward. It slammed into a car blocking it from reaching the breakdown lane, and then pushed the little Honda right across that space and off the highway.

"What the hell?" Sirois said.

The RV turned north on the breakdown lane and took off at a high rate of speed.

"Arrow 42 this is Bullet 13! Reel in your guys! We have an RV, off-white and brown, and green looks like. A big Fleetwood, I think. It slammed its way into the breakdown lane and it is hauling ass for Chicago. I'm breaking off to pursue," Sirois radioed. He pulled hard on the collective, and pushed the stick forward. The Little Bird nosed down and streaked forward after the RV.

McCall was on the intercom before Sirois was done with his radio transmission. "Hill! Get the Delta guys back aboard! Now! We've got a suspect RV up ahead!"

"Delta! Delta! Abort search! Double-time back to the bird!" Hill shouted into the loudspeaker. The Delta operators came back at a dead sprint, leaving the elderly couple with their hands up and terribly shaken. As the last of the commandos leapt into the helicopter, Hill called into the intercom, "We've got 'em, ma'am! Go go go!"

The powerful Black Hawk leapt into the sky and then nosed down just as Sirois's Little Bird had.

As the Black Hawk caught the RV, Sirois's Little Bird dropped down in front of it. His skids were less than a dozen feet from the front of the RV, when he spun in flight. Now flying sideways at more than sixty miles an hour, Sirois's copilot was waving for the RV to stop. Hill's voice came over the loudspeaker system again. "RV! Stop at once! Stop and be searched or we will open fire!"

Inside the RV, the man known as Todd looked out at the nimble helicopter flying sideways in front of him, filling the windshield. At first he was startled, but then he wished he could catch it, ram it. When the voice ordering them to stop sounded above all the engine and aircraft noises, Claudia thought it was time.

"We should detonate the device before they shoot!" Claudia shouted.

"No!" Todd shouted back. "Did you hear the voice? Little more than a teenager! For all they know right now, we are panicking elderly Americans! They will not shoot! Every kilometer, every half minute matters! We must wait!"

Claudia said nothing. Todd was right. If they were going to expend the weapon and give their lives, the closer they got to the city, the better.

Hill's voice came from above again: "This is the United States Army! Stop the vehicle, or I will open fire! You have five seconds to comply!"

"He's going to shoot!" Claudia shouted.

"Need more time!" Todd shouted back.

Claudia scrambled, found a large pad of paper and a marker, and scrawled some words on it. The she moved to the side door. She opened it and looked out at Hill. She held up the pad.

"It's a woman!" Hill said into the intercom. "She's got a sign!"

"What's it say?" McCall called back.

"Hard to read it!" Hill said, straining to see it. The RV and the aircraft were less than twenty feet apart, but with the wind and rotor wash, the dust, and everything else . . .

A Delta operator pulled binoculars to his face, and then jumped over to Hill. "It says, 'Help me! Kidnapped!' "

Hill nodded and relayed it.

"Bullshit!" McCall roared back. "How much of a coincidence is that? A woman happens to be kidnapped in an RV making a mad dash to Chicago?"

"Let's just shoot it up!" Arroyo offered from the opposite side. He was craning his neck to see what he could from his position on the bird, which wasn't much.

"Arrow 42, this is Bullet 13, what's going on, McCall? Let's shoot this thing!" Sirois called.

"Bullet 13, be advised, a woman just flashed a sign from within, claiming she is being kidnapped," McCall explained, knowing Sirois's reaction was going to be much like her own.

"That's a crock! There's no way! We have to stop this thing, we're coming up on thirty miles to downtown!" Sirois replied.

"Stand by," McCall answered Sirois, and then she radioed to Hartman, "Arrow 6, Arrow 6, this is Arrow 42." Sirois outranked McCall, but she had the Delta operators, and was given lead on the pair.

Immediately, the response came: "Go ahead, Arrow 42."

"Arrow 6, we have an RV here, on Interstate 57, headed north to Chicago, refusing to stop. Female in the RV indicates she has been kidnapped. We are three-zero miles from downtown. Please advise," McCall radioed.

If the RV had been an enemy military vehicle in the mountains of Afghanistan, McCall would have already ordered its destruction, but flying above a crowded interstate in Illinois . . . things were less black-and-white.

Just then, from his Little Bird, Sirois watched as a police cruiser turned out of the traffic and pulled out into the breakdown lane ahead of the RV, trying to slow its progress. The RV didn't slow down, it accelerated. The cop in the police cruiser realized the driver had no intention of slowing and he tried to retreat back into his position, but once vacated, his spot in traffic had been almost instantly filled. The RV rammed the cruiser. The car spun into the other cars, and traffic that had been creeping along came to a chaotic halt. The RV fishtailed, and came up on half of its tires.

"I think this might be it!" Sirois shouted hopefully.

But then the RV fell back to all its tires and was once again under control. It continued on its race toward Chicago in the breakdown lane. The considerable damage to the front of the large vehicle had down nothing to slow it down.

"Arrow 42, this is 6. Listen, I'm on the way, but I'm not there. You'll have to make the command decision on this one," Hartman radioed McCall. She knew Hartman was right.

McCall looked across at the RV and then turned to her copilot. Beyond the copilot, coming across their path, was a news helicopter, navy blue and grey, with "CBS 2 CHICAGO" and the large CBS eyeball logo painted on its side.

"Just what I need," McCall growled to herself.

49

"It looks like a war zone," Tiffany said softly to Lydia as they watched footage coming in from Detroit. People threw rocks and bottles at police shouting for everyone to return to their homes. Tear gas canisters were being fired into mobs to disperse them.

And then, even this incredible footage was superseded, when once again, the CNN *Breaking News* logo came floating into the center of the screen and Wolf Blitzer's voice broke in: "We leave these disturbing images from Detroit for a moment for some news that is just breaking south of Chicago. A CBS affiliate, WBBM, has a chopper in the air, and veteran pilot and journalist Christian Happerman is reporting, let's listen in . . ."

"And these military helicopters, army helicopters, including a Black Hawk familiar to many as the type of helicopter seen in the movie *Black Hawk Down,* appear to be chasing a large recreational vehicle. We are pacing them now, the Black Hawk and a smaller helicopter you can see here, and the RV. At this point, it is a complete mystery why this RV is being chased. It seems they want it to stop, but we have no way of knowing why. As you can see, the RV is driving very very quickly in the breakdown lane, which by itself is incredibly dangerous as the highway here is full of slow-moving cars and trucks." Happerman's voice was jittery from the vibration of the aircraft, the whine of its engine clearly heard behind. The images of McCall's Black Hawk and Sirois's Little Bird chasing the RV were riveting. Especially to the Night Stalker wives.

Wolf Blitzer's voice returned, unable to talk to the pilot directly. "Simply remarkable footage, coming from Chicago. It is not known at this time why the RV is being chased, but in these days of devastating terrorist attacks coming one after another, one can't help but guess this must be related. Let's listen in some more."

"So let's see if I can get around to the other side here." And the news chopper rose suddenly, slid over, and then dropped once more, so that the RV was between Happerman and McCall's Black Hawk. Sirois's Little Bird rose and descended behind the procession. In the footage, the crew chief, Hill, was clearly visibly in the door, waving for Happerman to get the news chopper out of the line of fire. To remove any doubt, the figure in the military helicopter, on live worldwide TV, reached out and in an exaggerated way, pointed to his minigun.

"I'm being waved off here! I think, as unbelievable as this might be, I think they intend to open fire on the RV!" Happerman reported.

Lydia, watching all of this unfold, and seeing Hill, who might have just as easily been her husband's crew chief Derek Cooper, came to the realization that she might even be watching her husband's aircraft. It was one thing, in the old days, when he would go on missions, but it was an entirely new sensation to be watching Night Stalker missions live on television.

"Not again," Lydia whispered.

50

"Arrow 42, this is Bullet 13, how do you want to handle this?" Sirois radioed to McCall.

She weighed the consequences. Worst-case scenario of destroying the RV would be a dead kidnapper and his victim. Worst-case scenario of not destroying the RV would be that Chicago would soon look like Warsaw. Chicago would stand in radioactive ruins.

"Bullet 13, this is Arrow 42. I will pull the news bird off of you and the target," McCall said. "And then I want you to take the target out."

"Good copy" was all Sirois said.

McCall's helicopter slid left, passing over the RV and crowding the news helicopter. The large Black Hawk slowly drifted closer and closer to Happerman's aircraft. The RV and the three helicopters were approaching Chicago at better than sixty-five miles per hour now, and McCall was inching in on the much smaller helicopter to Sirois's left. Sirois waited, ready to unleash the Little Bird's firepower on the RV. He waited for the news aircraft to give ground. It did not.

"The military chopper is intentionally trying to drive me away," Happerman's breathless voice came through. On the video feed, the Black Hawk loomed larger and larger, filling the television screens back in the CBS 2 control room and around the world.

"Back off, Chris, back off, give room," the director was ordering in Happerman's headphones.

"No way." Happerman responded not just to his director but out to the live feed. "I'm not moving."

"Arrow 42, this is Bullet 13, he hasn't budged," Sirois radioed.

"This is Arrow 42, I can see that," McCall replied. "A pretty cool customer, this guy."

Happerman's aircraft suddenly dropped, banked slightly right, and passed at car rooftop height beneath the Black Hawk. The air became terrible for both helicopters.

"Dammit! He's under me!" McCall barked.

"Confirmed, he is sliding right, beneath you," Sirois said, his jaw working.

"Pulling out!" McCall called as she applied collective, lifting away from the CBS 2 news chopper. Happerman rose slightly, steadied, and paced the RV once more. He had driven off the Black Hawk.

"He might be stupid, but he can fly the hell out of the bird," Sirois said.

"Bullet 13, the is Arrow 42, take out the RV now. We're getting too close to worry about the press," McCall radioed.

"Roger, engaging now," Sirois said, but just as he opened fire with his minigun and rockets, the right lane cleared and the RV swerved left from the breakdown lane into it. The rockets missed, but three of the large minigun rounds tore holes in the thin-skinned roof of the RV.

"Holy shit!" Happerman's profanity was broadcast throughout Chicagoland and beyond. Additionally, the video stream of an army helicopter opening up on a big, goofy-looking camper went out as well. At this point, Happerman did pull up and away, trying to put some distance between him and the target below. He understood now what McCall had been trying to accomplish by crowding him.

The roof had fist-sized chunks missing from it and the wind was whistling loudly inside the RV.

"We must detonate it!" Claudia shrieked.

"Not yet! Do not give in to your fear! Just a bit further! We'll get closer, Inshallah!" Todd screamed back.

Sirois lined up for another volley, this time all rockets. Just as he fired, the RV swung back into the breakdown lane as it caught up with the next block of slow-moving traffic. All of the rockets missed the RV. All of the rockets but one hit nothing at all, but that one struck right above the rear bumper of a Saturn Vue. The underpowered and lightweight SUV was thrown onto its side and the rear of it burst into flames.

Happerman was beside himself. "They just took out an SUV! It appears that the driver is climbing out, moving on her own, but that could have been much, much worse. One has to wonder what these military pilots are thinking. The collateral damage out here on I-57 could be enormous if this does not end quickly."

"Hold your fire! Cease fire, Bullet 13!" McCall shouted across the air net, and then into the intercom. "Hill, you're going to have to stop that RV. It's coming up on your side."

"Hooah, ma'am," Hill said through clenched teeth. Hill, the former Southside gang member, the kid from the tough neighborhood, was faced with stopping what looked like nothing more than an out of control vacation vehicle. As they came up alongside, the Delta operators took up firing positions in the large cargo door to the rear of Hill. He saw the door open, and the woman's form flashed there for a moment, and was gone. Hill decided he would stop the RV, but he would at least initially try to spare shooting up the whole passenger area where he guessed the woman was. He turned to the nearest D-boy and shouted above the howling wind, "Hold your fire! All of you! I got this!"

The word passed between them, and while none of them moved away from the door, they all lowered the muzzles of their weapons.

Hill knew he had just taken all of the responsibility on himself. The Black Hawk was impossibly low at this point, just barely clearing the roofs of cars they passed over. It leapt up over a truck and fell back to car height. Hill, the battle-tested crew chief, aimed carefully, and fired. An impressively aimed stream of rounds raced into the RV just above the front tire.

"What the hell are you shooting at?" Morrison, the copilot of the Black Hawk, bellowed into the intercom.

Pieces flew off the RV, there was some smoke, and the vehicle swerved a bit, but as Hill ceased fire the driver regained control.

"I'm shooting at the engine!" Hill yelled back.

"The engine's in the back, man! Come on! Stop this damn thing or a whole lot of people are going to die!" Morrison replied instantly, anticipating Hill's answer.

"Shit, I knew that," Hill hissed at himself, and he fired once more. This time the rounds poured into his best guess on the engine compartment.

"Arrow 42, Arrow 42, this is Arrow 6," Hartman radioed to McCall, "I'm on scene, I need an immediate SITREP!"

"Arrow 6, Arrow 42, we are engaging a target vehicle," McCall answered.

Hartman could see that. His aircraft was approaching from the north, on the west side of the highway. Hill's minigun was blowing huge chunks off the RV. Cars all along the engagement were crashing into each other at low speeds, trying to get whatever distance they could.

The Delta operators were shouting encouragement to Hill. The Black Hawk's undercarriage was lower than the RV was high. When the side door on the RV opened again, the woman was clearly visible once more. Her serious face, her clothing flapping in the wind. Hill ceased fire, picturing some horror about to unfold, like her throwing herself from the fleeing vehicle in a desperate attempt to escape her kidnapper and Hill's firing. Instead, she suddenly produced a 12-gauge shotgun and fired at the aircraft. She quickly pumped and fired again and again.

"Shit!" was all Hill said before he was hit in the vest and arm. He fell back. A couple of the Delta operators were hit, but all of the rest opened fire. Arroyo jumped up to move to Hill's side of the aircraft, but McCall pulled the Black Hawk away, before any of them could tell if they had hit anything.

Happerman, from the CBS 2 chopper, was shrieking his reporting now. "The woman is shooting at the army helicopters, shooting at them, driving off the larger of the two! I can only imagine the response will not be another attempt to disable the RV, but instead to destroy it outright!"

Hartman watched as McCall peeled away; he saw the woman blasting away at her aircraft.

"Rick, this is Colonel Hartman, I don't care what it takes, but take that RV out! Waste it!" the commander of the 6/160th roared.

"I'm all over it!" Sirois shouted back.

51

"Oh my God! Oh my God!" the wives were screaming as they watched McCall's Black Hawk gain altitude. The woman, Claudia, was visible even to them, and the shotgun blasts also easy to see.

Lydia sat down. She whispered only, "End this."

Tiffany sat beside her, and they held hands. In the kitchen a teapot began to whistle; nobody moved to pull it from the heat.

52

"I am going to detonate it now!" Claudia shouted.

Todd looked back and then up at the helicopters he could see. He nodded vigorously. *It was time.*

"Yes! Do it! We're close enough!" Todd screamed back. He swerved around a car that was a bit over the line and into the breakdown lane. The move caused Claudia to fall as she was working her way to the switch. She didn't bother to stand again, but instead crawled the remaining three feet to the switch. She picked up the switch box in her hands, cradling it as she rocked gently with the movement of the RV. She looked up front at Todd.

"Allah-u-akbar!" she shouted.

"Allah-u-akbar!" Todd shouted back. He was driving, but in that instant he closed his eyes tightly.

Above and from behind, Sirois streaked down on the RV. He loosed everything he had, rockets flying and miniguns blazing. This time there would be no missing. The skids on Sirois's bird nearly struck the top of the RV as it was disintegrating beneath him. The minigun and rockets ripped the RV open as if by a large can opener. The woman, Claudia, was blown out and under the tires just as the chassis itself came

apart and the wreckage began to tumble in a giant fireball.
Sirois pulled up and away hard, and then banked to watch.

The wreckage continued to tumble. If it weren't for the
occasional glimpse of tire, there would have been no
guessing the mass of metal and faux wood had ever been a
vehicle. A long, metallic, and cylindrical object also appeared and then disappeared, rolling as part of the total debris off the highway. Sirois's heart caught in his throat,
realizing what it was and wondering if it might actually go
off, and then all was still, amidst a large cloud of smoke
and dust.

"They blew it up! The RV is completely gone, completely
destroyed! It's just a pile of scrap smoking off to the side
of the highway!" Happerman shouted. "It appears this is
over. It's unlikely, it's impossible that there are any survivors in that."

Sirois wheeled around and then passed over the wreckage
of the RV.

"This is Arrow 42, Bullet 13 take up a racetrack pattern
above. I will insert my customers, they will secure the
scene," McCall called.

"Roger that," Sirois said, gaining altitude and setting a
new course. He was still breathing hard, beads of sweat on
his forehead.

"Arrow 42, this is Arrow 6, tell your customers to set up
a wide perimeter and not to get too close. We'll get a NEST
team out here ASAP. How copy over?" Hartman radioed.

"Good copy," McCall replied, and then in the intercom,
"Hill, you still okay?"

"Yes, ma'am," Hill said. A Delta medic had secured a
pressure bandage to Hill's upper arm, put it in a sling, and
Hill had returned to his position.

"Tell the D-boys to set up a perimeter, but to keep their distance, unless they want to glow in the dark," McCall said.

Hill even managed to smile, but Arroyo answered for him: "Yes, ma'am."

53

May 23
Barricade outside Family Housing
Ft. Campbell, Kentucky

Mike Ryan stood at a yellow barricade guarded by MPs, waiting to be allowed to pass. The forty-eight-hour quarantine was about to be lifted, and the Military Police were only waiting for the word.

The substance sprayed at Ft. Campbell was determined to be mineral oil, but no one regretted giving all the family members inside the prophylactic antibiotics. Everyone remembered the horrors of the bio attack on Manila.

A handheld radio squawked, an MP nodded, and the barricade was opened. The throng moved through, and Ryan at first walked quickly and then jogged to the front. The crowd, most of them fathers and husbands who had been forced to ponder the loss of their most treasured loved ones, kept pace. As they turned down into the main parking lot, women and children could be seen coming out of the buildings on both sides. The men broke into sprints. Names were shouted, and the cries of relief and reunion rang through the space. Wives jumped into the arms of their husbands, children pulled at clothing to be lifted up. Ryan was still looking. He was not sure where Tiffany and Scott Pangelinan lived. He knew which building, but it could be one of three stairway doors. He ran to the first, scanning faces. He saw nothing familiar, but then he heard her.

"Mike?" Lydia called.

Ryan turned, saw her walking across the grass. He ran to her, lifted her in a forceful embrace, fueled by washed-away fear and love reassured. As he spun her, she held his face in her hands, and then pulled his head to her. He put her down, and they kissed.

"I really do love you, you know?" she whispered.

"I love you too," he replied.

There was an incredibly shrill scream and then laughter. Turning to look, the Ryans saw Scott Pangelinan holding Tiffany as a groom might carry a bride over the threshold, headed for their apartment. No longer a room full of terrified wives, and once again their home.

Ryan looked over toward Lydia's car and asked, "You have the keys to that thing?"

She lifted them high in one hand and jingled them.

Ryan smiled. "Then let's go home."

He wrapped one arm over her shoulders, and then said, "By the way, when we move to Rucker, I've found someone to take care of the house while we're gone."

"Rent it, you mean? Who?" Lydia asked, looking up as they walked.

"No, not rent it, I mean just live there. Keeping it up, you know," Ryan said carefully.

"Hartman? Jack Hartman wants to freeload at our house?" Lydia asked.

"Not freeload!" Ryan laughed. "He'd be doing us a favor."

"What's that? Making sure we don't get honest rent for the place?" Lydia laughed back.

"Well, I could offer it to the Little Bird bachelors. They could treat it like a frat house," Ryan tried.

"Hartman told you to say that didn't he, about the frat house?" Lydia guessed.

"What? No," Ryan chuckled. "No, not at all. Anyway, what do you think of Jack living there?"

"Five hundred a month," Lydia said.

"What? He's our friend," Ryan replied.

They reached the car, Lydia hit the keyless entry, and they each opened a door. Lydia, of course, was climbing into the driver's seat.

"It's because he's our friend that I am offering such a fantastic discount. We won't even require a deposit from him," Lydia offered happily. "But I do want a one-year lease."

"Unbelievable," Ryan said, putting one hand to his forehead.

Lydia put the car in gear and drove away.

54

May 24
Night Stalker Picnic
Pennyrile Lake
An hour north of Ft. Campbell

Periodically, the 6/160th SOAR went to Pennyrile Lake for
battalion picnics. Pennyrile was a small lake, less than
sixty acres in all, but a somewhat secluded picnic area provided grills and open space. On this occasion, the Night
Stalkers were not only relieving tension, but celebrating.
Several of their family members, normally thought of as
noncombatants out of harm's way, had been directly and
deliberately attacked. Their battalion had also been the unit
to stop what would have been a nation-changing event, the
destruction of a major American city, and had saved countless lives.

Hill threw the football, with one arm in a sling, and it
fell back to earth into the arms of a running Derek Cooper.
The last of the sun's light was fading fast, and both men
laughed at the effort Cooper had had to make, adjustment
and readjustment, in order to catch the ball. He never threw
it back, however. Lara called for him, he dropped the ball
where he was, and took off at a jog. "We'll play again
later."

Hill shook his head in disbelief and started walking to
retrieve the ball.

Along the beach, Jack and Cat Hartman walked hand in
hand, detouring gradually and slowly around the fires.

Around each, another set of soldiers, wives, loved ones, and children sat, laughed, and some even sang. In the distance, from one of the fires, Jack could hear a radio playing the song "Lakeside Park" by Rush.

Out on the lake, a small floating platform loaded with fireworks waited. Luis Arroyo stood in a lightweight, button-down shirt, with very nearly a Hawaiian pattern to it, but not quite. He was discussing the intricacies of grilling burgers with Pettihorn who, unfortunately for Arroyo, held the only spatula.

Jack and Cat approached a fire they did not attempt to circumnavigate. Instead they sat down with the Ryans, Jeanie McCall, and Rick Sirois.

"Hey Captain Sirois," Pettihorn called, "you want another burger?"

Sirois looked back and waved Pettihorn off with a smile. Arroyo chimed in, "It's a good thing, sir, these burgers here are all burnt up. No good."

"What do you mean burned? These ain't burned. You're from Puerto Rico, what do you know about it anyhow. They isn't enough room on that whole island for a good herd of beef," Pettihorn retorted.

Arroyo laughed. "Oh snap! Good one. For an ignorant hick. You guys grow cows so you can have smarter friends and a love life."

Pettihorn froze. He was considerably larger than Arroyo, and there had been a time, just a month before really, that Pettihorn would have decided to settle the entire dispute physically. However, since being arrested for a bar brawl, and the Department of the Army not taking any stripes but reprimanding him severely enough to prevent future promotion, he knew as it was he would never see E-8. But their decision to leave him with his stripes and his security clearance had allowed him to stay in charge of his beloved C&E section. The men had cheered his return and apparent rebirth as if he were a conquering hero. He of course played it down, but he had been deeply moved. He had abandoned the bottle and returned to church. Things were improving for Pettihorn; his life was back on track.

"Good one, Arroyo." Pettihorn smiled.

Sirois, looking at the grill and Pettihorn, stood up. McCall couldn't believe it. "You're not actually going to have another one, are you?"

Sirois pulled McCall to her feet, and then turned to the crowd with a grin. "Everyone, listen up." McCall looked around at the frozen shapes in the half light. Even Pettihorn and Arroyo stopped bickering for a moment. And then Sirois fell to one knee.

"No way," Arroyo whispered.

"Jeanie, everyone here knows what an amazing pilot you are and what an outstanding soldier you are. They all know you are independent and driven. They know you are great to hang out with, and that you are as tough as you are funny. I've come to learn much more. I know that you're kind, sensitive, and warm. I know that you are, without a doubt, the sweetest and most generous person I've ever known. I know that neither of us believe that one person can or should try complete another, and I know that you do not need me. But right now, I'm asking you to try something with me. I want you and me to make a commitment to be partners, confidants, friends, and lovers for the rest of our lives," Sirois said.

McCall, as surprised as she was, held his gaze locked, searching for the slightest sign of insincerity. There was none.

"Jeanie, it would deeply honor me, and I would consider myself truly lucky, if you would marry me," Sirois said. Every set of eyes that had been on Sirois shifted at once to McCall's face.

She stood frozen for a moment, staring down at him, and Hill, still holding the football, half wondered if she might break out laughing at Sirois's proposal, but then in a very soft and unusually feminine voice, she said only, "Yes, Rick, I will."

Sirois rose, and they embraced. McCall, smiling and crying, wiped her tears on his shoulder, as every spectator suddenly came to life. They began cheering and clapping, and closing in on the two. Sirois and McCall kissed, and had time to exchange one set of "I love yous" before Sirois was wrenched away and hefted aloft by the other Little Bird pilots. He was grinning and pumping one fist in the air as if he had just won the state championship football game. McCall watched him, amused, until a hand fell on her shoulder. She turned and faced Jack and Cat Hartman.

"Congratulations," Jack said, shaking her hand. Cat pushed past her husband, and hugged McCall, both women laughing.

Lydia Ryan joined them and said, "We've got quite a wedding to plan!"

When Mike Ryan leaned in, in order to give his best wishes, McCall broke free of the women, and threw her arms around the major's shoulders. Ryan was surprised, his hands up awkwardly at first, but then hugged her back.

McCall pulled back and, looking into Ryan's face, asked, "Will you give me away, sir?"

Ryan's mouth fell open. Lydia's hands came together, and her head fell to one side. She knew what her husband was feeling.

"You want me to?" Ryan said, sounding shocked.

"Yes," McCall smiled warmly. "I'd love you to."

Ryan looked to Lydia for help. She nodded slowly, her face sweet. Ryan began nodding before he even looked back at Jeanie McCall, and then said, "I'd feel very privileged to give you away," as their eyes met. McCall hugged him again, tightly. Ryan was still stunned. He was going to give Seth McCall's daughter away at her wedding; he'd be standing in for Seth. He looked up at the sky, and whispered, "I'd be very proud to do this for you."

The Little Bird pilots were still parading around with Sirois held aloft, and he was cheering with them.

Cat snuggled up to Jack and said, "Remember how that felt?"

Jack smiled broadly, "I think about it all the time, baby." And he kissed her forehead.

55

President Rand sat at the large conference table across from Jeb Gould, his National Security advisor, and beside his chief of staff, Debra Pratt.

"Enough defense. I want some offense. New York will never be the same, they hit our military in their homes, and now two nukes stopped only by the grace of God. I want to know what you've come up with," Rand said.

Pratt shot Gould a look, and he announced, "Sir, we have a plan. It's twofold in nature. First, there is a council, a group running something called the Greater Islamic Consortium. We believe that it is this organization, and this council of twelve, who have ultimately been coordinating all of it. September 11, the attempt on Baghdad, the attacks on Warsaw and Manila, the Manhattan attack, the nukes, all of it."

"I thought that was Al-Qaeda, and/or the Iranians, and so forth. What evidence do we have that this council . . . ?" President Rand began.

"There is no hard evidence, Mr. President. That's why you haven't heard of it. Our system doesn't reward intelligence hunches, no matter how right they sometimes are. But there are dotted lines connecting these attacks all over the place," Gould said.

Rand considered this and then, "So what do you propose?"

Pratt dropped her head, and braced herself against that which she knew she would hate to hear.

"We propose, Mr. President, that you issue an executive order authorizing . . . no commanding, the termination of each member of this council of twelve," Gould replied.

Pratt lifted her head, and searched for a reaction on the president's face. She couldn't see one.

"Done. Next? What's the second part of this?" President Rand asked.

Pratt was stunned. "Mr. President, perhaps you might consider your position a bit more carefully. We are talking about the systematic hunting down and assassination of men who have not been connected to anything."

"By hard evidence," Gould interjected, "but there is a mountain of circumstantial evidence. So much so as to throw coincidence away as a possibility."

"But Mr. President, the other factor you might consider is, as difficult as it will be to track down these men and kill them, it wouldn't be nearly as difficult for our enemies to undertake a similar policy," Pratt said.

"You mean they could come after me?" President Rand huffed. "Let them. Bring it on. They are not going to cause the resolve of this great country to falter by making me afraid to step out of my car. That's why I have a vice president."

Pratt sat frozen for a moment. "You aren't the only possible target, Mr. President."

Rand laughed. "I'm sure they won't come after you, Debra."

She dropped her head again. "I'm not talking about me, sir. I'm talking about every diplomat stationed overseas. If this turns into a gang war, I get your guy and you get mine and so on, we have a lot more people in harm's way than they do."

Rand's voice softened. "First, let me point out that every person serving their country abroad should be aware that there are risks. Second, we aren't going to trade casualties one for one with them, Debra. We will dismantle what they have. By killing these men, we will be rid of those who are giving the orders that kill our people. This policy will save American lives, not cost them. In the long run. We are going to cut the head off the chicken. They will be left in disarray. If they do the same here, if I'm killed, we will still have order. We win in such an exchange."

Rand glanced at Gould, as if checking for approval. He got it. A slight nod of Gould's head.

Pratt said nothing.

"You still disagree?" President Rand asked.

"It's not up to me to disagree, Mr. President, only to advise," Pratt said.

Rand watched her for a moment, decided they could move on, and then asked, "What's the second part?"

Jeb Gould cleared his throat. "The second part is we track down those responsible for the nukes. We hunt down everyone involved, no matter where it takes us. If a bolt came from some factory in Pakistan, we hit the factory."

"What if the bolt came from a factory in New Jersey?" Pratt asked.

President Rand gave her a stern look, and went back to Gould: "Jeb, what if the trail leads to Americans?"

"It won't," Gould flatly said.

"How do you know?" Rand asked.

"We already have a good idea of where they came from," Gould said. "The radioactive materials came from Russia. The weapons appear to have been assembled in Iran, with plans supplied to the Iranians by a Pakistani scientist named B. R. Fazzir. We have reason to believe the nukes were smuggled whole into Guatemala, aboard a freighter under Liberian flag, and then into the United States, via Mexico, by a Guatemalan clique within a Central American mafia organization known as Mara Salvatrucha."

"Holy shit!" Pratt exclaimed. "Are you planning on starting another world war? Should we carpet bomb Liberia because their laws make it cheaper to register a ship there?"

"What is it, Debra?" Rand asked, frustrated now at not being able to understand what was truly bothering her. This of course only frustrated Pratt further.

"Mr. President," Pratt said, her tone hardly patient, "what is he suggesting? Should we actually carry out military action again Russia, Iran, Pakistan, and Guatemala?"

"You forgot Mexico," Gould added sarcastically. Rand held up one hand.

"What would you do?" Rand asked Pratt. It was her opening, her one chance. Gould knew it too, and rolled his eyes before she began, irritated that the president was going to give her advice a hearing.

"Go to the UN with this information. Go there personally and make a stand. Reveal to the world that we had nuclear weapons here on our soil, in the hands of terrorists, and we prevented another Warsaw only by a few minutes. Europe and Asia have already been hit; they will be sympathetic to a plan to root out those who make these attacks possible. Let local authorities, working as a web, seek out and apprehend these people. With the backing of the United Nations," Pratt pleaded.

"And what will you do when Russia vetoes it? What will you do with situations like we have in Pakistan where a scientist, whose sale of nuclear weapon technology may be responsible someday for the murder of millions and who almost assuredly was actually working on behalf of the Pakistani government, is arrested, confesses, and then given a sentence of comfortable house arrest? That's a pretty good-sized hole in your web," Gould said.

"Enough, enough," President Rand said, holding up one hand. He paused, stood, and walked around the small room.

"What can we do about B. R. Fazzir?" Rand asked.

Gould jumped on the question. "Nothing. We desperately need to stay on the good side of the Pakistani president. If we assassinate Fazzir, or even arrest him, that will put the Pakistani leadership in the position of either harshly criticizing us, or acquiescing to us in the kidnapping or murder of a scientist considered a national and cultural hero, which would risk the stability of the entire country. Besides, Fazzir is probably just the visible and intellectual tip of a much larger government-sanctioned program."

Rand turned to Gould and said softly, "How good is your intel on the twelve men and the other targets? Is it actionable?"

Gould could not help but smile. "Yes, Mr. President, absolutely. A slam dunk."

Pratt whispered, "God help us."

"I think He has been, Debra," President Rand responded. "You ever hear the story about the man and the flood?"

"Noah, sir?" Pratt asked, bitterly.

"No, not that flood," Rand smiled. "See, there was this guy, and there was a flood. So he went to the upstairs bedroom to get above the water, and as it rose, a boat came by outside his window. A firefighter in the boat offered to rescue the man, but the man refused, saying, 'God will save me.'

"The water kept rising, and the man climbed on the roof. Another firefighter came by with another boat, but could not convince the man to get on board. The man just insisted, 'God will save me.'

"So, finally, the man was on the peak of his roof, clinging to the chimney in the rising water. A helicopter came by and threw him a rope. The man refused to take it, shouting, 'God will save me.' Well, Debra, the man drowned, and when he met our Lord, he asked Him, 'Lord, I waited for You to save me, but You never came.'

"To which the Lord answered, 'I sent two boats and a helicopter, what more did you want from Me?' "

Pratt stared and said nothing.

President Rand sensed he needed to continue. "Don't you see? He's provided all this intelligence, all this opportunity. We can change the world, rid it of these people who would use science to wipe out a nation."

Pratt said nothing at first. There was a pause, a heavy silence, and then she asked, "What if the Lord gave you the United Nations?"

Gould sneered, "God wouldn't give the UN to Job."

Pratt had had enough. "Okay Gould, look, you know what? Cute religious vignettes aren't going to cut it here. This is too complex a set of issues to be solved with bedtime stories and sermons."

"Remember where you are," Gould hissed.

"It is precisely my understanding of my situation and location that causes me to stand now, to say these things, and to offer my resignation, Mr. President," Pratt said, speaking at first to Gould, but then turning to Rand.

Rand had at first a confused look on his face, and then he broke out in a warm, reassuring smile. "Debra, I need you as my chief of staff. It is precisely this kind of fierce honesty and intelligence I need around here. Please reconsider. Go home, get some sleep; it's been a long day. We'll discuss it in the morning. If tomorrow afternoon, you still want to resign, well, we'll deal with that then. But I do hope you'll change your mind." He walked her to the door, his hand on her shoulder.

"Yes, Mr. President, good night," Pratt said in a low voice as she stepped out and a large Secret Service agent closed the door behind her. Rand was left alone with Gould in the Situation Room.

"Where do we start, Jeb?" Rand asked.

"Let's start with the easiest. The Central American mafia. We're already there. We can track down and destroy the terrorists there all in the name of drugs," Gould said happily. "The attorney general made this all easier when he went on television and told the American people that a known al-Qaeda member and suspect in the planning of the September 11 attacks was seen in Guatemala meeting with leaders of the Mara Salvatrucha, securing entry routes into the United States along the Mexican border. The Mara Salvatrucha has established a major smuggling center in Matamoros, Mexico, just south of Brownsville, Texas, just for this purpose. They were already attacking us, in one form, and now we know they smuggled nuclear weapons into our country. These Central American terrorists are a clear and present threat."

"But doesn't the Mara Salvatrucha . . . don't they have gangs here in the United States?" Rand asked.

"Mr. President," Gould said, "in the coming days, we should consider and treat those 'gangs' as domestic terror cells. But for right now, we need to go after the specific clique that allowed, no enabled, the attack that almost destroyed two of our major cities."

"Very well, Jeb. Let's do it. The buck stops here. I want this Mara Salvatrucha stomped out, and I want them squeezed for every bit of intel we can get. If we have to, we'll hold every member as an enemy combatant," Rand said.

56

May 24
Al-Istiqlal Mosque
Jakarta, Indonesia
Greater Islamic Consortium

"A devastating failure," a nasally voice said. "We have been set back twenty years in our struggle."

"The Americans will not be on the defensive now," the gravelly voiced one added. "They will tear the Earth apart searching for those who carried out these attacks. They were expending a great deal of their resources protecting their homeland. But at this point, with the bridges falling in New York, the attacks on the families of their military, and the two nuclear weapons they managed to intercept, they will come. They will come with all their might. There will be nothing that will be able to slow the juggernaut that is about to be unleashed upon the world except for the direct intervention of Allah."

"If it is the will of Allah that we be swept away, it will be so," said an older man, "but we must leave this place and seek refuge. We must not try to contact each other, and we must blend back into the societies from which we came."

"Agreed," said a deep voice. "We must disband the council, at least for some years."

"One advantage we have," said the nasally voice, "is that the Americans almost assuredly do not know of the existence of this council. Oh, they might have heard rumors, but they will have no details. If we go to our homes, and lead normal lives, it is very unlikely they will ever find any of us. Also, with some luck, we might yet strike a mortal blow against the Americans. All is not lost."

57

Martin Bragdon hadn't been back to the United States in years. The idea that he had been summoned made him more than a little curious. What in the world would cause his superiors to recall him? he wondered. He had received missions in Europe upon which the lives of hundreds of thousands had depended. What could make them insist on speaking to him here in the U.S.?

Two weeks before, he had had his bell rung hard with a piece of lumber; the healing scar on his tanned forehead was still pink and fresh. He had woken up the next morning with symptoms that would have rivaled the worst college hangover, but he had made his way out of the safe house, out of Doha, out of Qatar, and here he was back in the States.

It wasn't especially warm, but it was humid and sticky in the late Virginia spring. He entered the air-conditioned building, looking exactly like a middle manager stepping into the low but sprawling office building. In the lobby, the only sign that this wasn't just one more high-tech firm was, in the place of the usual cute receptionist, a man of considerable size and of extremely serious countenance. No toothy grin, just a matter-of-fact inquiry into whom he was hoping to see.

"Say that again," the man said.

"I'm here to see Mr. Lance Faucher," Bragdon said, holding the man's stare without so much as blinking.

"And your name is?" the man asked.

"Stephen Wrisley," Bragdon said, again without the least bit of hesitation.

"Please have a seat over there," the man said, pointing. No promise of seeing anyone, just instructions on where to sit. Bragdon nodded and walked across the dark marble floor to a small and oddly carpeted area bordered with cheap armchairs.

Bragdon had scarcely been in one of the chairs for a minute when another man, dressed much the same as the first, approached. "Mr. Wrisley, please follow me."

Bragdon rose and walked past the reception counter. They turned down a wide hallway, stopped at an ordinary-looking door, and stepped through. Not twelve feet beyond the first door was a second, but this one was at least a foot thick. Entering through this door, Bragdon followed his guide into a very ordinary-looking cubicle farm. None of the women sitting in these cubes bothered to look up as Bragdon entered. From the look of it all, he could have been in an office anywhere, except for the utter lack of windows and small talk. Everyone in this cube farm was working with a look of grave determination.

The man led Bragdon past the cubicles, and into a small office. Without a word, he abandoned Bragdon there with two other men, one seated behind a desk, another standing near a nearly empty bookshelf. Neither of them was Lance Faucher. There was no real Lance Faucher. Bragdon had simply been told to ask for Faucher. Bragdon did not know the names of the men with whom he was about to talk, nor would he ever likely know who they really were.

"Please, have a seat," said the man near the bookshelf, gesturing to yet another armchair.

Bragdon closed the door himself, and walked over to the seat offered to him.

"Can I get you a coffee?" the bookshelf man asked.

"No, thank you," Bragdon replied. He'd just as soon get this over with. Instincts that had kept him alive for years were screaming in his head for him to get out of there. Intellectually, he knew he was safe, but his gut was pointing out that the thick security door meant thick walls, and the men, like his guide, were surely armed.

The man behind the desk took a deep breath and brought one hand to his face, as he began to speak. "Have you ever heard of the Greater Islamic Consortium?"

Bragdon cocked his head. "I've heard rumors of it. A overarching conglomerate of Islamist extremist groups, organizing all of it. But it's considered by most to be wishful thinking on the part of the Islamists, built on the desire that even their setbacks and suffering are all part of a grand plan."

"Well," the man behind the desk said, "it's not just a rumor. It exists."

"What really exists? The council or the consortium?" Bragdon asked.

The men shared a quick look, and the man behind the desk asked, "You've heard of the council?"

"Again, just rumors," Bragdon said nodding.

"The council exists, and the council is why you were called to this meeting," the man behind the desk said.

Bragdon sat forward just a bit, just enough to indicate his interest.

The man continued, "The council is made up of twelve men from around the world. Some are clerics, some are intelligence operatives, some are ministers in government, and some are businessmen. They have scattered, gone to ground, returned to their mundane everyday lives."

Bragdon said nothing; he just listened.

"The mission is to seek out each of these men, whom

we believe are ultimately responsible for the attacks in Warsaw, Manila, New York, Washington, and the military installations, among many others. You will seek each of them out, and you will terminate them," the man said.

The word *terminate* hung in the air. Bragdon squinted at the man behind the desk, turning this over in his head.

"You would have no cover from us," the man went on. "If caught, arrested, whatever, we'll deny you or your mission ever existed."

Bragdon nodded, and then asked, "How soon?"

"You'd start today. We'll set you up with the usual. Cash, contacts, weapons, passports," the man answered.

There was a pause. The men stared at Bragdon, waiting for what might come next. He couldn't really decline the mission, even if he had wanted to, which he didn't.

"I ask one thing," Bragdon said finally. "Let me work solo on this. Do not put another operations officer on this mission. Once I've terminated a few of these guys, the others will get even more scarce. I will have to smoke them out, and having someone else out there could be very counterproductive and dangerous. Like two hunters, facing each other, flushing out birds."

"Agreed," the man at the bookshelf said too quickly. Bragdon looked over at him for a moment. It was never a good thing when someone like him agreed too quickly with anything. It always had the sound of a door to a trap slamming shut.

"One other thing," the man behind the desk said. "Once you complete this mission, your time with us is over. We will arrange a new identity for you, set you up with enough to keep you comfortable, in any city you choose. But you'll have to leave the agency and the rest of your life behind. Not only for your safety but also because we need to maintain security over this whole thing."

Leave the CIA? Bragdon was stunned. He hadn't considered it for a moment. He loved serving his country.

"You've done your fair share already," said the man behind the desk, reading Bragdon's face. "If you accomplish this last mission, your country will ask no more of you except for you to disappear and retire."

Bragdon stood and walked over to a set of window curtains hanging in the office. He pulled one back to reveal a cinder-block wall where a window should have been.

"Agreed," Bragdon said. "I'll take this mission as my last." He'd retire to Prague, take up photography or something mellow like that. Hang out in pubs, play some chess, read. Maybe get to know his neighbor a bit better.

"Excellent," the bookshelf man said.

58

May 25
Headquarters, U.S. SOCOM
Tampa Point Boulevard
MacDill AFB, Florida

Lieutenant General Bizzocchi returned Jack Hartman's salute, and offered him a seat. A major, wearing the insignia of the U.S. Army's intel corps, sat off to Hartman's left. Bizzocchi remained standing.

"Hartman, we're sorry to bring you all this way without explaining why. I'm also going to apologize in advance because I am going to task one of your pilots, and I'm afraid I won't be telling you what the mission is. You are going to have to accept that it is all need-to-know. Are we clear?" Bizzocchi said.

"Yessir," Hartman said, a knot forming in his gut.

"Good. I need you to recommend a pilot for me. He must be an excellent pilot, of considerable courage, perhaps a bit of a risk taker," Bizzocchi continued.

"General, you just described my entire battalion," Hartman said impassively.

"Yes, Hartman, I know, I know, but there must be someone who stands out as not only having great skill as a pilot but also as having a wild streak in him. Mind you, I'm looking for someone who is very dependable, but I'm also hoping you have a cowboy of a pilot up there at Campbell," the general said.

"Most of my pilots are quiet pros, family men. But I do

have a couple of pilots who might fit your bill," Hartman said. "What type of helicopter do you want this person to be checked out on?"

"I want that pilot, from among all your pilots, who is the one most likely to be able to fly the living hell out a helicopter type he's never been in before," Bizzocchi said.

Hartman squinted at the general. What is this all about? Hartman wondered. The choice, of course, became clear to Hartman. He just wished he knew what, where, and why.

"I've got a pilot for you, sir," Hartman said. "Will he receive written orders? How long will I be without him? When your tasking out is over, will he be allowed to return to the 160th SOAR?"

"We won't keep him a day longer than we need him, and upon successful completion of the mission, we'll give him the option of returning to you. If he decides not to return to your command, we will let you know that too. If he is KIA, your command will be informed. I think that's fair," Bizzocchi said. "As for written orders, he'll get none. He simply needs to report, in civilian clothing, to the Richard B. Russell Federal Building in Atlanta in two days. Tell him to leave the uniform and dog tags at home."

Civilian clothes? Hartman wondered.

"Is that clear, Hartman?" Bizzocchi asked.

"Yessir," Hartman replied.

Hartman saluted once more and left, nodding his respects to the major as he went. Walking down the hallway, Hartman wondered what it was he was about to volunteer Sirois for. He had heard stories of army helicopter pilots being farmed out to the CIA and other agencies. He knew that pilots who were shot down under such circumstances were often never heard of again because the United States government immediately disavowed all knowledge of the man and the mission.

However, the pilot the general described he needed was almost a dead ringer description of Rick Sirois. There were perhaps better technical fliers, and the battalion was filled with people who could quote FMs and TMs better than Sirois, but when it came to seat-of-the-pants flying, Sirois was the best. Maybe better even than Hartman had been.

Hartman had a feeling that this was a turning point in Sirois's life, and the young captain didn't know it yet. Even if Sirois came back in one piece, he would likely not want to return to the normal everyday life of being a soldier. The mission or missions that the general wanted him for were likely to be all the best of being a Night Stalker without any of the garrison regulations.

Another factor: Sirois was romantically involved with another member of the unit. What would Sirois's mysterious new assignment do to Jeanie McCall?

Hartman sighed. Too many unknowns to worry about it, he thought to himself.

59

May 30
Defense Intelligence Analysis Center
Bolling Air Force Base
Washington, D.C.

"Hey Jason, I got one," Tom Phillips called across the room.

"It's Justin. Who is it?" The intern sighed.

"Whatever. It's target nine," Phillips said. "He's on his cell phone, the idiot."

"Where?" the intern asked.

"Sofia. In Bulgaria," Phillips replied. "Write it up."

60

They were coming out of the setting sun, heading east toward the village. The stone buildings, reflecting orange and red, clung to the hillside above the lake. Mountains all around the lake, including a towering volcano named San Pedro, formed a bowl holding the lake in place, off to right of the approaching helicopters.

"Standby," McCall announced into the intercom. Hill and Arroyo got ready. It was a tricky mission, and Arroyo had more than the usual anxiety. Not because of how deadly the mission might prove to be, but instead because this was not an enemy village. This was a normal, poor, Guatemalan village, sure to be filled with children, where gangster terrorists had chosen to hide and live. They would insert their customers, Rangers and Delta operators, who would then try to sort out innocent from monstrous, snatch or kill the bad guys, and then get extracted.

But sitting in the Black Hawk, Arroyo knew it would not be that simple. He knew that it was one thing to try to capture Central American guerillas from a hillside camp when all they were fighting for was money. It was going to be something wholly different to come into the homes of one of the fiercest gangs in Latin and North America and steal them away. Arroyo knew most would believe that capture

equaled death, and would fight that way, not to mention
just the disrespect they would feel at having strangers rush
into their homes and try to overpower them. Arroyo just
hoped the number of noncombatants killed would be low.

The village itself was nestled into a spot where the
slope became severe on two sides. This meant there were
only two ways to approach it: from over the lake, which
would put the volcano behind them, or from the west. With
the bright Guatemalan sunset behind them, it would be obvious that helicopters were approaching, but for the enemy
to get an accurate count or even to aim at dots in the orange
glow would be difficult.

McCall's voice in Arroyo's ears announced, "Coming
up on the target."

Here we go, thought Arroyo. As he had always done, at
least when Hill had been with them, Arroyo checked back
over his shoulder and saw Hill sitting at his gun. It was always reassuring. Although Hill had been through some difficult times, and had lost his way temporarily, along with
some rank, Arroyo counted on the big Chicagoan. Hill sat,
unmoving, ready.

Hill, for his part, was less sure about his steadfastness.
Nothing had been the same since Iran, since he broke his
back and had to learn to walk again, and then he lost his
stripes. He thought he was on the road back to where he
once was, but then there was the breaker bar. He had care-
lessly forgotten it, nearly caused the bird to fall, and then
he had lied about it. Despite his now being called a hero for
the mission south of Chicago where he stopped the RV,
Hill just felt like he'd never be as clean as he once was. To
him, stopping a nuke from getting to Chicago had been his
job, and any crew chief in the battalion would have done at
least as well as he did. The breaker bar was him screwing
up at his job, and he felt like right now he was the only
crew chief who could make such a mistake.

The Delta operators on the Black Hawk were ready to

go. Quiet professionals, like the pilots carrying them into the village, but eager to get in and accomplish the mission. Intense in their silence.

The Fast Rope Insertion/Extraction System, or FRIES, was attached and the FRIES master among the Delta operators stood up and shouted, "Standby!"

Four of the ten seated operators rose and began one more check of each other's equipment.

The aircraft came in at about forty feet, moving just under ninety miles per hour, and just as it arrived above the target house it slowed in a deliberate and controlled manner to a hover.

The ropes were thrown, and they fell to a stone path below. Arroyo spoke into the intercom, "Ropes deployed." The path ran uphill along the edge of the village. It appeared to be fieldstones, sunken into a bed of concrete. Sunken so deep that the surface of the path was more like holes with a fieldstone in each, filling it, than a length of bumpy sidewalk.

Arroyo watched as other Black Hawks, and a couple of Little Birds, streaked by on the way to their own insertion points. And then one of the larger aircraft pulled into a hover not three hundred meters from Arroyo, and the ropes deployed.

Delta operators were exiting his Black Hawk silently. Not because this was a stealthy insertion—with the rotors of the helicopters it certainly wasn't. The D-boys just did it this way, silent, businesslike. The first four were out very quickly, and Arroyo called, "Ropers out." The D-boys followed close behind them, including the FRIES master. They quickly spread out on the path below, and as a wave over a seawall, they went over the ancient stone wall surrounding Santa Cruz.

Arroyo's voice: "All ropers away."

"Jettison ropes," McCall immediately answered.

Arroyo pulled the pins holding his rope, and looked back once more. Hill was doing the same.

The ropes fell away.

"Ropes clear!" said Hill.

"Ropes clear!" Arroyo echoed.

"Arrow 6, this is Arrow 42, coming out," McCall radioed to Hartman.

Aboard the C2 aircraft, Hartman circled above the village. It was not quite dark yet, but there was no longer much direct sunlight, and what little was left was casting long shadows in the narrow streets.

"Arrow 42, this is Arrow 6, good copy," Hartman replied. The streets below had emptied at their approach, but then the reverse occurred. Frightened villagers, especially mothers with their children, fled buildings being stormed, or even buildings too close to target buildings. Hartman watched a woman, running with a little girl clinging to each hand, move downhill away from McCall's insertion point. He shook his head. He hoped intel had gotten this one right.

Incoming rounds suddenly ricocheted off the cargo door nearest Hartman. He flinched, raising an arm.

"Well, someone's got guns down there, Glen," Hartman said into the intercom to his pilot, CW3 Glen Arsten.

"Yessir," was all Arsten said in response.

At McCall's insertion point, the Delta operators kicked in the door nearest the wall they had come over. The first two sprinted to the back of the small room they entered, while another four came in after them, fanning out to the sides. The remaining four split into pairs on either side of the street outside the house, scanning for approaching threats.

"Clear! Clear! Clear!" came through their earpieces as they found no one in the home.

The team leader, Greg Cohen, began giving instructions. "Parker, you guys clear the other rooms. The rest of you, let's sweep for anything of intel value."

"Moving" was all Parker said, and he and his partner were gone through a darkening doorway into the rear of the house.

The others searched quickly, and not carefully. The furniture was demolished, pulled apart to see if anything was hidden inside.

"I've got something here," a voice announced.

"What is it, Melanson?" Cohen replied, dropping what he was doing and moving that way.

"The cupboard doors beneath this sink basin won't open. They're nailed shut," Melanson said, turning to show Cohen as he arrived. The doors would not budge. Cohen grabbed the basin, bracing himself to kick through the small wooden doors, but then the basin itself shifted. Cohen shot Melanson a look, and then shook the basin once more. It moved easily, too easily.

Before Cohen could say anything, heavy rounds exploded up through the bottom of the basin, cracking it. Melanson and Cohen hit the floor.

The radio came alive: "Cohen, you need a medic?"

Cohen quickly looked over Melanson, who was doing the same, until their eyes met. "Negative, but we have hostiles here. Possible tunnel beneath the sink basin, radio that around, England. Tell people to look for tunnels."

"Roger that." England's voice.

Melanson and Cohen got to their feet as the other team members got to the sink.

"Back up," Cohen said, and everyone complied. He extended his arms, and his MP5, and fired a burst straight down into the basin. It cracked further, and then much of it fell away. They heard the impact of its parts far below the floor.

Melanson stepped forward and dropped a flash-bang grenade into the hole. At the sound of it, Cohen and Melanson reached forward and pulled what remained of the basin away in two large chunks. Parker stepped between the men, and looked straight down, MP5 near his face. He nodded. "I don't see anyone, about a ten-foot drop."

"Melanson, Parker, you're going, flash it again first," Cohen said.

Another flash-bang grenade was dropped; it went off, and into the smoke dropped Melanson and Parker. They stepped forward.

"We've got lights down here. It's clear from what we can see in the hanging smoke," Parker radioed back. The tunnel was obviously hand-dug and was braced with four-by-four timbers. It was apparent that a great deal of labor had gone into digging the tunnel, clearing the dirt, bracing it up. Parker and Melanson peered through the smoke and could see the tunnel go on and then abruptly turn.

"Pull half the outside security team into the house," Cohen said, looking over his shoulder, "and leave two men outside. Then follow us."

With that, Cohen dropped into the hole, followed by another, and then another two. Cohen nodded at Melanson, and they were off, moving swiftly through the tunnel, but chasing someone with a five-minute head start, who knew the tunnel, and who must be running like mad.

Or so they thought.

Turning a second corner in the tunnel, Parker and Melanson, leading the six Delta operators, were suddenly fired upon. Parker went down hard, and Melanson dove back around the corner from where he had come.

"Parker!" Melanson called.

Melanson took a step past the corner to try and reach Parker, stealing a quick look down at who was firing at them, but he was met with withering fire, and he threw himself back behind cover. He had no idea how they had missed him.

"Melanson, hold up, don't do that again," Cohen said. "Anyway we can throw a couple frags down there and do some damage?"

"Naw, it's not far, but they're dug in, with cover. I'm not sure, but it looks like they dug grenade sumps around their positions. Anything we throw down there, except for a miracle shot, will just fall down in the sumps and do nothing. They expected to have to run down this hole and defend themselves someday," Melanson said. He looked out at Parker, who was not moving, and knew he was dead. There was no cover on the far side of Parker, just smooth tunnel wall.

"Did you see another way out?" Cohen asked. They both knew he actually meant another way in.

"I didn't see one. I'd want one if I were them, but I don't know if they were that smart. They might be just hoping we'll be convinced to leave, or maybe they're deadenders," Melanson said. "I'm sure they thought the worstcase scenario down here was going to be some patchwork Guatemalan state police team. The space down there is maybe ten feet by ten feet. It looked like a dead-end but I don't know. What do you want to do?"

Cohen thought for a moment, and then called into his mike, "England?"

The response from the surface, from inside the house, was immediate: "Go ahead."

"England, there's a five-gallon can, looked like diesel, near the door. Do you see it?" Cohen asked.

There was a pause, and then England's voice was there again: "Got it, but it's pretty much empty."

"Take it outside, fill it at that big pump with water, maybe two-thirds full, then toss it down here," Cohen said.

"Standby" was England's response.

Melanson looked at Cohen questioningly.

"Let's find out if they have another way out," Cohen said flatly.

Within a couple minutes: "Here's the can, stand clear."

"Drop it," Cohen replied.

An old metal can, rectangular and apparently painted at one time, fell into the tunnel. Two Delta operators ran it forward to Cohen's position. The liquid inside, by far mostly water, sloshed as it came.

Cohen took it, and then asked Melanson, "How's your Spanish?"

"Not as good as Parker's," he replied.

Cohen nodded, and then said, "Give it a try. Tell them that if they don't give up, we'll smoke them out or else seal them in."

Melanson looked at the can, and then at Cohen. He turned, approached the corner, and yelled, *"Saído lá."*

Cohen jabbed Melanson in the back. "Spanish, you idiot! Now they're going to think the Brazilian army has them pinned down!"

"Oh right, my bad." Melanson winced, and then tried again. *"Usted debe salir allí con sus manos sobre sus cabezas."* Melanson shook his head at his own Spanish and listened, heard nothing, and said, *"Usted debe salir o nos quemaremos le. Usted morirá del humo grande."*

Cohen hissed, "We'll burn you? Big smoke? Come on man!"

"You want to try?" Melanson turned on him. "Spanish isn't my thing."

Still no response from the men in the holes. Cohen stepped forward with the can, loosened the screw-on cap, and with a mighty heave and step tossed it down the tunnel toward the men dug in. They fired a single burst at Cohen, but then stopped, seeing what he had and not wanting to ignite it. The can fell to the floor of the tunnel, fairly close to the foxholes the men were in, and liquid could be seen sloshing out around the loose cap.

"Lanzaré una granada en cinco segundos," Melanson yelled.

Nothing. No response.

"*Cinco . . . cuatro . . . tres . . .*" Melanson began his countdown, and pulled a grenade.

"Will you really throw it?" Cohen asked.

Melanson never had a chance to respond.

"*Nos entregaremos*, we are surrendering," a voice came from the end of the tunnel, the English better than Melanson's Spanish.

Melanson shot Cohen an angry look, and then shouted, "Come toward my voice, one at a time, hands above your heads!"

"Okay" was the response.

The first man appeared, shirtless, and was pulled back to the opening of the tunnel. Among other extensive tattoos, on one shoulder he had a huge *13* drawn in black. A sign of membership in Mara Salvatrucha. He was zip-tied and then lifted up to arms that pulled him into the house, as was the next prisoner. The two were brought near the door of the home, along with everything found in the house of possible value: papers, maps, a journal, and even a computer CD in a house without a computer. Parker's body was also carefully carried to the door. The two punks from Mara Salvatrucha sat uncomfortably next to Parker while Melanson stood over them, his MP5 leveled at their heads.

"Arrow 6, this is Hunter 4, we're ready for extraction. We have one KIA, and we have two guests," Cohen radioed.

"Hunter 4, this is Arrow 6, good copy, your ride's on the way, move to extraction site," Hartman replied, and then to McCall, "Arrow 42, pick up your customers at extraction point, plus two, one KIA." Eleven, Hartman thought, the two McCall will pick up makes a total of eleven prisoners.

"This is Arrow 42, on the way," McCall responded. She lowered the collective, gave a little pedal, and pulled the cyclic left. The bird's nose fell and the entire aircraft banked. One KIA, McCall thought, that sucks.

"Hope you're alright, Rick," she whispered to herself, thinking of the dead American she was about to pick up, but it carried throughout the bird on the intercom.

The Black Hawk came down quickly, almost straight down in the cramped space, and a couple of Delta operators were first to board. They pulled the prisoners on next, and then Parker's body. Finally, the remaining D-boys climbed on.

"We've got 'em," Arroyo said, and the Black Hawk lifted skyward again.

61

"My name is Pablo Eurgenia," he said, squinting at the first light he'd seen in six hours. In addition to the large *13* tattooed on one shoulder, he had several others running up his chest and down his back. He had a teardrop tattoo near each eye. There was no mistaking a member of MS-13, of the Mara Salvatrucha.

"You've told us your name already," said the interrogator. He was an American, of Latin descent, short and thick. He arms filled the short sleeves of his button-down shirt; the khaki pants were a bit too big and hung loose on him.

"I'm not telling you anything else," said Pablo.

"Listen, stupid," the interrogator said, sounding not like a professional who specialized in getting information from the unwilling, but instead with the tone of a tough-love high school guidance counselor, "you've got a choice here. You're going to answer my questions, and then we'll tuck you away nice and safe in a detention center, maybe even rehab you, have those tattoos taken off if you like. Or, you're not going to say anything except your name again and again, like some parrot, and we will release you to authorities at Quezaltepeque prison in El Salvador."

"El Salvador?" Pablo sat up straight. "Why El Salvador? I'm from Guatemala."

The overcrowded prison in Quezaltepeque in northern El Salvador is a warehouse for Salvadoran and deported U.S. members of Mara Salvatrucha, plagued by murder and riots. The conditions inside were abhorrent.

"We have your attention now, eh?" the interrogator said. "With your tattoos, we turn you over in El Salvador, and you won't last a week. Not even on the street, let alone in the prison. The only mystery will be who kills you first. So how about telling me more than your name? Like, who first mentioned smuggling the nuclear weapons into the United States."

"We did not know what they were," Pablo said to the floor.

"Long, metallic eggs," the interrogator said. "Sure, you might not have known they were nuclear weapons, but you must have known that they weren't just some harmless goods."

"For all I knew, those things were filled with just cocaine," Pablo offered.

"Come on, Pablito," the interrogator said mockingly, "have you ever seen someone take cocaine, which is relatively easy to smuggle into the United States, and put it in a huge, unique, and bomb-shaped container in order to sneak it somewhere? Does that make sense to you?"

Pablo paused, and then, "This detention center you mentioned . . . you mean Guantánamo?"

"No, no," the interrogator waved his hand, "Alamosa, in Colorado. We take illegal aliens there, we'll keep you safe there. Enable you to straighten out your screwed up and pathetic life."

The interrogator made it sound as if Pablo would be safe in Alamosa, but just recently a judge there ruled that a sixteen-year-old member of Mara Salvatrucha, who had letters vouching for his rehab and relatives promising to give the boy a home and a fresh start, must be forcibly returned to Central American streets. His advocates told the judge it was a death sentence, that just the fact that the boy had had some of his MS-13 tattoos removed was enough to get him killed. The pleas fell on deaf ears, and the judge had his ruling carried out. The boy was killed in the street within two weeks of his return. No one cared nearly as much about Pablo; at Alamosa there would be no one to fight for Pablo, but Pablo seemed to be thinking it over.

"What's to think about? Colorado or Quezaltepeque prison. It's a clear choice. You have no other," the interrogator said.

"Okay, okay," Pablo said, "but you have to keep me safe. Once I leave Mara Salvatrucha, I cannot go back."

"Pablo, you already have left MS. Even now, we are leaking it out on the street that you left Mara Salvatrucha and are cooperating with the Guatemalan government," the interrogator said matter-of-factly, "so you are correct, you cannot go back. By now, you've already been 'green-lighted' by your old friends."

Pablo sat stunned for a moment, cut loose from everything he knew, and he understood he really only had one choice. To listen to this man, cooperate, and then pray he was not being deceived.

"The weapons were brought to us by a man, I never knew his name. I rarely talked to him. He had a scar on his forehead, like a cigar burn. He wanted them brought to the United States, through Mexico. He knew that we had operations smuggling weapons, drugs, and people north. He also knew that we smuggled handguns and cars south. He said that the weapons were from Iran, proud that they were built in a place called Shahviran, or something like that. He joked that they were built in a food processing plant and that everyone in the area knew no food was made there, but that he hoped the Americans would choke on this product," Pablo said, forming the oblong shape of the weapons with his hands.

"Why would he tell you all this?" the interrogator

asked. "Why not just tell you to mind your own business, and just have you deliver it?"

"This guy would not shut up," Pablo said, getting animated at being doubted. "He was like all keyed up, all excited about what we were doing. He smiled all the time, but it was like a terrible smile, you know? Like a psycho smile."

The interrogator stood silently for a moment, considering this, and then asked, "Where did you say it came from?"

"From Iran, like I said," Pablo repeated.

"From where in Iran?" The interrogator looked puzzled.

"Man, I don't know," Pablo said, really getting worked up. "Like Shahrivan or some shit."

"Pablo, you just said *Shahviran,* now it's *Shahrivan.* Which is it?" the interrogator asked, looking very skeptical.

Pablo felt El Salvador had just gotten closer. "I told you! I don't know for sure. I don't speak Arabic, you know?"

"Arabic? I thought you said he was from Iran. And who was he speaking Arabic to?" the interrogator said.

"He wasn't speaking Arabic to nobody!" Pablo shouted, scared now. "I was just saying that because I got the name of the place wrong."

"He wasn't speaking to anybody?" the interrogator continued.

"Yeah, he was, but not in Arabic," Pablo replied quickly.

"Well, what language then?" the interrogator asked.

"Spanish, man, he spoke Spanish," Pablo said, becoming exhausted at the effort and stress.

"Well, then how do you know where he was from?" the interrogator asked, getting up, walking.

"Because he told us, Shahviran or whatever, he told us that," Pablo said.

"In Spanish?" the interrogator asked doubtfully.

"Yes, yes, in Spanish," Pablo said.

The interrogator waited a moment, looked at Pablo intently, and then said, "Pablo, start over. Where did the nuclear weapons come from?"

Pablo felt the air rush out of him. "Start over?"

"It's either that, or we can pack for El Salvador. Or I could just drop you back in your village. Of course, we're spreading the news of your turning your back on MS get out first."

"This guy, man," Pablo said, "he came to us. We thought for drugs or something, but he said he had something he needed smuggled to America. We set up a transfer station at Matamoros in Mexico for this."

"And where were the weapons from? Iraq?" the interrogator asked.

"Yeah. No, wait Iran. That's different, right? Iran. From Shahviran," Pablo said.

"From a supermarket?" the interrogator asked.

"Stop it man!" Pablo shouted. "You're messing this up on purpose. It was a food processing plant, okay?"

"Why would they make nuclear weapons in a food processing plant? Never mind, skip it, you want me to believe that this guy from Iran comes all they way over here, and gives you both of his nuclear weapons to smuggle north?"

There was silence.

"Well?" the interrogator pushed, trying to keep Pablo on his heels, wanting to keep the pressure on.

"Both? You mean like two?" Pablo blinked.

"Yeah both; don't try and tell me you didn't know there were two," the interrogator said.

Pablo was still, and then said, "There were three."

"What?" It was the interrogator's turn to be stunned.

"Three, man, three. There were three of those things," Pablo said.

The interrogator looked over at the mirror. On the other side, six people, all employees of different departments and agencies within the United States government, despite three different recordings being made, took copious notes.

62

Lieutenant Colonel Hartman stood at the podium as the pilots took their seats.

Hartman cleared his throat. "People, most of you have memories of our recent missions in Iran. Many of them you'd just as soon forget. But we are going back, to a place called Shaherviran. Consider yourselves in iso as of now."

There was a grave whispering among pilots in the back of the room.

Hartman continued, "As most of you know, officially and unofficially, we stopped a nuclear weapon on its way to Chicago. As it turns out, there was another weapon, virtually identical, stopped only because of the heads-up work of first responders near Dallas and some good luck."

Behind Hartman, a slide appeared on a screen, an aerial view of a small building surrounded first by some parking spaces and grass, and then by a small town.

"This," Hartman said, "is where those nukes came from. It is supposedly a food processing plant, but closer examination . . ."

The picture on the screen was replaced, in quick succession, by four increasingly close shots of the area, zooming in on a high fence topped with razor wire.

"We see that this building is strangely well-protected for processing food," Hartman finished. What followed was a series of shots, showing cameras, guards with dogs, and more wire.

"We even suspect that this area here," Hartman pointed, "may have land mines buried beneath the soil.

"Standard stuff. We will insert Rangers in a four-point perimeter around the plant, and then insert Delta operators here and here," Hartman said, indicating with a laser pointer spots outside the building but inside the fence.

"We are not going to have to be as cautious about collateral damage on this one. There are no civilians to be concerned about. This is an intel mission. The Rangers will set up security; the D-boys will run in and grab whatever intel or prisoners they might, take some photos, and if they happen to see anything worth setting charges on, they will. Then, they will un-ass the plant and we will let the air force knock it down," Hartman said.

All of the pilots were leaning forward, listening intently.

"We will stage in Iraq, in Irbil," Hartman said, and then he lowered his voice. "People, we are not going to Iran to get payback. Intel tells us there is another nuke."

At this there was groaning. They had been led on WMD goose chases before.

Hartman held up one hand. "This time it's different. We are not going to this plant expecting to find the nuke there. The nuke is reportedly in the United States. We don't know where it is. Our sources of intel in this hemisphere have apparently dried up on this one, because they are sending us into Iran on a Hail Mary pass. They are hoping with this mission, we'll discover even the smallest clue as to where the third one is. It's a safe bet that it is not in an RV now. We need to go to Iran to save an American city. To me, it seems well worth it."

There was a general mumbling of approval, and then Hartman said, "Major Ryan will give you the details."

Hartman stepped away from the podium and let Ryan take his place.

"People," Ryan began, "we will be coming in fast, at oh-dark-thirty. The intent is to be in and out of there before anyone who gets a phone call has time to even completely wake up. McCall, you and Gowdy will insert the D-boys. The rest of the Black Hawks will insert Rangers or will stand by for extractions. The Little Birds will fly patterns in support of the Rangers at the four points. Now, the target city is in a narrow valley. We will have to . . ."

Jeanie McCall was struggling to focus. Every mention of Little Birds had her wondering where Sirois was, and if he was in one piece. She noticed she had drifted mentally, cursed herself for it, tried to listen, and then drifted again.

She remembered a time they had gone camping. They had driven far out into the country, saw a hill they thought would be perfect, and went on up. They drove as far as they could and then humped it the rest of the way. It was beautiful. The forest, wildlife everywhere, climbing the hill, avoiding an old trail, looking for a place of their own.

They had found a small space not quite at the top, but out from under the trees. The tent had gone up quickly, and they had dined on MREs and a bottle of wine. They sat outside with a small fire, cuddling under a blanket until the sky was absolutely black. They talked of childhood memories, high school stories, past loves, sports, and army tall tales.

McCall smiled at the memory, and then snapped out of it and reflexively answered, "No" to Ryan asking if anyone had any questions.

A few people turned to look at her, Ryan among them, looking down from the podium. "Good, McCall, good. That's it."

All was movement. McCall stood, collected her clipboard and bag, and was stepping out when Ryan cut her off.

"I'm sure he's fine, McCall," Ryan said.

"I know, sir." McCall half smiled.

There was moment's pause and then Ryan said, "We need you focused on this."

"I know, sir, I will be. I am," McCall said.

63

June 6
Near the Banya Bashi mosque
Sofia, Bulgaria

Bragdon was across the street from the mosque, a couple floors up from the street. The mosque was built of tan stone, with a large dome, and a brown minaret standing off to one side.

Bragdon was set far back from the window, behind a large net draping from the ceiling. The wall behind him was a pale blue, as was the net and strips of cloth tied in it. His breathing was slow and deliberate. His cheek was welded to the stock. And then his target came out.

A tall, dark man stepped out of the mosque and walked toward a waiting car. He had a bodyguard with him, and at least two waited with the vehicle.

Bragdon whispered, "Reap the whirlwind," and then fully exhaled, sighted in center mass on the dark man, and gently squeezed the trigger.

The report of the rifle surprised him, just as it should to prevent anticipation of the shot ruining his concentration, trigger squeeze, and placement.

The dark man was thrown on his back, in a spray of blood, and his chest went immediately red. Bragdon immediately began disassembling his rifle to pack it in the open case. The man's bodyguards opened fire, spraying the building Bragdon was in with bullets. Glass flew inward from four windows. Bragdon covered his head and fell over onto the floor. A shard of glass the size of a man's thumb embedded in the back of Bragdon's hand.

The bodyguards stopped firing and threw the dark man's lifeless body in the car. With tires screeching, they attempted to pull away, but the street below was suddenly filled with police. Blocking their escape was a large van carrying soldiers in tactical gear and assault weapons, members of the Bulgarian National Security Service. The domestic antiterror forces.

Bragdon finished packing his rifle into the case, without making a sound and without taking the time to either pull the glass from his hand or to bandage it. The blood dripped down off his fingers as he carefully peeked down into the street where many eyewitnesses were pointing up toward his window. Within seconds, the Bulgarian NSS team was storming the floor below him. Bragdon grabbed the case and ran up the stairs.

"Pegasus, Pegasus, this is Vejovis, I need extraction, and I need it fast," Bragdon called into his headset. He could hear the police right behind him, one flight down from him. They had spotted Bragdon now, and were shouting for him to stop.

"Vejovis, Pegasus, ETA twenty seconds," a voice came back.

Bragdon hit the roof door, but it didn't open. It was padlocked from the outside. Bragdon had no real desire to fall into the hands of the Bulgarian NSS. He turned, drew a handgun from the back of his trousers, and fired four quick shots down the stairs. The NSS men took cover, and Bragdon then fired four more shots at where he guessed the padlock was. When he threw his body against the door, it flew open, and the sound of approaching rotor greeted him.

Bragdon ran to the center of the roof and got there just as the SA341J Gazelle helicopter descended to pick him up. He pulled the door of the aircraft open and threw in the case. He scrambled in after it, just as rounds began pinging the thin metal skin. The three blades above changed pitch and the pilot gave the old bird throttle. It pulled away from the rooftop and dropped into the city.

The Gazelle, while old, was every bit as quick as any helicopter on Earth. They were soon out of range of the NSS weapons.

Bragdon looked over at the pilot, his civilian clothes and his week's growth on his face, and nodded a thank you.

Rick Sirois nodded back, eased the collective down a bit, and headed for the countryside rendezvous point. He and Bragdon had been working together now for only four days, but a deep respect had formed between the two. A friendship really. Something Bragdon, the longtime loner, was not particularly used to. Except for a young lady in Prague, Bragdon rarely took the time to even think about other people on a personal level. Sirois was different, a fraternal spirit somehow.

64

June 6
Midnight
Irbil, Iraq

The Little Birds lifted off first, and then began a long, circuitous flight path around the airfield. Into the center of the circling flock of AH-6Js, the Black Hawks took flight. Their noses dropped, and with tails high, they moved forward and disappeared into the eastern night. With no lights, they were soon gone, and even the sound of more than twenty rotors soon faded.

Into the dark the Night Stalkers went. Hill sat at his minigun, behind him sat ten Delta operators, and Arroyo was on the opposite side. Hill sat there, looking out at the night, once again worrying if he had forgotten something or screwed something up. His confidence was shaken, and he knew it. Much as one can keep himself awake worrying about how late it was getting, Hill was gnawing at his own self-confidence because he knew he lacked the confidence he once had.

"Hey Hill." Arroyo's voice came through on the intercom. "You start reading that book yet?"

Hill rolled his eyes. "No, Arroyo, I haven't had a chance. Been a bit busy and all."

"Come on, man, Reading Is Fundamental. You don't remember that stuff?" Arroyo added.

"Leave me alone, I'll read it when I get a chance," Hill said.

"What book?" Morrison, the copilot, asked.

"Sympathy for the Devil," McCall answered. "Arroyo's always had a thing for that book. Isn't that right, Arroyo?"

"Yes ma'am," Arroyo said, "and I'm trying to spread the wealth to Hill."

"I'll read it if Hill doesn't want to," Morrison offered.

Hill roared into the intercom, "I said I'm going to read it! Alright! Just give me a chance and I'll read the stupid thing!"

The helicopters rose and fell. The formation seemed to ripple over the ridges and hilltops. They flew nap of the Earth, at almost two hundred miles per hour, and they did it completely without light thanks to technology, training, and guts. The distance between Irbil and their target was about one hundred miles, and they would be there within minutes.

As if just to remind Hill of a mission he'd just as soon forget, in the dark and through his NVGs he saw a small lake reflect the starlight just as they dropped down from a mountain ridge. Different body of water, but seeing that sort of image again, while smelling, hearing, feeling all the same things, and being on the wrong side of the Iranian border, was more than a bit unsettling. Hill gripped his minigun's handles a bit tighter.

"You know, Hill, you don't have to read the book, man." Arroyo's voice on the intercom.

"Shut up about the book, Arroyo," Hill said.

"Standby, approaching Shaherviran and target," McCall's voice cut in.

Everyone tensed. McCall, Morrison, Arroyo at his gun, and even Hill found a way to get just a bit more jacked up. The Delta operators actually became still, like springs wound to the point of immobility, sitting at capacity with all the potential energy that could possibly be stored within them.

Hill felt the Black Hawk lose airspeed, allowing the other Black Hawks, save one, to rush forward and insert the Rangers. Then, the nose dipped once more and Hill knew this was it. Across from him, he could see the Black Hawk that Lieutenant Gowdy was piloting, Arrow 47, mirror his own aircraft's movements. They gained speed, but lost altitude until they were skimming across the ground. The target building suddenly filled the space between Hill and Arrow 47, and his eye level was lower than the roof. The aircraft flared only slightly, McCall wary of striking the ground with the tail, and then the D-boys were gone. They raced silently across the space to the building, buffeted by the rotor wash.

"Clear," Hill said.

"Clear," Arroyo confirmed.

"Arrow 6, this is Arrow 42, customers inserted, coming out," McCall radioed.

Not a shot had been fired. Not an enemy combatant had been seen. Not until McCall had climbed to fifty feet, and a single man ran out from a shadow, with an RPG. Hill and Arroyo did not see him. He was directly to their rear. To him, the Black Hawk was in essence a stationary target, albeit growing smaller. He aimed and fired. The rocket had hardly left the launcher when Gowdy's crew chief cut the man down, and nearly in half, with his minigun. But it was too late. The rocket streaked toward McCall's Black Hawk.

Hartman saw it.

"Arrow 42!" was all he managed to say before her aircraft was struck.

The tail boom came apart in the impact. Inside, there was no way for McCall to fight it, no way to minimize the risks or damage. It felt as if a giant boot had kicked the helicopter square in the ass.

At the first sign of spin, McCall shouted, "Cut the power!"

Morrison complied immediately, and McCall flattened the rotor disk. The helicopter fell from altitude as if it had been pushed from the roof of a six-story building. It fell and landed toe-to-heel, with much of the initial impact striking beneath the feet of McCall and Morrison. The floor came up under them.

Hill and Arroyo, who had gone weightless, and then were caught in what felt like a centrifuge, were suddenly slammed into their seats.

The aircraft rolled slightly, not completely over onto its side, but enough so that the rotor blades struck the ground and beat themselves apart.

Inside the building, the Delta operators had immediately come under fire upon entering. They had fanned out behind cover of the heavy milling and metalworking machinery, but were pinned down by a much larger force. If it was a food processing plant, someone had decided they needed fifty or more soldiers guarding it, even in the middle of the night.

"Roadrunner 4, this is Arrow 6, Black Hawk down. Can your men get to her to secure the crash site?" Hartman's voice came down over the radio to the D-boys.

"Ah, that's negative, Arrow 6, we are currently fully engaged with at least five-zero enemy troops. We're coming in from both sides, so I think this will go our way, but right now, I'm pinned behind a metal-lathe and I've got nowhere to go. Sorry," Roadrunner 4, the team leader of the men who came from McCall's Black Hawk, replied.

"Understood," Hartman radioed back, and then on the air net, "I want all Black Hawks to back off the insertion sites. Bullet 18, come on in here and provide cover for McCall. Keep anyone from getting near Arrow 42."

"Ah roger, this is Bullet 18, on the way," the reply came. Within moments, an AH-6J was circling the crash site as if tied to a rope that was staked on the other end to McCall's helicopter.

Hartman's Black Hawk circled in a wider orbit than the Little Bird. He was praying for some sign of life, and he got one. It was clearly Hill, his large frame unmistakable. In the NVGs, Hartman could see him reach back into the aircraft and pull another person free. Most likely Arroyo, Hartman thought.

"Come on Jeanie," Hartman whispered.

Down at the crash site, Hill laid Arroyo down gently and ran back to the aircraft. Climbing in, he shouted, "Morrison! McCall!"

"Here!" Morrison said. "We're here. McCall is unconscious, maybe dead. I can't reach her, I'm pinned, I'm bleeding."

Hill started working his way to the cockpit. The self-sealing tanks were doing their job: Hill couldn't smell fuel in any quantity to be worried about.

"Is she bleeding? Can you tell?" Hill called forward.

"Yes, I think I see blood on her face." Morrison coughed, and then, "Blood, I'm coughing up blood."

"You'll be fine, sir, I'll be right there." Hill looked toward the pilots and realized that while he might be able to squeeze his way through, it would be nearly impossible to get them out this way. It might be easier to go around from the nose, he thought.

"I'm going to go around," Hill shouted. "You're going to be alright!"

Hill scrambled back out the cargo door as the Little Bird circling passed directly overhead. Hill immediately wondered why the AH-6J had changed its flight track. Dropping down to the ground, he looked up just in time to see

Hartman's Black Hawk pass over him and then drop flares from his position out to the fence and beyond. They popped and hissed to life, and illuminated what was clearly more than two hundred members of Iranian infantry moving quickly his way.

"God help us," Hill said simply.

The Little Bird passed directly overhead next and strafed the approaching enemy. Some went diving and others fell dying, and immediately after the pass, they were on their feet and closing on Hill again.

Hill sprinted to the nose of the ruined Black Hawk and pulled hard at McCall's door. It gave way, but opened only a mere four inches. Hill reached in, and felt for a pulse. There was one.

"McCall's alive!" Hill announced, as much to himself as to Morrison.

Other Little Birds were arriving above Hill.

"That's it sir, keep those guys off me for a while," Hill said as he pulled frantically on McCall's door again.

"Bullet elements, I want run after run after run. I don't want to hear a pause in the firing. Just pour it in there. All Arrow elements, be prepared for hasty extraction," Hartman ordered, and then, switching to the ground net, "Roadrunner, Roadrunner, be advised, situation tenuous at best. Nearly a battalion of ground pounders on the way, approaching from the west. The Rangers have shifted and are fully engaged, we can slow them down, but this might be just the first wave. Time to think about getting out of there. I still have people on the ground waiting to be rescued as well. I am—"

Hartman's transmission was cut off. An SA-7 antiaircraft missile came corkscrewing up past his aircraft and destroyed one of the Little Birds in midair. The other two Little Birds, including Bullet 18, immediately wheeled and strafed the Iranians, flying abreast. Two more missiles

raced skyward, and another AH-6J was turned into a ball
of flame, and plummeted to the ground.

"Break off!" Hartman roared into the air net. Bullet 18
broke right and fell to a man's height above the ground. A
missile flashed in the dark and took off after the nimble
aircraft, closing incredibly fast. Hartman watched as Bullet
18 leapt up and over the building, and the missile clipped
the peak of the roof, not detonating but spiraling into the
dirt of the far side and then exploding.

"All Arrow and Bullet elements, we are out of here! Arrow 47, I am sending Roadrunner to your LZ. Arrow 43,
join Gowdy and pick up the customers. All Bullet elements
avoid the crash site. I'm going down to pick up the survivors myself," Hartman ordered.

"Uh, Arrow 6, this is Arrow 5," Ryan radioed. "I'm already on approach to pick up Arrow 42 crew."

Ryan flew in the space before Hartman could even tell
his pilot what they were going to do. Hartman watched
him, and could see the amount of fire the Black Hawk began taking almost immediately, could see the flash of
Cooper's minigun, and said, "Protecting the old man again,
huh Mike?"

Cooper was trying to shout over the rotor wash for Hill to
run, but Hill couldn't hear him and wouldn't have complied anyway.

"Coop! Go get them!" Ryan shouted in the intercom.

Cooper was instantly up and moving. He leapt down to
the ground and ran to Arroyo, checked for vital signs, felt a
pulse, and picked his fellow crew chief up in a fireman's
carry. Cooper began running back to his aircraft, and Arroyo moaned. The dirt churned around Cooper's feet with
incoming rounds. He threw Arroyo in through the cargo
door and then ran back for Hill.

Reaching him still pulling at the door, Cooper shouted, "We gotta go!"

Sparks flew as bullets ricocheted off the downed Black Hawk.

"They're still alive!" Hill shouted back.

Cooper looked out at the approaching enemy and the Rangers fighting their way backwards, fighting with everything they had, just trying to buy time and praying with all their might that they wouldn't be left behind. Cooper ran around to Morrison's side and reached in through the missing window.

"No pulse here!" Cooper shouted up to Hill.

Hill stopped, Morrison had just been talking. He reached in and checked again for a pulse on McCall.

"She's still alive!" Hill shouted back.

Cooper ran back to McCall's side. Just then, an RPG streaked into the nose of the helicopter, through the windscreen without detonating, through Morrison's chest, and finally exploded through the back of his seat. Hill and Cooper jumped clear. Fire ignited in the back. Hill was semiconscious as Cooper rose and began dragging the much bigger man toward extraction.

Rangers retreated into their crash zone, but none stopped at McCall's Black Hawk. No one could be alive in there, they thought.

Rangers grabbed Hill, who came to his senses and began struggling. "Let me go back for her! We don't know she's dead!"

Enemy soldiers were streaming in through the gate now, not twenty feet from McCall's helicopter.

"No way man, forget it! Nobody lived through that!" a Ranger shouted into his ear. Hill was thrown aboard next to Arroyo, and Cooper jumped on the minigun and began blazing away at the infantry as Ryan lifted off.

Black Hawks came down in a swarm to pick up the

Rangers and Delta operators, and the Little Birds made a big pass over the infantry, spraying them with minigun and rocket fire.

A single SA-7 missile streaked up into the night sky, but missed and then kept right on going, climbing like a fireworks rocket until it disappeared.

"Arrow 5, this is Arrow 6," Hartman radioed. "Do you have Arrow 42 actual?"

A quick check with Cooper confirmed the bad news. "This is Arrow 5. We don't have her. Copilot KIA, pilot MIA assumed captured."

Hartman's heart sank. If she was alive, she was a female POW from a covert border crossing mission. That might be worse than dead.

Another missile corkscrewed into the night sky, and a Little Bird tumbled to Earth, exploding on impact.

"All elements! Disengage and return to base!" Hartman radioed, and then on the ground net, "Roadrunner, I hope this was worth it."

"This is Roadrunner, we took some photos and filled a bag with docs, but it's not much. We set charges on some high-end metalworking equipment and some centrifuges, but nothing the airstrike wouldn't have done for us," came the reply.

"Good copy, out," Hartman replied. That was also a dilemma. Hartman should call in an airstrike immediately, but what if McCall was alive, what if they moved her into the target building?

"Arrow 6, this is Arrow 5, you have to call it in," Ryan radioed on the air net, reading his commander's mind.

Hartman hesitated.

"Arrow 6, this is Arrow 5, did you copy my last?" Ryan asked.

"Good copy, now shut the hell up," Hartman hissed back.

He held the mike to his forehead for a moment, and then switched nets. "Shepherd, Shepherd, this is Arrow 6, we need an airstrike at target golf-one-one. How copy, over?"

The response was immediate. "This is Shepherd, good copy. Be there in five mikes."

"Roger, good copy. Arrow 6 out," Hartman said softly.

Back at the target building, the Iranians pulled McCall's Black Hawk apart; the flames in the rear were not a raging fire yet, having not yet reached helicopter fuel. The men pulled the windscreen off, looking for maps, radio frequency information, any kind of intel, when McCall suddenly coughed. Immediately, there was the shouting of many men, as they extracted McCall. Throwing her on the ground, they began kicking her, until the man that had pulled her out of her seat came out shouting for them to stop. He knelt beside McCall, and removed her helmet, revealing her long hair and her feminine face. The Iranians crowded around, staring.

"Get her a medic and get her out of here!" an officer among them barked suddenly, and all was movement. She was quickly loaded into a vehicle and driven away.

The two F-15E Strike Eagles came streaking across the night sky. They each unloaded their explosive payloads, five two-thousand-pound JDAMs each from level flight at ten thousand feet at 0.8 Mach. They were headed back before the munitions reached the building.

When the ten formerly dumb-bombs, each fitted with the new tail kits and guidance to make them smarter, came into the target site, the building and its contents were utterly destroyed. Along with the Iranian soldiers still guarding it. With the first good luck of the night, the last of the ten bombs landed three feet from Morrison's side of the

Black Hawk, destroying what was left of the aircraft as well.

McCall began to regain consciousness, just as the vehicle entered the prison grounds. She was taken to the infirmary, where she was brought fully awake by a man who set her broken leg within a minute of her arrival.

65

June 8
Van Air Base
Van. Turkey

Rick Sirois, shaven-faced and still wearing civilian clothing, lay on an army cot, reading a book. They had been here for twenty-four hours, and Sirois didn't know if this was just a place to rest or if they would launch from here. He didn't know if they'd be here for another day or another week. It wasn't his job to know. He just flew the bird. Whatever bird they gave him. Although, he had to admit, he had enjoyed the Gazelle.

Bragdon came into the small one-room building. The walls were framed and sheathed, but the studs were visible on the inside. It was not built for the Turkish winters, or at least not yet. A small, wooden folding table, painted olive-drab green, three small chairs, two cots, a cable running out to a generator. A couple of five-gallon cans of potable water, and a chest full of ice and bottled water. A few Pepsis tossed in for color. That was it. They were set off by themselves, within the security of the air base, but far from the curious.

"Sirois, I've got some news. Back-channel stuff. Someone out there thought you would want to know," Bragdon said, sitting down on his cot. He had to break bad news to this guy he hardly knew. Sirois was the closest thing to a "buddy" he'd had in decades, and now he had to tell him

something hard, something about the fiancée he had heard
so much about in the past week. Bragdon tried to conjure
up some long-forgotten sugarcoating for the bitter news,
but could not.

"Jeanie McCall is MIA, captured by Iranian military,
and is reportedly being held in the Shaherviran region,"
Bragdon said in a rush of breath.

The news tore Sirois's breath away. He sat up and stared
at Bragdon, trying to assess whether or not this was some
sort of sick prank.

"What?" was all Sirois could manage.

"That's all I know," Bragdon said.

Sirois rose to his feet and paced a moment, Bragdon
watching him. Then, the pilot grabbed a rucksack and began to pack.

"What are you doing?" Bragdon asked, truly perplexed.

"Going to Shaherviran," Sirois answered without turning around.

Bragdon's eyes widened. "Listen, man, you can't go in
there. You think you can fly down there, getting fuel from
who knows where, land in Iran, and start asking for directions to your girlfriend?"

Sirois turned around suddenly. "I've been there."

"Shaherviran?" Bragdon asked.

Sirois stopped. "No. I've been held by the Iranians. I
know what that's all about. I have to go get her. There's no
choice."

Bragdon stood up. "Look, Rick, you're not going to get
anywhere near her."

"I can't stay here and not try. How do I live with that?"
Sirois asked.

"You made it. They rescued you," Bragdon said.

"Only because I happened to be in the same convoy as a
nuke on its way to Baghdad, man," Sirois said. "They
weren't coming for me, and they aren't going to go after
Jeanie. I have to go."

After another moment, Sirois added, pointing southeast, "She's right there, like two hundred miles that way."

Bragdon watched him resume packing, looked at the floor, and then said, "I'll go. I'll go confirm exactly where she is first. Then we'll work on getting her out. We have to recon this first. She wouldn't want you to go get stupidly killed, especially if she really is counting on you to get her out of there."

Sirois froze, and then said, "What about your mission? Won't people notice you're missing?"

Bragdon grinned. "I think half of them wish I *would* go missing."

Sirois thought for a moment, and then asked, "Why would you do this?"

"So you'll owe me big," Bragdon said. "And because going to save someone is always a better gig than going to kill someone."

"You think we can pull this off?" Sirois asked.

Bragdon's face fell serious once more, and he said, "No. No, I don't think we have a chance in hell, but I do know that our chances together are loads better than your chances alone."

Sirois extended his hand, and Bragdon took it.

"I won't forget this," Sirois said.

"Yeah, I hope not," Bragdon replied.

"What do you want me to do?" Sirois asked, releasing Bragdon's hand.

"First, unpack. Second, lie down and start reading your book again. Don't say anything to anyone, no matter who they say they are, no matter how important they say it might be to find me," Bragdon said. "I'll be back in a few days. Just stay here, mellow out. I'll go recon this. I know you're worried and all, but for the next few days, you're going to have to be cool."

Sirois sighed. "This is going to kill me."

"Hopefully not," Bragdon said, turning to leave.

"Wait, where are you going?" Sirois asked.

"Iran. Where else?" Bragdon chuckled.

"Just like that?" Sirois was dumfounded.

"I could go by way of Miami if you'd like, but I thought I'd see about hitching a ride to the border, slipping across, making my way to where she was captured, and seeing what's up." Bragdon smiled.

"You sure I can't come with you?" Sirois asked.

"I'm way sure. By myself, I have a shot. With you along, we're guaranteed dead. You tell anyone about any of it, me and your girlfriend are sure to be killed. I'll be back in a couple days. Stay cool," Bragdon instructed.

Sirois nodded, and Bragdon walked out. Sirois sat down on the cot and dropped his head into his hands. It was going to be a long wait.

He remembered being a prisoner in Iran all too well, how he'd been tortured. How he'd regained consciousness in a strange room and two men had walked in, one small and one huge. The larger man had walked over to a loop of chain hanging limp from the darkness above. Sirois had tried to see where the chain led, when the man had begun pulling. The chain rattled as the loose loop turned, half of the visible chain being pulled down, the other half rising into the unseen. There had been a sudden tug at Sirois's hands. A searing pain had ripped the remaining fog from his head as he was pulled to his feet by his bound wrists. As the large man continued to pull, Sirois was lifted to his toes. The agony in his hands, arms, and shoulders had been overwhelming. Sirois waited for that terrible moment when his feet would be lifted from the floor and he would swing free by the wrists tied behind his back.

The smaller, older man had unexpectedly barked a few words, and the man on the chains stopped pulling. Only Sirois's toes remained in contact with the floor.

The older man had had his back to Sirois, and when he turned he was holding a ball-peen hammer.

"Aw man, listen, there is no reason to use that. I don't know anything. How about we just get a beer, huh?" Sirois had said.

The old man had approached and said something in Farsi.

"What does that mean?" Sirois had pleaded. Kneeling in front of Sirois, the old man had tapped lightly on Sirois's right toes with the hammer. His toes' grip on the floor had been the only thing keeping him from swinging, and his breathing became shallow as fear welled up.

Without lowering his eyes, the old man had swiftly brought the ball side of the hammer down on Sirois's foot. His toes had came off the floor and he twisted slightly; the pain had been unimaginable. He struggled to maintain his balance and contact with the floor with his uninjured foot. Pain shot through his shoulders as they took some of his weight in the attempt to steady him. His left foot held fast to the stone, and he gingerly brought his broken right toes back down. Sweat had run down his face. Sirois remembered that he could taste the hatred. He looked down again, and the old man was still there, looking up impassively.

The older, smaller man had kept saying things in Farsi, things Sirois had not understood. Mercifully, after Sirois had said a few insulting things about Islam and Khomeini, the larger man had put him out of his misery. He had come over, lifted Sirois's head by his hair, and driven a giant fist into his face. As consciousness had slipped away, and all went black, Sirois was grateful.

He sat on that cot in Turkey, his head in his hands, and pictured Jeanie in their hands, enduring the same kind of treatment, or worse. It was killing him, and like anyone in his position, he wished that he and Jeanie could just switch. That he could take her place.

66

"I'm going blind on this shit," said Jen Parmenter, rubbing her eyes. She had been an intel analyst for more than ten years, and in that ten years she had decided that intel collectors did it on purpose: they buried the good stuff in the most boring material they could find.

She sat among six other intelligence analysts, all brought here to Irbil to work on this one haul, all too busy to respond to her complaint, translating and scouring the documents seized in the raid on the Shaherviran site.

After four hours of checking every mark that may or may not have been made by a typewriter or pen, she picked up a scrap of paper that looked no more important than a grocery list. Written in Farsi, it read: *Destination Nappanee, Indiana. Destination San Angelo, Texas. Destination Bridgeport, Connecticut.*

Parmenter blinked, and strained to read it again, lifting her glasses. "Holy crap."

The other analysts stopped and looked up.

"Holy crap," Parmenter said again. The scrap of paper went on to list addresses, but it was torn. Most of the Connecticut address was missing. All that was left was the word *Barnum*.

A street name? wondered Parmenter. She wrote it up, scanned it in, and passed it up.

67

June 8
Late evening
Airfield
Irbil, Iraq

Mike Ryan sat out on the tarmac, looking up at the night sky. Jack Hartman came out and stood behind him.

"I can't believe we have to go through this again," Ryan said.

"It comes with the job, Mike," Hartman replied.

Ryan knew that was true, but it didn't make it a bit easier. "Jack, this is Jeanie McCall. She's out there, maybe taken all the way to Tehran like Sirois was. Who knows what they're doing to her."

"Look, Mike, you aren't helping her by imagining the worst that could be happening to her," Hartman said.

"How can I help her?" Ryan said, looking down between his feet.

"A few prayers couldn't hurt," Hartman said softly.

Both men fell silent for a moment, and then Ryan spoke again. "We will never get orders to go get her. She's stuck in there, and even with the forces we have right here, we won't get orders to get her back."

"True," Hartman said, "and without a precise location, we can't even go in of our own initiative."

"Tehran on our own?" Ryan asked, trying to look back.

Hartman stepped forward. "No, not Tehran, but I have a

feeling, in my gut, that she's closer than that. We just don't know where."

"Might as well be Siberia," Ryan grumbled. "You know, a while back I found McCall sitting out on a tarmac wondering why her dad had to be lost. And now, I'm sitting out here wondering why Jeanie. I mean, Maggie McCall has paid her dues, ya know?"

"I know," Hartman agreed. "We'll do whatever we can, Mike, I promise."

Ryan looked up at Hartman and nodded, believing him.

Hartman nodded back, and walked away, leaving Mike Ryan with the stars and his prayers. Ryan remembered Seth McCall, Jeanie's father, as the leader of his flight the night Seth McCall was lost. That night in Operation Desert Storm at the battle of Medina Ridge, so many of them were shot down. Of the crew members of the numerous downed aircraft, Ryan had been the sole survivor. Picked up by a dust-off helicopter flown by Jack Hartman, no less. Seemed like a million years ago.

Ryan had once told Jeanie McCall that her dad would be proud of her, and Ryan was sure he would be, but he wondered as he sat out on that tarmac if Seth McCall wouldn't have rather seen his daughter become a doctor or a lawyer or any other job that didn't include bad guys shooting at her.

68

June 9
Attack site
Shaherviran, Iran

Bragdon had hitched rides with truckers, including once in the back with a load of sheep, on the roof of a bus, and even on a tractor, but he had covered the two hundred miles in great time. As darkness fell, he worked his way across the valley floor toward huge lights spotlighting the wreckage of a building. Crews were out, clearing the debris. There were obvious signs of a past pitched battle of some size, and Bragdon knew he had arrived at Shaherviran.

He worked his way through the shadows toward a series of low-slung buildings outside the fenced perimeter, and then, having gotten to within a couple hundred yards, stopped to watch. There were guard shacks, but no visible guards. The only person he could see was the silhouette of a man in a tower beyond the building. He could hear dogs in the distance, but could not see them. Until he saw something other than structures and someone other than the tower guard, he'd have to wait. He lay down behind a string of boulders and watched.

Within a couple of hours, a single man appeared. He walked the route of a guard, but with the complacency of a conscript. Bragdon rose to a squat behind the cool rock. The guard was going to come within twenty feet of Bragdon's position if he followed the worn path he was on, right along the edge of the light. Guards often do this, thinking they are extending their perimeter beyond the lights. While this was true, it also put the guards on the fringe of what could be seen, and what could not.

As the guard closed on his position, Bragdon froze absolutely still. The guard kept coming, looking at his feet more than looking out into the darkness. Even with the sounds of the clearing of battle debris behind him, the soldier simply strolled past Bragdon. When the guard was a couple steps past, Bragdon quickly moved out to the man, seized him by the mouth in one hand, and grabbed his rifle in the other. Bragdon dragged him into the dark shadows, and fell on top of him. He dropped the guard's rifle, pulled a knife, and pressed it against the guard's throat.

There they froze, both waiting to see if anyone had spotted the flurry of activity on the edge of their perimeter. No one had.

Bragdon said in Farsi, "Be very quiet and I will not kill you."

The man nodded. Bragdon let his mouth go, but kept the blade at his throat.

"The other night, a helicopter crashed . . ." Bragdon began.

"Many crashed, but I did not shoot them down, and I stole nothing!" the man interrupted.

"Quiet," Bragdon said calmly, and the man fell silent, so Bragdon continued, "A helicopter went down and a woman was captured. You will tell me where she is."

"They took her away," the guard said.

"To where?" Bragdon asked.

"I don't know," the guard said.

Bragdon applied more pressure to the blade pressed against the man's throat.

"Orumieh!" the guard hissed in fear. "Orumieh Prison! I've heard people say she is in Orumieh." The pressure on his neck lessened.

"Is it a big prison? What does it look like?" Bragdon asked.

"It is not very big, and from the air it is a large square with a great courtyard in the middle," the guard answered immediately.

"How many guards?" Bragdon asked.

The guard said, "I'm not sure perhaps . . ." and then he looked toward his left hand. Bragdon looked that way as well, just in time to see a softball-sized rock catch him in the eye. Bragdon went rolling off, moaning in pain, badly dazed.

The guard leapt to his feet and ran toward the light. Bragdon could not catch him. The tower light swung toward the shouting guard. Just before it got there, Bragdon grabbed the AK-47 rifle the guard had left behind, aimed, and fired a burst at the tower. The running guard never hesitated, but kept on running into the light. As soon as he broke out of the shadows, the tower guard returned fire and dropped the running guard dead in his tracks. The tower spotlighted the man's body, and Bragdon threw the rifle down toward it. He then turned and ran back up the valley, disappearing in the draws and boulders as several soldiers ran to their fallen comrade to wonder what could have possibly led to his death.

69

June 9
Maggie McCall's home
Alpharetta, Georgia

The white Chevy Blazer pulled into the narrow driveway. Two men, both officers in Class A uniforms, stepped out— one a chaplain, the small cross on his lapel, and the other a full-bird colonel, from army aviation.

A maroon sedan sat neatly parked under the carport beside a concrete porch. Beyond the carport, a rugged bluff overlooked the Chattahoochee River. Royal blue shutters framed the windows on the white house. The landscaping was perfect.

The men approached the door with a solemnity reserved perhaps for no other occasion, with a purpose they wished wasn't theirs but one which they would not trust to anyone else. The colonel rang the doorbell.

Inside, it was the first sign that something was wrong. No one ever rang her doorbell—no one she knew. Everyone just knocked lightly and entered calling her name.

The colonel rang the bell again, and the door opened wide.

Maggie McCall's mouth dropped wide, her bright green eyes filled with fear. She tried to step back, but couldn't seem to lift her feet. She fell hard to a seated position in the middle of her dining room.

The men rushed in to help her, but she twisted, as if trying to escape them. She had been here before, had had these visitors over a decade ago. *Not again, not Jeanie too,* was all that ran through her head.

A wailing began, a deep guttural moan, a sound of such intense grief as would have stilled a man in his tracks if he had not served on a notification team as long as the chaplain and colonel had. The men lifted Maggie McCall to her feet and helped her to a sofa in the living room. There, laying her down, the chaplain fell to one knee and took one of Maggie's hands.

"Ma'am," the colonel began, "I'm so sorry, but we are here to let you know that your daughter, Jeanie McCall, is missing in action as the result of action on June 6, in Iraq."

The chaplain understood that the words had to be said, but as Maggie squeezed his hand, he wished they did not. Maggie sobbed uncontrollably, inconsolably.

"Now now, Mrs. McCall, she's missing. There is still some hope," the chaplain offered.

Maggie slowed her sobbing and fixed her gaze on the priest in uniform, and softly said, "Missing?"

"That's right. Nothing is sure except she is at this moment missing," the chaplain said, hoping he was making progress.

Maggie said nothing for a moment, and then, "Her father has been missing since 1991."

"Yes, I know," the chaplain began.

"No you don't," Maggie said, her sobbing coming to an end. "You have no idea what it means that when I go to Arlington, when I go to Memorial Headstone 520 in Section H, and see his name etched in stone, I also know that there is no one there beneath it."

"Ma'am," the colonel interjected, "is there anything we can do for you? Is there anyone you'd like us to call for you?"

Maggie just shook her head, and began to cry again.

"We'll stay here with you, ma'am," the colonel offered, the chaplain stepping back. As the colonel knelt beside Maggie, she rolled suddenly into him, wrapped her arms around him, and let the grief of a widow and the grief of a parent who has almost assuredly lost her only child wash out of her and over him.

The colonel, a man of battles won and lost himself, of many notifications like this one, could not help but be moved. He held her, as if she were his, and cried with her.

70

Her wrists were chained together, and then to a large bolt in the concrete wall. She sat on a wooden bench, her back against one wall, her right leg throbbing from her hip to her toes. It was broken and set, with no broken skin, not a compound fracture. She was grateful for that at least, but without painkillers, the slightest adjustment of the limb blurred her vision with the pain.

To her right was a Turkish toilet and a bucket, presumably of water, but she couldn't reach it anyway. There was no window, no way of knowing if it was day or night. She pulled at the chains in frustration. She noticed the ring, and started to cry. Fighting off the tears, she began to examine the chain carefully again, as if freeing herself from it would set her completely free. There was nothing else to do, other than sit and contemplate the pain in her leg. She began to pull at the chain again, this time furiously, wildly, screaming with rage at her situation, knowing it would only get worse, until the sobbing came. She just couldn't help it, she needed it. She wept deeply. She knew what this would do to her mother, she cried for plans not yet executed and Rick, she cried for children she'd not yet had, she cried for the feeling of sun on her face, the feeling of wind in her hair, she cried for feeling free and whole.

She remembered how she felt when Rick was downed and captured. The motorcycle ride she took, interstate therapy she had called it.

Straddling the black and maroon Suzuki Hayabusa, Rick's prized 1300cc motorcycle, she had raced down the interstate, thinking of Rick, held in some Iranian prison, being free for him and raging against her own helplessness. The wind had howled past her ears and clawed at her sunglasses. She accelerated past 110 miles per hour. She cut off a large truck and swooped down into the breakdown lane to get around two cars blocking both lanes. She swerved back into the fast lane in front of the honking sedans. She had reached back with one hand and vigorously flipped them off. She continued to accelerate. Exceeding 140 miles per hour, she had shifted into fourth gear.

This was not a ride of sentimentality. At 160 miles per hour, the bike redlined again and she shifted into fifth, leaning low against the tank. A car had pulled out into her path to pass a bus. McCall blasted between the two, exceeding the speed of the car by one hundred miles per hour. She caught herself screaming.

And in her cell, she screamed again. The same sort of angry, cathartic, scream. She opened her eyes, and saw the ring again, and it became an anchor of her resolve. She decided she would do whatever it took to make it back, to her mother, to Rick.

She heard the door open, and looked up. Three men in Iranian military uniforms came into her cell.

"Hello," said the oldest of the three. "I am Hamid. What is your name please?"

The three men stopped, standing side by side along the bench, looking down at McCall. She knew already this would not be pleasant.

"Chief Warrant Officer Jeanie McCall," she said, leaning her head back against the wall.

Two of the men stepped back, but Hamid did not move.

"Why were you flying a helicopter in the army?" Hamid asked.

"Someone had to," she said, closing her eyes.

"A woman pilot in combat? Are the Americans that desperate?" Hamid asked.

McCall said nothing.

"What was your mission?" Hamid asked, knowing the answer.

"I can't tell you, it's a big secret," McCall said, taunting, wanting to get the niceties out of the way. She knew what was coming; she had been awakened by Sirois's nightmares and had listened to his stories.

Hamid looked confused. He didn't realize she was being sarcastic, and immediately thought that not only did he have a woman on his hands, but that she was perhaps mentally retarded. As if her being a woman was not complicating enough.

"You can tell me—it is over now," Hamid offered.

McCall laughed at his sincerity. Hamid realized he was being laughed at, and all of his problems melted away. He was not a man to suffer this sort of lack of respect lightly, even from a man, but especially not from a woman. Hamid stepped forward and took hold of the foot on McCall's broken leg. She gasped, and then clenched her teeth.

"It is perhaps less funny now?" Hamid said.

She said and did nothing. Hamid gave the foot a shake, just to punctuate his point. The movement did not last a complete second, but the pain was incredible. McCall's back arched, and even with her eyes closed, her vision flashed white.

As soon as Hamid stopped, she opened her eyes. A single tear fell from one corner, but she hadn't made a sound. Hamid stared at her.

"Perhaps now you will show some respect?" he said. He released her foot, stepped forward, and sat beside her on the bench. He sat there and looked at her as a doctor might after a scary surgery.

"Now, tell me why you came into my country. Why you attacked a food processing plant. Tell me these things, and nothing will happen to you," Hamid said.

"I . . . ," she said very softly. "I . . ."

"Yes?" Hamid leaned in.

McCall balled her fists around the chain and drove them both upward into his mouth and teeth with all of her might. She felt the teeth breaking away with a satisfying crunch. He may kill me, she thought, but he'll remember me.

Hamid rolled to the floor of the cell as the two other men jumped over him and onto McCall. One grabbed and pinned her arms against her chest, while the other landed on her hips. The proximity to her broken leg was enough to cause new waves of pain. She struggled beneath them both, but was not able to lift them off. Hamid jumped up and leaned into her face; she could smell his breath, could see the blood from his wrecked mouth, bloody spit spraying as he shouted, "You bitch! I was prepared to simply talk with you, but you decided to be arrogant, even here, a true American patriot! This is fine with me."

He moved away. McCall strained to see where he was; she knew where he was going. She felt the bench shake as he stepped on it. She felt his feet between her legs, and then above the two men, she saw his bloodied face. Hamid looked absolutely mad, evil.

"You will learn to respect me, and you will give me whatever I ask!" he shrieked, and then, raising one foot, he stomped on her broken leg.

McCall screamed in agony, and then promptly and mercifully passed out.

71

Sirois's feet were on the cot, but his hands were on the floor. He extended his arms again and again, and his body rose stiff as a board. Sweat dripped off the end of his nose and fell to the floor in front of his face, creating a small wet stain on the unfinished wood.

The door opened and Sirois froze. Bragdon came in, dressed like a Kurdish goatherd, and sporting a black eye. Sirois pulled his feet under him and stood.

"She's alive," Bragdon said.

"Where is she?" Sirois sighed with relief.

"In a prison not far from here, not far from where she went down. They haven't moved her to Tehran. She's still close," Bragdon said.

"What's next?" Sirois asked eagerly. Waiting for two days had been absolute murder. He half hoped Bragdon would just announce it was time for the two of them to go get her.

"Next, we report it. I'll call higher on the Sat phone, they'll go get her," Bragdon said confidently.

"I doubt they'll go into Iran for a single person shot down on a covert mission," Sirois said, shaking his head.

"Look, man, she's not in Tehran like you were. She's like a stone's throw from the border. They might move her, but they haven't yet. It's not even a big prison, I've seen it. Not a tough gig, zip in there with some of your Delta guys. They went after that guy in Panama, and he was like a civilian," Bragdon said.

"They?" Sirois sniffed. "That was 'we' and we didn't just go there alone, we had to get that guy, Muse, out because there was an invasion coming. And as much as I think Iran could use a good invasion, I don't think one's coming anytime soon."

Bragdon held up his hands. "Fine. Sit tight, let me pass it up, let's see what happens. Be right back. Don't go after her yet."

"I can't. You haven't told me where she is," Sirois replied dryly.

"Oh, right, good. Be right back, man, stay cool. Ten mikes, that's all."

Sirois went back to his push-ups. At least now, Sirois thought, there was some real hope.

Bragdon strode out into the morning sun. His eye hurt, but the orbital socket was not broken. There was an abrasion and a contusion, but that was about the extent of it. He was lucky the Iranian guard had not been a bit stronger, or more determined.

Bragdon went to the Gazelle helicopter parked not fifty feet from the small outbuilding they shared, and pulled open the door. He climbed inside, pulled a pack open, and removed the Iridium 9505A portable satellite phone. It wasn't much bigger than a cordless phone you might find in someone's kitchen, but this phone was set up for end-to-end encryption, and direct uplink to the Defense Information Systems Network or DISN.

Bragdon let the antenna extend from the charcoal gray handset.

"Blue, blue, black. Number 9567-GOLF-2-BRAVO,"

Bragdon said into the receiver, looking out over the plain of concrete that was the airfield. Mountains in the distance rose up in white-capped ruggedness.

"Yes, it's me. The 160th SOAR, out of Ft. Campbell, struck a site in Shaherviran the other night. One of their pilots, a female pilot, was shot down and captured. She's being held at Orumieh Prison in Iranian Kurdistan, western Azerbaijan province," Bragdon said, and then listened.

"Yes, that's confirmed. By who?" Bragdon didn't like how this was going. "By me. Pass it along to DoD. Confirmed."

Bragdon saw movement off to his right, and turned to see Sirois approaching.

"Listen, man, she's in there. She might not be there for long, pass it along to DoD and let them go get her. They got like a million helicopters within thirty minutes of her, with a bunch of Delta operators sitting around doing nothing," Bragdon said.

Bragdon fell silent, his eyes closed. Sirois stood watching at the helicopter door.

"Yeah, I get it, but I didn't compromise anything. Bottom line, you going to pass it along or what?" Bragdon asked.

He heard the answer and then looked at Sirois. It was obvious the answer had been in the negative.

"Alright, then let me go," Bragdon said. "I said let me go. I'll go get her."

A pause, and then Bragdon said, "Compromise this," and hung up.

Bragdon stared at Sirois in silence for a moment and then dialed again.

"I'd like to speak to Colonel Kelly Patrick, please. Yes, I'll hold," Bragdon said.

Sirois nodded his understanding.

"Sir, this is Bragdon. Fine, sir, how are you?" Bragdon said.

Sirois waved his hands in impatience.

"Sir, I need a favor. What else is new? Come on, sir," Bragdon said, shrugging at Sirois. "Sir, I need to get word to Colonel . . . Wait one."

"Hartman, Jack," Sirois offered.

"To Colonel Jack Hartman at the 160th SOAR, likely still deployed in Iraq," Bragdon said, then paused, nodded to himself, and said, "Message follows: McCall is being held at Orumieh Prison just over the border. Confirmed as of 9 June. You got it, sir?"

"No, don't run it through channels. Use the buddy system, get word to him. Tell him Sirois is on his way to get her," Bragdon said, looking back at Sirois, who stood gravely, ready to go as soon as Bragdon hung up.

"Sorry I can't tell you any more than that, sir," Bragdon said. "Yes sir, next time you're in England, we'll get in some golf. Yes sir. Thank you."

Bragdon hung up and packed the phone. He climbed out of the bird and walked past Sirois into the shack. Sirois followed him in. Bragdon was pulling maps from a bag, spreading them on the field table. Sirois approached and his eyes followed Bragdon's finger as it dragged around the line representing the Iranian–Turkish border.

"Let's get our shit together and go do this," Bragdon said sternly.

Playtime was over; Bragdon had already slipped into mission-mode.

"It's about time," Sirois said, and leaned in.

72

McCall's eye was swollen shut. Her hair was matted to her head with grime and blood. She was wearing nothing except for her army T-shirt and her underwear, and a rough wooden splint on her leg. It was so hopelessly loose, it did almost nothing for her injury.

She had not been raped, as she feared she would. They seemed to be satisfied with stripping her down, having her live with a constant fear of it instead of the actual assault.

It was working. She could feel herself slipping, her strength and resolve fading. She knew that she was only expected to stay silent for a few days, that no reasonable military today expects indefinite withholding of information. The intel she might provide would be largely worthless within a week. Any nonperishable information they might get out of her was available on the Internet.

The ugly, black bruise and swelling surrounding the break in her lower leg had spread up to the knee and down to the ankle.

She lay on the floor, on one elbow, her hair hanging about her face, and she stared at the engagement ring they had inexplicably left on her finger. She lay there and thought of Sirois, of making love in Pennyrile Lake, of playing pool at the Mae West, of nights riding with the top off of her Jeep. She remembered the motorcycles, each having their own these days, the racing on the interstate. She remembered when Sirois proposed and had given her the ring.

She remembered all of them, the picnics at Pennyrile Lake, the time she wore a sundress and felt like a woman, felt feminine and sexy. A weightless and short sundress, strings over each shoulder, with light sandals. Her hair was loose, with a breeze blowing through it.

How a football thrown by Hill had sailed down and struck Cooper in the head, because Cooper had been gawking at McCall in a sundress. They'd never seen her dress this way before. As the first female pilot to be accepted into the 160th SOAR, the first woman Night Stalker, she had always tried to be one of the guys.

Cooper had thrown the football hard back to Hill, and it went long, and instinctively McCall had broken into a sprint, jumped high, with her arms above her head, and made a beautiful catch. In the effort, her dress had ridden up, exposing her underwear for all the world to see. When she landed, she had immediately tugged her dress back into place. Hill and Rick had stood with mouths hanging open. Cooper and Arroyo just stared. A few wives whispered jealously amongst themselves.

Arroyo was the first to speak. "Ma'am, that was about the coolest thing I've seen since I joined the army."

McCall had blushed and was very embarrassed, but then Major Ryan had come and saved her, asking her what she wanted to eat, taking her and Rick to his picnic table. McCall wished she could be there right now. With the sun on her shoulders, eating grilled food, laughing with Rick, the Ryans, and with Colonel Hartman.

The door of her cell suddenly swung wide and two men came in. She barely had time to lift her head when they doused her with a large metal tub of ice water. She screamed and fell to the floor. The men did not say a word and walked out, relocking the door.

She would've cried, but she'd run out of tears. She rose to her elbow again, and looked once more at the ring.

"Rick, help me, tell me how you got through this," she whispered.

Outside, on the valley slope, Martin Bragdon looked down on the prison. It wasn't especially large, not for being on the outskirts of a city of nearly half a million inhabitants. The Iranian who had brained him with a rock had not lied about its layout and size. It was clearly well-guarded, however. There were four towers, fences topped with concertina wire, searchlights in the half dark of early evening, and dogs. There would be no sneaking in the back way, no overpowering a guard or two.

Then Bragdon heard it. The tiniest of sounds. Maybe just the compression of moss on the stones behind him. He spun, drawing his handgun as he turned. Looking right back down at him was a boy, still a teen, aiming an old Russian-made SKS rifle at Bragdon's head. Very slowly, Bragdon lowered his pistol and laid it on the gravel.

Smart kid, thought Bragdon, most people will walk right up on you, but the kid stayed well out of my reach but close enough to kill me with his eyes closed.

The boy lowered his rifle. "Who are you? You are dressed like us, but you are not one of us."

Azeri, Bragdon thought. Figures he'd run into a language one day that he just couldn't get by in. If he tried Farsi, the kid might kill him as an Iranian. If he went Arabic, the same sort of thing might happen for different reasons.

"I'm just looking at the prison. Someone I care about is in there," Bragdon said, in Kurdish.

"You are not Kurdish," the kid instantly said. "Russian?"

"No, I'm not Kurdish. I'm not Russian, I'm not Iranian. Does it matter so much?" Bragdon asked, his Kurdish very rusty.

The kid tilted his head and asked, "You want to speak Persian Farsi?"

Bragdon smiled, and switched to Farsi. "Yes. Please."

The boy smiled back, and then asked, "Who is in there?"

"A woman friend of mine," Bragdon said.

The boy's eyes narrowed. "You are an American who has come for the pilot."

The boy's astute analysis and excellent intel startled Bragdon, but then he nodded in the affirmative.

"I can help you get her out, but you have to help me," the boy said after a moment.

"I have no parents, but my uncle is in there. He is all I have left here. You promise to get me and my uncle to Kirkuk, to the house of his friend, and I will get you in there," the boy said, pointing at the prison. His tone and demeanor were very businesslike.

"How will you do that?" Bragdon asked.

"So we have a deal?" the boy asked.

"What's your name?" Bragdon prodded.

"Elyar," the boy said, "and yours?"

"Stephen," Bragdon said.

"This is not your real name," Elyar announced.

"It is as far as you are concerned." Bragdon smiled.

Elyar considered this and then nodded, "Yes, very well, get up."

Bragdon stood, taking the handgun with him, and slipping it back beneath his shirt.

"So, we have a deal then, Stephen?" Elyar asked again.

"Yes, we have a deal. How will you get us in there?" Bragdon asked.

"I go in there almost every night. I go and sell cigarettes

and hashish. I go often, and they expect me. Sometimes, when I have a lot of hashish, I bring help. I have a lot of hashish tonight." Elyar smiled.

"How will we get your uncle and my friend out?" Bragdon asked.

"That," Elyar said turning and walking away, "was not part of the deal. I only said I would get you in. You are supposed to get them and us out."

Bragdon dropped his head, shook it, and followed after the boy.

"Where are we going now?" Bragdon asked.

"To get the merchandise," Elyar replied.

73

"We have received a completely self-serving op order. For the first time in the history of this unit, we are going on a mission that serves this unit more than any other single group. We are going to hit Orumieh Prison just over the border in Iran, insert our customers, who will infiltrate the building, and then we will extract them. Among their number on the way out will be our very own Jeanie McCall," Hartman announced. The op-order had not been completely blessed. When he'd received word of McCall's location through Colonel Kelly Patrick, a man he only vaguely knew, he tried to get a mission approved. The Pentagon approved it with a single, and yet ominous, caveat. If the operation were successful, no sweat. If the mission to rescue McCall went bad, and then went public somehow, DoD would call the whole thing a rogue op concocted by Hartman out of desperation to get one of his pilots back. The other pilots did not know this, and perhaps another leader might have told them, but Hartman claimed this burden as his own, and kept it to himself.

At hearing that they would be going to attempt to rescue McCall, there was no cheer, no talking. This was deadly serious, and these were quietly professional warriors, undertaking a mission to save one of their own.

"We will surely lose, among our crews and our customers, more than one life, and so those outside our culture might question why we undertake such a mission," Hartman said. "But we know it is because we cannot allow one of us to be held captive while the rest of us breathe free. We will leave no one behind."

"We leave within a couple hours," Hartman concluded. "Here is Major Ryan with the details."

74

"Why would they believe you need help to carry in this much hash?" Bragdon asked, looking down at a dark brown brick, about twelve inches long and four inches thick, wrapped loosely in paper, with paper dividing many layers within it.

Elyar rolled his eyes. "I don't need help to carry it! But when I have this much, I need protection getting there with it. And you will not be able to bring your gun."

"You're bringing yours?" Bragdon asked.

"My gun looks like it belongs here. Your gun looks like it belongs somewhere else," Elyar explained.

"Where can I leave it?" Bragdon asked.

"Hide it in the box, where the hash was hidden," Elyar said.

Bragdon hesitated.

"Hurry, we are going to be late," Elyar said, motioning.

Bragdon shook his head and slipped his gun into the simple wooden box. There was no lock on the box, and no real door to lock either. Bragdon knew that in this part of the world, putting a lock on anything was just announcing to thieves that there was something worth stealing there.

"Come, come!" Elyar said.

"I'm on a schedule too, Elyar," Bragdon said. "Our ride

out will get here at a specific time. We don't want to be sitting around with all your hash sold, with your uncle and my friend, and have to wait for our ride to arrive."

"Come, Stephen," Elyar said, ignoring his timetable information, pulling on Bragdon's arm.

"Should I speak Kurdish to the guards?" Bragdon asked.

"Do not speak at all. You say the dumbest things when you talk. Act feeble-minded but fearless. If you must speak, say only one word at a time, and speak Kurdish, yes. And you do not understand Farsi," Elyar said. The tone in the boy's voice was one of such exasperation that he made Bragdon, the veteran field officer from the world's most famous intelligence organization, feel a bit feeble-minded at that.

They walked down the slope to the first gate, Elyar first and Bragdon immediately behind. Bragdon saw the guards surveying him, and practically ignoring the boy they knew, even though it was the kid who had a weapon. Bragdon wished he had his handgun; he felt unbelievably vulnerable like this. For all he knew, the enterprising teen was about to sell him for a profit. They had roughly an hour and a half until Sirois would show up to extract them. The prison, empty of guards, could be searched in half that time. But the prison wasn't empty. As they stopped at the gate, and Bragdon scanned with his eyes, there was literally an armed guard in every direction, and at three different elevations.

"Ah, it's the Azeri bandit," the closest guard said in Farsi.

"I have an especially fine product tonight, gentlemen," Elyar replied, also in Farsi.

The guard suddenly lowered his rifle, aiming it at Elyar's head. "Maybe I will just take it all, for free tonight, eh?"

Bragdon couldn't believe how badly things had gone so quickly. Stupid kid's going to be lucky just to lose his hash, Bragdon thought.

"Yamil, you idiot, don't point that thing at me," Elyar said, pushing the muzzle of the rifle away.

The guards began laughing, and the guard named Yamil slung his rifle back over his shoulder with a grin. "I want the same amount as usual. Just leave it on my bunk, under the pillow."

"I will leave you a wad of hashish hairs if you are lucky," Elyar said, pushing his way past the two guards and into the gate itself. Bragdon tried to follow, and immediately two AK-47 muzzles were pressed against either side of his chest. Bragdon looked down, and then up again, and grinned broadly, laughed stupidly a bit, and then fell stone-faced and open-mouthed, staring at Elyar.

"He is with me, Yamil. I need him to protect the product from all the criminals in the prison," Elyar said calmly.

"The prisoners are locked in their cells," Yamil answered.

"I was not talking about the prisoners," Elyar chuckled.

Yamil laughed at this too, and the guards stepped back from Bragdon, who quickly stepped over to Elyar.

"Keep him with you, Bandit, don't let him roam about by himself," Yamil said.

Elyar waved without looking back, leading Bragdon into the prison. Elyar was still holding his rifle, and the hashish. Bragdon felt utterly useless walking empty-handed behind the teenager.

They walked through two chain-link fences, each topped with spiraling razor-studded concertina wire. Between the fences walked guards with dogs. The search-lights from the towers worked back and forth across the space, across the fences and back, and still there were many sets of eyes watching them. Only half interested, but watching.

Bragdon and Elyar walked on, into the building itself, through immense steel doors. Somewhere inside, Bragdon thought, was a woman he was coming to rescue, whom he'd never met, and of whom he only had a verbal description. Sirois had not even had a photograph. Bragdon knew they would need more than a little luck.

Elyar led Bragdon down a hallway, with no visible signs that it was a prison. In fact, the hallway looked more like some of the third-world hospitals he had been in. Cold, without feature, not dirty but not clean either. He had expected a more military appearance.

They entered a room, and inside were a set of bunk beds. The beds were made up, but not crisp. More like the room of a conscientious American teenager. Elyar put his rifle down, and lay the brick of hashish on the bottom bunk. He tore off a piece the size of a standard cassette tape, and slid it beneath the pillow.

"For Yamil," smiled Elyar.

"When does he pay you?" Bragdon asked.

"Yamil does not pay me. He is the one who created this business for me, and ensures I get in. The hashish is his payment," Elyar said.

Bragdon nodded and picked up the rifle.

"Put that down!" hissed Elyar. "They do not care that I carry it, but they will shoot you on sight if you pick it up again."

Bragdon quickly complied, but said, "You need a holiday, Elyar. Listen, you need to show me where the cells are, and you need to show me the easiest way out to the courtyard, the center area, from the cells. Do you understand?"

"Of course I understand; you're the feeble-minded one, remember?" Elyar said, pushing past Bragdon.

The boy was pushing past amusing now, thought Bragdon.

The two walked down the hall further, and turned the corner. Up ahead, they faced a locked door made of steel bars. Elyar approached the bars, and said, "I've got hashish tonight."

"You always have hashish," said a voice, and then a surprisingly large man appeared. "Who's this?" The guard looked Bragdon over carefully.

"This is my security," Elyar said.

"Lift up your shirt," the guard told Bragdon, in Farsi. Bragdon stared blankly.

"Lift up your shirt," Elyar said in Kurdish. Bragdon looked down at the boy, and then picked up the front of his shirt, exposing his abdomen as a two-year-old might.

The guard shot Elyar an understanding look, and opened the gate. Elyar broke off another like-sized piece, but this time, after taking a good sniff of the hashish, the guard gave Elyar some money. The money went promptly into Elyar's pocket, and then Elyar turned to Bragdon, pointed at the guard, and said, "Kill this one."

Bragdon wasn't sure who was more surprised, he or the guard. The guard looked at Bragdon and then at Elyar, and then made a move, reaching for a pistol holstered on his hip. Bragdon stepped forward and struck with incredible speed and force, punching the guard in the throat. Elyar heard the crushing of the windpipe, the strange wheezing sound the guard made, and did not even look away. The guard's hands immediately went to the injury. Bragdon grabbed them both, and the guard's ruined throat, and drove the man onto his back. He held the man down until he passed out, and then stood as the man died.

"Why didn't you tell me in advance?" Bragdon growled.

"I just thought of it," Elyar answered calmly. "Might as well kill him now. There is no other guard looking into this part of the prison for another hour until his relief arrives. By then, we'll be gone, correct?"

"How do you know she is in this section?" Bragdon asked, pointing at the cells.

"I don't, but I know my uncle is in this section," Elyar replied.

Bragdon grabbed the teenager by the shirt with both

hands. Elyar struggled to keep hold of both the rifle and hashish.

"I have done things your way until now, but if I fail to find my friend because of your little tricks, I will kill you myself. Is that clear?" Bragdon hissed.

"Yes yes, you will kill me, can we go now?" Elyar asked. Bragdon released him, and ripped the rifle from the boy's hands. He pulled the pistol from the dead guard's holster, and used it to indicate he was ready to move, pointing into the cellblock with it. He then slipped it into the back waistband of his pants.

Elyar ran forward, and began standing on his toes to peek into each of the door windows. The rooms were dark, and what light was inside was intended to be just enough for the guards to ascertain whether or not the occupants of the cells were indeed still present. Of course, they always were.

Bragdon sprinted down to the other end of the cellblock and began checking cells himself, and then he heard it. The sound of a woman crying.

Elyar suddenly yelled something in Azeri, dropped the hashish, then ran back to the fallen guard, and returned with keys. He was still working one of the locks when Bragdon found her. A feminine form on the floor within.

"Elyar, hurry up with the keys!" Bragdon said, and then into the window he called, in English, "Jeanie? Jeanie McCall?"

The woman inside looked up with one eye, her face a mass of bruises and cuts. Her arms were black-and-blue, one entire leg was a dark color, almost blending in with the floor. She said nothing. Bragdon stood Elyar's rifle against the wall.

"Rick sent me. Rick Sirois sent me, he's coming," Bragdon said, and then, "Elyar! Bring me the keys!"

The door to the cell Elyar had been working was wide open, and the keys were still in it. Bragdon went down to retrieve them, and when he glanced inside, he could see Elyar holding the emaciated body of an old man. Elyar was rocking and crying. Bragdon stopped fiddling with the key, and went in.

"He is not alive, my uncle," Elyar said.

"Yes, I see," Bragdon replied softly. The man was a skeleton. He had been dead for at least a couple of days.

Elyar just kept rocking the old man.

"I have found my friend. I am going to get her. Elyar, we still have to get out of here. I am sorry, but we will have to leave your uncle," Bragdon said.

"Yes, I know, it is not him anyway, just his body. But you must still bring me to the friend of my uncle's. In Kirkuk. I cannot stay here, in my village, any longer," Elyar said, as if the death of his uncle had somehow altered the arrangement. "Not after we killed the guard and free your friend."

"Of course, Elyar. Let me help you," Bragdon said, and then the two of them gently lifted the body onto the cot, and Elyar covered it with a meager blanket. The body couldn't weigh a hundred pounds, thought Bragdon.

They closed the cell door, locked it once more, and ran to the door of McCall's cell. They opened the door, and Bragdon rushed in.

Bragdon checked his watch. "We have about ten minutes to be in the center of the courtyard. A helicopter will pick us up."

Bragdon pulled the pistol from the back of his pants with his right hand, and lifted McCall in his arms, with his right arm under her thighs. In this way, he could somewhat aim the pistol and carry her at the same time. She groaned in pain, but didn't scream as Bragdon had expected. She was past that.

Elyar snatched up his rifle. "This should be a neat trick. There are at least two towers that will be able to fire on us in the courtyard, not to mention any guards on the ground outside. And then once we get into the air, it will get much worse. I hope he is a good pilot."

McCall said nothing, but began to cling tightly to Bragdon, instead of simply hanging as dead weight. It made carrying her much easier.

"He is a good pilot, but we'll need some of your luck, too," Bragdon said. "Which way?"

Elyar pointed down further into the cell block. "There's the way we came and there is that way. That's it. Let's go." The teen gave one last look back at his uncle's cell door, and took off at a jog, the rifle held in front of him.

Bragdon followed, matching his pace, stopping as he did at a corner.

"There are always two guards in this hallway, each with a Kalashnikov. You will have to shoot them," Elyar said.

Bragdon tried to lay McCall on the floor. She whimpered and would not let go.

"Shh shh shh, it's okay, Jeanie," Bragdon said. She smelled terrible. He couldn't believe, looking at her injuries, that she was not unconscious from the pain, dead from shock. He stood, and instead backed to the corner, and then with a quick movement, leaned back and then forward again. In the split second when he could see, he had established where the guards were, and how hard it might be to take them out.

"I've got to put you down, Jeanie, just for a second," he whispered in English. She began to whimper again as he lowered her to the floor. Bragdon rose once more, sighed, looked at Elyar, and said, "This pistol is going to make a lot of noise. As soon as I use it, anyone anywhere near us will know something is wrong. Elyar, the door, halfway down the hallway, is that the door out to the courtyard?"

"Yes." Elyar nodded.

"Good. We'll wait until we hear the helicopter. Then, we'll shoot our way to the door and then out. You and me. Both of us will shoot, understood?" Bragdon said.

"Yes," Elyar said again.

"When we get outside, do not stop to aim or for any

other reason. Just run to the helicopter, as fast as you can. Understand?" Bragdon said.

"I understand," Elyar said. Elyar was still nodding when they heard the approaching helicopter. McCall suddenly looked up.

Bragdon looked at Elyar, and then took two quick steps out into the hallway. The guards had moved to the door in an effort to see why a helicopter might be landing at this time of night. Bragdon fired twice, from beneath McCall's legs as he carried her, hitting the guard closest to the door. The man fell without making a sound. The report of El-yar's rifle echoed off the walls, and the rounds impacted inches from the head of the second guard. Chips of con-crete sprayed his face as he spun and fired a burst from the AK-47 in their direction. Bragdon fired once more, and the man's head rocked back and led him to the floor. McCall was gripping Bragdon fiercely, but was not making a sound.

Bragdon hit the door first, and it opened. The three of them ran out into the courtyard. Spotlights from the towers had the helicopter illuminated, but no one was firing at it. They assumed that someone within Iran, flying a helicop-ter into a prison courtyard, must have authority to do so. Since the helicopter came in with confidence and in no par-ticular hurry, with its light on, it seemed they might be hav-ing a visitor of importance. No one recognized the type of helicopter, but they were prison guards, not intelligence soldiers or even line troops.

However, when Bragdon appeared carrying McCall and followed by Elyar, it became immediately apparent that something was wrong. A guard in one of the towers imme-diately ordered them all to stop.

"Get on the ground, or we will fire!" he ordered over a loudspeaker in Persian Farsi first, and then in Azeri.

The door of the helicopter opened, and Bragdon pushed McCall inside. She still would not release him.

"Let go of me, McCall! We gotta get in here!" Bragdon yelled in English.

"Let me in!" Elyar was shouting in Farsi.

"Oh my God!" Sirois exclaimed, seeing McCall's injuries.

"Let go of me!" Bragdon insisted, prying her fingers loose. She began to whimper and then scream. Sirois pulled her from Bragdon, as he batted away her hands.

"Get on the ground!" the tower guard shouted again, and this time it was punctuated by a burst of automatic fire across the ground not ten feet from Elyar. He decided he had been patient enough, and pushed in past Bragdon. Bragdon grabbed the rifle as Elyar climbed in.

"No! Get in the back, you idiot!" Bragdon shouted at Elyar.

McCall was in the front seat beside Sirois, curled up in the fetal position, whimpering loudly, as Elyar moved into the back. Bragdon put one foot inside, climbing into the back as well, when rounds suddenly stitched across the aircraft just above him. He ducked, and then turned, firing at the tower. McCall screamed, and Elyar joined her. There was no way of knowing the effect of firing at the tower— the light was still lit and aimed right at them. The tower was just a shape behind it.

"Get in!" Sirois roared.

Bragdon leapt into the back and was not yet seated when Sirois lifted off. The bird spun, its light went out, and it passed over the outer wall and fences of the prison.

The amount of fire the helicopter was taking just seemed to steadily increase. Glass was flying inside the aircraft. Bragdon lay over the top of Elyar. McCall had gone into full-fledged shrieking at this point.

"Jesus!" Sirois shouted. "They're ripping the bird apart!"

Sirois could tell the helicopter was not going to take them to Iraq, or Turkey, or anywhere all that far. In fact, he was not even sure if he could land it. As the number of rounds impacting the aircraft dwindled, Sirois fought with it long enough to put perhaps a mile between them and the prison. The pedals vibrated violently beneath his feet. The stick controls were sluggish.

"We're going down," he said flatly.

"How far can you get us?" Bragdon asked. Just then, there was a terrible crunch sound to the rear. The helicopter immediately began to spin.

"About this far!" Sirois shouted back. He cut the power and the Gazelle came spiraling down. It impacted hard, and rolled completely over, the blades snapping off and flying in all directions. The aircraft nearly righted itself before all movement ceased. It became quiet in the dark. No fire. No sound.

"Bragdon!" Sirois called from the front seat.

"Bragdon!" Sirois called again. Still nothing.

"Jeanie," Sirois said more softly.

He heard a whine first, and then, "Here."

"Kid?" he asked in English, trying to check on Elyar. No response. He fought with his door, and surprisingly, it opened. Sirois slid out. He leaned back in and felt for McCall. He found her hair first; it felt like nothing he could remember, except a different version of how his had once been. He worked his hands down to under her shoulders. He could see she was pinned, and didn't know if her back or neck were broken, but he was out of time. He could already see the headlights of trucks approaching. Over the rough terrain, they had maybe two minutes. Not much more. He pulled, steadily increasing how strongly. She moaned.

"I know baby, I know it hurts, come on out here with me, okay?" he said softly. She was free. He pulled as gently as he could and brought her out onto the moss-covered rocks.

He moved to the back, and pulled open the door. The kid sprang out, startling the hell out of Sirois, and he never made a sound. Elyar came out, walked a few steps, and sat down hard next to McCall. Sirois felt inside for Bragdon, and found him. He was unconscious, blood in his hair, but alive. Sirois pulled him free and laid him next to the kid. Then, he went back to the front and found his MP5. Joining the others, he checked his weapon.

The kid turned and said something Sirois couldn't understand, but the meaning was clear enough. The trucks were approaching fast. They had closed half the distance already. Sirois took a look at McCall and decided neither of them was going to go through that hell again. He would make a stand right now, and if he had to, he'd use the last bullets on himself and Jeanie.

He half aimed at the oncoming trucks, two large five-tons, sure to be full of troops. He set his teeth, put his finger alongside the trigger and waited.

The ground suddenly boiled in front of the lead truck, and then rockets streaked down on both of them. Sirois looked up just in time to see a pair of Little Birds pass overhead. The first truck swerved, and then rolled, throwing its occupants everywhere. The second truck caught fire and ran into the first, both exploding with the impact. A Black Hawk pulled into a hover directly above them and Delta operators began fast-roping down to his position.

The Black Hawk slid left, dropped the ropes, and then descended to a few feet above the ground. The Delta operators lifted Bragdon and McCall and began running to the waiting Black Hawk as the Little Birds ran in a circle above them.

Sirois stood up, ran to the kid, grabbed him by one arm, and pulled him to his feet. He ran and dragged the stumbling teenager to the Black Hawk and threw him into the back. Sirois climbed in, and looked over at the crew chief. It was Derek Cooper.

"We got them all, McCall's here. And for some reason Captain Sirois, and two people I've never seen before. All D-boys are onboard," Cooper said into the intercom.

"Roger that," Ryan's voice came back, and then over the air net, "This is Arrow 5, coming out. We have McCall, Sirois, and then some. Returning to base."

"Arrow 5 this is Arrow 6, keep it low and fast and get back here double quick. Nice work. Arrow 6, out," Hartman's voice came back.

The lone Black Hawk and the two Little Birds flew less than twenty feet all the way back to the Iraqi border and Irbil Airfield. Sirois lay beside McCall the entire way, gently stroking her hair as she sobbed. Elyar just sat and stared at them both, his left hand on Bragdon's right foot.

75

Bragdon walked with Elyar, across the street, past several taxis painted two-tone flat orange and white. An ancient bus came through, coughing diesel. Black flags with Arabic scrawled in blue, white, and gold paint were hanging between a light pole and a street sign.

On they walked to tan buildings, looking surprisingly new, with a shop downstairs sporting a freshly painted Pepsi logo. The windows of the shop were covered with lowered panels, not unlike small garage doors, and these were painted in two tones as well. Tan on one half, dark brown on the other, with the line between running diagonally across the panel.

Bragdon and Elyar walked into the shop, through it, and up the stairs in the rear. Reaching the top with Elyar leading the way, they knocked on the door. There was no response. Elyar knocked again.

The door suddenly opened, and a woman peered out.

Elyar looked puzzled, and in Kurdish asked, "Is Berzan at home?"

The woman said nothing, looking at Bragdon.

Bragdon asked in Arabic, "Is Berzan at home?"

The woman answered in Arabic, "There is no Berzan here."

Elyar looked at Bragdon, who shook his head.

"But this is were he lives," Elyar insisted.

"Go away," the woman said, "or I will call them."

Bragdon waved one hand in acknowledgment, knowing he did not want any trouble with whomever "them" turned out to be, and said to Elyar, "He does not live here anymore."

"Well, then we have to ask her where he went," Elyar replied.

"She doesn't know," Bragdon said. "She doesn't even know him. And if she did, she wouldn't tell us how to find him."

"What will I do?" Elyar asked.

Bragdon asked, "How old are you?"

"I'm eighteen years old," Elyar answered.

Bragdon waited.

"I do not know how old I am. Maybe fifteen years?" Elyar tried again.

Bragdon nodded, thinking that was probably about right. "Come with me."

Elyar followed Bragdon down the stairs, and then asked, "What is your real name?"

"What's wrong with Stephen?" Bragdon smiled.

"Nothing. What did your mother name you?" Elyar asked.

Bragdon only smiled and kept walking.

"Where are we going?" Elyar asked.

"How's your French?" Bragdon asked in response.

"I do not speak French at all," Elyar replied.

"That's okay, you can learn," Bragdon said.

"I'm going to France?" Elyar asked.

76

Jeanie McCall lay in the bed, surrounded by monitors, connected to tubes, and covered in bandages. A cast on her leg included a long steel rod connected to the broken bone with pins entering the cast and passing through the skin.

She was clean, her face bruised and her untied hair pulled back, with one eye bandaged over. The other eye began to flutter, and then it opened.

"I'm still in the hospital?" McCall asked.

"Hi again, you've only been here for a couple days. This is the new hospital, you are at Walter Reed," Sirois answered, rubbing her left shoulder. It seemed the only part of her that wasn't bruised, bandaged, or plugged in.

McCall began to cry softly, but not in pain. More in confusion.

"What's wrong with me?" she asked.

"You're going to be just fine. You leg was badly broken, and needed surgery. You're going to need a couple more operations on it yet. But you're going to be fine, and you're going to walk, run, all that good stuff," Sirois answered with a gentle smile.

She was still crying softly. "Will I fly again?"

"Let's take one thing at a time," Sirois said, still smiling.

She looked away, tried to focus on the windows with her

one available eye. "Oh Rick, I know what it's like now. Since you went down, since I got you back, I've been living and flying with extra apprehension—more fear of being captured, and tortured."

Her crying became more intense, bending the last syllables of what she was saying.

"I know." Rick leaned in and lay his forehead on that same shoulder. "I know. I'm so sorry you went through this. And I'm sorry for what you went through when I was in Tehran."

She turned her head back and lay her cheek against his short hair, her tears falling into it.

Then her crying slowed a bit and she asked, "Is Morrison . . . dead?"

Sirois had given her the bad news twice already. This was the third time she'd asked, but she also seemed more lucid this time.

"Yes, Jeanie, Morrison was killed after the crash by Iranian ground troops," he said, hoping this answer would allow McCall to take on less guilt about losing another copilot.

Her crying once again intensified. She just quietly wept, her face pressed in his hair.

Slowly and unexpectedly, the door to the room opened. In walked Maggie McCall, the woman who thought that years after burying her husband and one true love she would now have to bury her daughter.

Maggie's face went from one of fear of hope to one of unadulterated joy and relief.

"Jeanie!" she squealed.

Sirois looked up, startled, and then pulled back as Maggie ran past him and, not nearly as cautious as Sirois had been, threw herself across her daughter.

Jeanie McCall winced at the pain from her mother's landing, but then she reached out one weary and intravenously connected arm and laid it across Maggie's back. At the touch, Maggie McCall cried even harder.

Jeanie began to soothe her mother, in spite of her own tears, and Rick came to both of them, laying a hand on each. He looked away, blinking tears of his own from his eyes, and saw her ring on the bedside table. The ring the Iranian interrogators had not removed had been taken off by the staff and lain on a faux-wood table. Sirois reached for and lifted the ring with one hand, lifted Jeanie's left hand with his own, and slipped the ring back on where it belonged.

Jeanie smiled through her tears up at Rick.

"I love you. You're going to be fine. We'll be fine," Rick said.

"I know," Jeanie replied as her mother stood, holding the other hand. "I know we will."

"You'll both have to stop flying," Maggie said suddenly, but matter-of-factly.

"One step at a time," Sirois said again.

"No," Maggie said. "No, Rick. This is enough. Enough. You can't have a marriage this way. Can you imagine if you had little kids, seeing their mommy this way? Or worrying because one of you has disappeared? Or how about just the deployments, the being gone."

"People make it work," Rick said softly, not wanting to discuss this now.

"For some it works, for many it doesn't, and none of them have two Night Stalkers in the family. No, it doesn't make sense, enough already. Go fly some CEOs around, wear a nice suit, enough of the suicide missions. Enough," Maggie insisted. She was tightly gripping Jeanie's hand, as if Sirois were there to take her away.

"Look, I don't think now is the best time to discuss this," Sirois said.

"We might as well, because I need you both to know, I can't take it anymore. I won't be made to worry for another twenty years because you two have these adventures you want to go on, or you feel a call to serve your country, or whatever. You can serve your country in other ways. I've had more than I can take. I don't want to have to help one of you through the loss of the other. I don't want to watch another child grow up with the ghost of a war-hero parent in the home," Maggie said.

"Listen, I understand how you feel, but I'm not going to get into an argument about this right now, right here—" Sirois began.

"You don't know how I feel, I'm trying to prevent you from understanding how I feel—" Maggie interrupted.

"Okay, okay, stop it," Jeanie interjected. The other two stopped and turned, their faces frozen, waiting.

Jeanie McCall looked at one and then the other. "Look, Rick, I still want to fly. I know I'm meant to fly, but maybe Mom is right. Maybe this won't work. Maybe we should consider other things. Maybe it's time to stop being a Night Stalker. I mean, look at me, and what did we really get? Did we find any useful intelligence in that raid at all?"

"Yes, we did," a voice said at the door. They turned to look, and in walked LTC Jack Hartman, with a bouquet of flowers.

"It appears that there was valuable information about another potential terror attack on our soil," Hartman said. He walked in and took a spot standing beside Jeanie's bed, across from Sirois and Maggie McCall.

Down the hall, in another room, Arroyo's beside area was less crowded. His ribs were wrapped and an IV dripped painkiller into his arm. Still, he was having fun.

"Ow, ow," he laughed. "Don't make me laugh!"

Hill laughed also as he continued reading aloud about a monkey shrieking in terror aboard a cargo plane over Vietnam. Hill turned the page in the book that Arroyo had kept insisting he read, and he read further, aloud.

Arroyo interrupted, "I can't believe I'm in here again."

"I can," Hill grinned. "Some of the nurses here are hot. That one that you were joking with, about getting you some Chinese food . . . wow."

Just then, a beautiful young woman, dressed in scrubs and a ponytail, came in with three white boxes scrawled on with red Chinese letters.

Arroyo shot Hill a look, no trace of a smile on his face, and said, "Want an egg roll?" His eyebrows jumped up and down smugly.

Hill sat stunned. The nurse gave Arroyo a wink, smiled at Hill, and left with a twitch in her step. Arroyo began laughing again, and then once again grabbed his ribs in pain.

Hill reached into the pack he had brought along and pulled out a cribbage board and a deck of cards.

"Aw man, I don't feel like giving you cribbage lessons right now," Arroyo said.

"You teach me? Who do you think taught you?" Hill said.

"I told you man, Kannenberg taught me, T.K. the master himself," Arroyo said.

"Come on, I'll spot you ten pegs," Hill said.

"Oh, you keep your charity, I'll whip you without it," Arroyo said, wincing as he raised his bed a bit.

Hill set the board on the small lunch tray table, wheeled it closer to Arroyo, and then began dealing the cards.

77

June 16
Predawn
Self-Storage warehouse
"Planned Self Store"
Bridgeport, Connecticut

They made no secret of it. There was no sneaking up on it, no stealthy approach. A Bell Jet Ranger helicopter flew above, navy blue, almost black, with huge white letters on the side, FBI. From every side, from every street, from every angle, cars and vans came screeching into the parking lot surrounding the warehouse.

From every vehicle poured out heavily armed men, wearing a variety of colors and numerous symbols of their authority. They all ran to the warehouse's exterior walls, and were there only long enough for a lightly armored and similarly navy blue vehicle to drive forward and through the large garage-type door facing the street. The door came down with a crash, and the vehicle retreated, pulling the door away with it.

The law enforcement agents streamed in, weapons at the ready, and fanned out. Shouts of "Clear!" echoed in the cavernous building, and the men broke into pairs to search each of the partitioned areas rented by clients of Planned Self Store.

FBI Special Agent Danny Clough ripped a padlock off the door of one such unit with a pry bar. He let it fall to the floor, pulled the door open, and stepped into the space with a sheriff's deputy right on his heels. On the floor, standing by itself, was a large crate, covered by a tarp. He went to one end of the crate, and pried it open as well. There wasn't a thought given to warrants or search procedures. If they found a truckload of heroin, there would be no arrests, no prosecutions. They were not there to lock someone up. They had come in force to save a city, and probably not the lovely but relatively insignificant Bridgeport. They were a sixty-mile drive from Manhattan.

Clough leaned in, shining his Mag-Lite into the end. A water heater. Just an ordinary water heater, sitting by itself, in a crate. The tags still on it, the copper still shiny. Clough thought about dismantling the water heater to make sure it wasn't a camouflaged weapon of mass destruction when he heard shouting from the other end of the warehouse.

"I think we've got it!" the voice came again as Clough sprinted down to see. The NEST and LGAT team members were there as quickly.

Wedged between two long sofas and hidden under their matching covers was the same cylindrical type of object found in Texas and Illinois. What was different about this one was the timer.

A timer, with a countdown of cheap, red LED lighted numbers, was running. After looking and looking again, Clough could see that unlike movies they did not have a matter of seconds; they had found this apparent nuke with thirteen hours to spare.

Clough knew this meant that someone had likely meant to pick the weapon up within a few hours and deliver it, but if they could not, they were willing to let this one go off wherever it happened to be when the time expired.

The NEST and LGAT members moved in and roared for everyone to get back; still no one retreated more than ten feet. If the weapon was a nuke, and it detonated, they all understood that unless they were given a forty-five-minute driving head start, it would not matter.

The lead NEST member stood and walked back to

Clough. "Listen, Special Agent Clough, right? My name is McMurray. It seems we have hours to play with here, so while we will hurry to make this thing safe, there is no sense rushing to a mistake. We have to plan this out. Right now, we're trying to decide if we should attempt to make this safe here, or if we should transport it to a more remote location. Like out to sea."

Clough listened intently. *Out to sea?* he thought. They want to chance picking this thing up?

"Why not simply disconnect the clock?" Clough asked. "I know there is some risk in that, but it seems the natural course."

"Because," McMurray replied, "it could be as simple as the clock not counting down to when an electric charge will be sent to *close* the circuit. It could be that the clock is ticking down the time until an electrical current keeping a circuit *open* is turned off. If we cut the power to the timer, we might just instantly close the circuit that detonates the device."

The timer was attached to the device by two wires that looked exactly like the one attached to the toggle switch on the nukes they had dismantled, and those had been real enough, but this one was different. The people who had been in charge of this one had thought enough to set a finite amount of time it would spend sitting around, so they may have also set it up to detonate if tampered with.

Clough nodded. "Okay, so what can we do to help?" He swept one arm at the crowd of law enforcement personnel, all standing by for what was next.

"Nothing," McMurray said. "Just set up a perimeter, secure the area, until the military gets here."

"The military?" Clough asked.

"Of course. When we find something like this, we need it secured. The army is on the way," McMurray said. "The 143rd Military Police Company is on the way. Until they get here, if you and these men could just move on outside, and keep everyone else out of here, that would be great. Thanks, Special Agent."

"You want me to pull guard duty?" Clough asked.

"I want you to simply do your job while I do mine," Mc-Murray replied.

"Listen, I'm not going to pull guard duty for you—" Clough began.

From over next to the device, the last words anyone wanted to hear were shouted loud and clear: "We have a problem here!"

Clough and McMurray ran to the man. Before they could ask or he could explain, the man moved back to reveal the timer ticking down at a mind-numbing speed.

"What did you do?!" McMurray shouted.

"Nothing! It just beeped and started racing like this!" the man said. His hands were visibly shaking. To Clough it was all surreal. A nuke that had been dormant, at least for another half day, was now ticking down to presumably detonate within a minute. And one of the men sent to dismantle the nuke had the shakes so bad, he wouldn't have been able to shave.

"Cut the wire," Clough said.

"We need to know what you did!" McMurray roared at the man.

"I don't know what I did! I did nothing! I was just kneeling next to it and the timer started to go nuts!" the man replied.

"Cut the wire," Clough said again.

"Well, you must have done something! Why else would it just speed up?" McMurray said.

"Cut the wire!" Clough barked.

Snapping his head around to Clough, McMurray said, "I already told you, that might set it off immediately!"

"McMurray! That thing is going to go off immediately anyway if you don't cut the timer off. We have a fifty-fifty shot, and about twenty seconds!" Clough insisted.

McMurray looked at Clough and then at the man with the shaky hands, and said, pointing, "Do it."

"Screw that!" the man replied, backing away.

Clough jumped past McMurray and lifted the timer in his hand, just as the last few digits left were not even numbers but a blur. Clough wrapped his fist around one of the wires leading from the elongated steel egg to the timer box, and yanked hard. He felt the wire come loose and saw the LED digits go black. And there Special Agent Danny Clough stood, with a wire in one hand, the box in the other, and his legs straddling a nuclear weapon. He let out a rush of air, and felt his shoulders and head drop.

"Can someone please take these from me?" Clough asked without turning. Men, until that moment frozen in place, rushed forward to relieve him.

Clough pulled out his cell phone and called King in the Newark temporary office. "Sir, we apparently have found the device and are in the process of making it safe."

"Let's hope that's the last one," King replied.

Clough held out one trembling hand and said, "Yes, sir."

78

June 16
McLean, Virginia

Cassie Thompson, formerly of CEEBIC and currently of the U.S. Department of Commerce, walked into the plain-looking office building. She had been called in for an interview. After her experience with the attack on the Metro at Federal Triangle, she had spent a couple of days crying. Then, she became angry.

She decided that she would leave behind her job of trade agreements and showing foreign trade negotiators around Washington, D.C., and instead would get into the fight that almost took her life and had stolen the lives of far too many of her countrymen.

She pulled the door open and felt the rush of air-conditioned air as she stepped in. She checked in at the desk, and sat among several nervous-looking people roughly her own age. She was the only woman and certainly the only one with a nose ring. Still, she was determined to see if she had the stuff to be an operations officer for the Central Intelligence Agency. She wasn't going to wait for the fight to come to her again. She was going to go out and find it.

"Cassie Thompson?" a young lady with a clipboard called.

"Yes?" Cassie said, and then felt stupid. She stood and

followed the young lady into a small office. There, she was offered a chair on one side of a cheap desk, while a chair waited empty on the other side.

"She'll be right with you," clipboard girl said and then left.

Moments later, a woman in her midforties came in and took a seat.

"My name is Ms. Brown. It's very nice to meet you. I'd like to start with a hypothetical question," the woman said, smiling.

Cassie swallowed, and then said, "Okay, go ahead."

"Pick a city outside the United States," the woman said.

"London," Cassie said immediately. She loved London, and had even done some summer program work on Shakespeare at Cambridge.

"Fine. Imagine you are in London, you've rented a car and picked up your contact, he's really excited to give you information. He passes you documents and is hurriedly telling you great stuff, when he suddenly develops difficulty breathing, and grasps his chest. He's apparently having a heart attack. What would you do?" Ms. Brown asked.

Cassie took a deep breath and answered, "Well, I would . . ."

79

Jack Hartman lay on his back, one hand behind his head, the other arm under and around Cat. She lay with her head on his bare chest, the sheet pulled to her shoulder, her hand on his abdomen. She could feel the strength there, could sense the power he still had, and admired how hard he worked at staying fit.

"Do you think Jeanie McCall will stay in the unit?" Cat asked.

"If you would have asked me a month ago, I would have told you I couldn't imagine anything that would keep Mc-Call from flying a Black Hawk. Now, I'm not so sure," Jack said, moving a hand to play with Cat's hair.

"Being engaged, seeing marriage right around the corner, it changes things," Cat said softly.

"Do you think they'll actually get married?" Jack asked.

"I think they'll get married," Cat said, "but I'm not sure they'll get married as soon as they once thought they would."

"Hmmm," Hartman hummed in agreement. "Mike Ryan's going to go though. He and Lydia have had enough—they want to start slowing down, start planning that retirement."

Cat nodded against Jack's chest, but said nothing.

"Lydia will like that, right?" Jack asked.

"Lydia will like anything that risks Mike less and gives her more time with him," Cat answered.

Jack smiled in the dark. "I can really see Mike going fishing all day, playing golf, maybe writing a book."

"Yeah, but the names would all be fictionalized, to protect the less than innocent," Cat chuckled.

Hartman smiled even more broadly, and Cat snuggled into him, tighter, closer.

"I'm not going to retire, Cat," Hartman said softly, but confidently. "I'm not going to retire and you're not going to retire, and it will all work out just fine. We'll have the rest of our lives together, but for now, I think we can make it work. I was being selfish before, but we can make this work. And then, when God's ready for us to be together again, he'll work it all out for us."

Cat smiled. "It took you long enough to figure it out."

"Oh come on." Hartman looked down at her. "It's not like you were totally calm, cool, and collected about all this. I suggested a break and you immediately thought there was another woman."

Cat grinned up at him, and said in her best official voice, "I can neither confirm nor deny that."

Hartman laughed. "What can you confirm?"

Cat paused and said, "That I'll always love you, Jack."

She climbed up, bringing her face to his, her mouth to his, and they kissed deeply, and then rolled in the sheets.

80

June 21
Rowan, Iowa

They turned left onto Main Street from Bingham Avenue and then right onto Emerson. The house was tan, with dark brown shingles. The shutters were an earthy dark green, and there was white trim neatly painted around each window.

A cracking paved driveway went into the lot on the left side of the house, and a concrete walkway curved through the grass from the drive to the front door, making a crisp ninety-degree left-hand turn along the way.

The lot was small, but there was room for a garage as well, with a basketball net hanging above the wide door.

Cooper pulled in and threw the car into park.

"This is it," Cooper smiled. "Ready to meet the fam?"

"No," Lara grinned back. "I'm nervous."

"What's to be nervous about? My folks have hated most of my girlfriends. You can't do any worse than them," Cooper said.

"Stop it! You're making it worse!" Lara laughed.

The front door opened and a woman with graying hair and an apron stepped out, and waved them in with a dish towel.

"Oh my God, she's so cute," Lara gasped.

"Yeah, she's cute," Cooper said, pushing his door open, and stepping out. "Hi Mom!"

Lara exited the car as well. Cooper came around and took her hand, and led her toward the house.

"Mom, this is Lara," Cooper said.

"Hi, Lara, I'm Christine; it's so nice to finally meet you, heard so much about you," she said, extending her hand. Lara took it, a firm handshake.

"It's nice to meet you," Lara had time to say before being swept into the house.

"You're right, Derek, she's the prettiest thing," Christine Cooper said.

"Mom, please," Cooper replied, hugging her. Lara blushed. His mother laughed at the big hug Cooper gave her, patted his back, and the front door to the house finally closed behind them.

81

June 22
Ain El Remaneh suburb of Beirut
Lebanon

Bragdon was parked in a Renault Laguna, in his hand a device that looked like a garage door opener.

He had brought Elyar to Paris. The boy had been terrified
at first. Not just on the flight to France, jumping at every
noise and every bit of turbulence, but also of plunging into a
new culture, and a new language, and a new beginning.

Bragdon knew he couldn't leave the kid in Iraq, and he
knew he couldn't create a home for him, so he found a
small year-round residential school for Elyar. A place used
to supporting kids from the Middle East, with little or no
French skills. A school where they would catch him up
with reading and other skills quickly, but where they would
also provide a nurturing environment.

Elyar had made him promise to visit regularly and write
often, and in exchange Elyar promised to stay at the school
and work hard for him. Sounded fair to Bragdon.

And in the Renault, sitting in Beirut, Bragdon wondered
how Elyar's first week was going. He'd run up to Paris before autumn and check in on the boy.

Just then, a man came out of the building he had been
staking out. The man wore an expensive suit and was
flanked on all sides by a security detail. They moved as a

herd to the waiting limo. The rear door was opened for the man, and he climbed in.

No sooner was the door closed than Bragdon pushed the oversized button in the middle of the device he held in his hand. The limo detonated.

A massive explosion, blowing every visible shop window out. The man, his driver, and the security men who were standing too close had not a chance of survival.

Bragdon tossed the remote control onto the floor in front of the seat, and put the Renault in gear. He pulled out and drove through the intersection and away from the fire.

He watched in his rearview mirror as a crowd began to form. Bragdon caught his own eye in the mirror and said, "Only ten more to go."

82

June 22
Black Lake
Two hours north of Syracuse
Upstate New York

Special Agent Danny Clough leaned back in a seat on his twenty-three-foot bass boat. Bass season had just opened, and he needed the break. He cast out, set the rod down, and pulled out a bag of Doritos and a Diet Pepsi.

Munching on the chips, he looked out at the beautiful lake from the shallow bay where he sat. He was fishing with a plastic worm, and should have been working it, but instead he just let the bobber hang it out there.

Clough looked out at the lake and processed what he had been through, what he had accomplished in the last month, and without warning jumped to his feet, threw one fist in the air, and shouted like a teenager winning the state championship. Doritos flew from his mouth and his voice echoed across the water. Some birds called back.

The bad guys might win some of the time, but he'd won a big one in the later rounds. Clough grinned, and slowly took his seat again.

MICHAEL HAWKE

Night Stalkers
They left no man behind at Mogadishu.
They chased the Taliban out of Afghanistan.
Now the Black Hawk pilots of the 160th
Special Operation Aviation Regiment must
locate and destroy weapons of mass
destruction smuggled into Lebanon.
And failure is not an option.
0-425-19992-4

Night Stalkers #2: Coercion
The Night Stalkers have taken prisoner one
of Al Qaeda's most prominent leaders—and
his capture sparks a bloody string of attacks
in Europe and Asia. Now, the Night Stalkers
must finish the fight they began, and stop
the devastation before it takes aim at home.
0-425-20392-1

Available wherever books are sold or at
penguin.com

B038